I0775710

The Value
in Our Lies

a 509 Crime Story

by Colin Conway

The Value in Our Lies

Original Cover Design by Zach McCain
Updated Cover Design by Rob Williams

First Edition – 2020, Second Edition – 2023

ISBN: 978-1-961030-09-1

Original Ink Press, an imprint of High Speed Creative, LLC
1521 N. Argonne Road, #C-205
Spokane Valley, WA 99212

Visit the author's website at www.colinconway.com

What is the 509?

Separated by the Cascade Range, Washington State is divided into two distinctly different climates and cultures.

The western side of the Cascades is home to Seattle, its 34 inches of annual rainfall, and the incredibly weird and smelly Gum Wall. Most of the state's wealth and political power are concentrated in and around this enormous city. The residents of this area know the prosperity that has come from being the home of Microsoft, Amazon, Boeing, and Starbucks.

To the east of the Cascade Mountains lies nearly two-thirds of the entire state, a lot of which is used for agriculture. Washington State leads the nation in producing apples, it is the second-largest potato grower, and it's the fourth for providing wheat.

This eastern part of the state can enjoy more than 170 days of sunshine each year, which is important when there are more than 200 lakes nearby. However, the beautiful summers are offset by harsh winters, with average snowfall reaching 47 inches and the average high hovering around 37°.

While five telephone area codes provide service to the westside, only 509 covers everything east of the Cascades, a staggering twenty-one counties.

Of these, Spokane County is the largest with an estimated population of 506,000.

Lies are not freedom.

Arkady Renko (played by William Hurt)
/ *Gorky Park*

The Value
in Our Lies

Chapter 1

Parked nose-first into the rear of an abandoned industrial building, the red brake lights of the Subaru Outback shone brightly into the night.

The security lights attached to the structure's exterior no longer functioned. The last of them burned out long before the building finally vacated. Darkness blanketed the parking lot while a series of broken pole lights provided no illumination.

The Subaru's brake lights resembled the eyes of an angry monster hiding in the blackness. When the brake lights winked on and off several times, it was as if the terrible thing in the darkness blinked—a warning to approaching interlopers.

Even though this stretch of the city experienced redevelopment recently, this property, along with those to the immediate east and west, avoided it since they were hung up in litigation. Hard times had fallen on the cluster of properties that formed a small manufacturing plant, and a bankruptcy petition was filed. The ownership, now consisting of the original partners' eleven adult children, filed multiple lawsuits against the company and each other, all of which were still in court. Even the IRS was involved, having demanded payment of back taxes and subsequent penalties. When those demands were not met, the government began the process of seizure. To say the properties were stuck in a legal quagmire would put it mildly.

The occupants of the Subaru were unaware of the manufacturing plant's history and, frankly, they wouldn't care. They only knew this to be a quiet location to conduct personal transactions, the kind that polite society kept hidden in dark places like this.

The location was not a secret for this type of activity. Many private dealings had occurred in this same spot over the years, even while the manufacturing plant operated at full capacity, and the parking lot remained well-illuminated at night.

With its headlights off, a black Dodge Charger pulled slowly behind the building. Gravel crunched under its tires. From its hiding place behind a large clump of weeds, a feral cat burst into the open and sprinted across the parking lot.

Despite the movement behind the Subaru, its brake lights continued to wink on and off—the monster cautioning potential intruders from nearing.

Hip-hop music played from inside the car and rattled its license plate cover.

Spokane Police Detective James Morgan stopped his car and placed it into Park. As he watched the monster blink its warning from the shadows, he was unafraid.

Morgan did not notify dispatch where he was. In fact, his police radio was turned off. With a mini-Maglite in hand, he slid out of the car, leaving his door open. The in-car light did not turn on, as this feature had been previously disabled for moments like this.

The detective deliberately walked toward the driver's door.

A white male in a dark suit, his tie loosened, reclined in the driver's seat. His eyes were closed, and his face twisted in a mixture of pain and pleasure.

Stretched across both the passenger and driver's seats was a woman with her head down in the man's lap. Due to her short afro and long skinny frame, Morgan felt confident it was the woman for whom he was searching.

He pulled his badge from his belt and tapped it several times against the car's window. As the music continued to thump from inside, neither of the vehicle's occupants looked up. Morgan clinked his badge against the window again, this time clanking his flashlight against the side of the car door in a matching rhythm.

The man's eyes opened then, and he dreamily looked toward the detective. The woman, however, never broke her pace, her head and hand bobbing together in the same determined tempo.

With his flashlight, Morgan illuminated his badge.

It took a moment for recognition to occur to the man. When it did, a flurry of activity suddenly happened inside the car. The man grabbed the woman by the shoulder and yanked her back. He then tucked himself away and zipped his pants. As the woman adjusted herself, the driver returned his seat upright and clicked the radio off.

A nearly silent calm suddenly returned to the night.

Morgan clipped his badge back to his belt.

The man behind the steering wheel began to lower the window. As it dropped, he placed his face near the glass and asked through the ever-widening opening, "What can I do for you, Officer?"

"License and registration," Morgan said.

The man glanced at the woman before facing the detective, the window now completely down. "But I wasn't driving."

"License and registration," the detective repeated.

With apparent resignation, the man muttered, "Yes, sir."

Morgan bent down to make eye contact with the woman. With a frown, she shook her head. Then she turned forward in her seat, crossed her arms, and stared at the concrete wall in front of the car.

The man pulled his wallet from his rear pocket, dug his license out, and handed it to the detective. He dropped the wallet into his lap, reached across the car, and opened the glove box. He quickly retrieved some paperwork. When he settled back into his seat, he handed the papers to Morgan.

The detective's eyes flicked over the driver's license. "Erick Dupree?"

"Yes, sir, that's correct."

Morgan compared the address on the driver's license to that on the vehicle registration. "Still live up north?"

"Uh-huh. That's right."

"A little far from home, aren't you?"

Dupree didn't answer but quietly watched the detective. His Adam's apple bobbed several times as he nervously swallowed.

Morgan removed his cell phone from his pocket and initiated its camera function. He held the mini-Maglite between his teeth, the license in his left hand, and activated the phone with his right. When he finished snapping a picture, he put the phone away.

"Tell me, Erick," the detective said, "what are you doing down here?"

Dupree glanced at the woman again. "We were... you know."

"No," Morgan said. "I don't."

The man put his hands on the steering wheel and stared ahead at the block wall. "Well... I guess... you saw, right?"

"You going to tell me she's your girlfriend?"

Dupree blinked repeatedly but didn't turn to the detective.

"Because she's not," Morgan said.

The man's tongue wetted his lips, and his blinking turned into several scrunches of the face.

"She's a prostitute."

The man's facial contortions stopped, but he still refused to look at either Morgan or the woman.

"I'm not telling you anything you already don't know, am I?"

Dupree now resembled a mannequin—a crash test dummy waiting for a collision test to end so he could be removed from the car and returned to the safety of a factory shelf.

"Have you paid her?"

Frozen in panic, the man stared straight ahead.

Morgan bent to look at the woman. "Has he paid you?"

The prostitute rolled her eyes before saying, "He paid me."

"How much do you have left in your wallet, Mr. Dupree?"

Turning to face the detective, the driver asked, "Sir?"

Morgan glanced around the darkness before repeating his question. "How much is in your wallet?"

The man opened the leather billfold in his lap, and Morgan shone his flashlight upon it. Several bills were tucked orderly inside, and Dupree quickly thumbed through them. "About four hundred," he said.

"About?"

"Four hundred," Dupree weakly said.

"Give it to the girl."

With surprised eyes, Dupree peered up at the detective. "I already paid her."

"Pay her," Morgan said. "*Again.*"

"But that's more than she's worth," Dupree muttered as he examined the money in his wallet.

The prostitute looked out her side window and shook her head. Morgan noticed this movement and felt a surge of anger toward the man behind the steering wheel.

"Hey, Erick?" Morgan said, his words coming quick and loud now. "How about I arrest you and haul your ass to jail?"

The man shook his head. "Wait—"

"You can call your family to come and pick you up—you got a family, right? A wife, maybe? Some kids?"

Dupree's face slackened.

Morgan's smile was cruel. "Thought so."

"I—"

"When I'm done with you," the detective continued, "you won't have either. How about I also do this? I'll issue a press release. Something that says I ran a sting to catch johns like you. We'll put your name in the paper." Morgan stood upright and yelled into the night sky, "Erick Dupree has sex with prostitutes!"

When the detective bent down again, the driver's eyes filled with tears, and his mouth hung open.

"And when you're convicted," Morgan continued, "because you will be, you'll have to register as a sex offender. You won't pick your kids up from school ever again. Your friends and family will know. The people at church—"

Dupree shuddered.

"Now that we understand each other, is keeping this whole thing quiet worth something? Is that woman over there worth an extra four hundred dollars?"

"That's extortion," Dupree mumbled through trembling lips. His hand shook as he fingered the bills in his wallet.

His voice low and threatening, Morgan said, "Give the money to the fucking girl."

Dupree thought about it for a moment further, then reluctantly handed the money to the woman. She snatched it from his hand and tucked it into her purse.

"Out of the car," Morgan ordered the woman.

She sighed heavily, but still climbed out. The door slammed behind her.

"Mr. Dupree," Morgan said, bringing the man's attention to him.

"Sir?"

"Go home," the detective said while politely handing Dupree his driver's license and registration. "And have a nice night."

The driver tossed the paperwork into the passenger seat, started the car, and reversed fifty feet with the engine whining. When it was far enough back, the Subaru turned around. The brake lights winked several times—a monster blinking away its fear before scampering out of the darkness.

When the silence of the night returned, the prostitute put her hands on her skinny hips. Her large purse lay on the ground next to her feet. She wore a yellow T-shirt, brown shorts, and dirty tan Converse tennis shoes. Her T-shirt featured the likenesses of Muhammad Ali and George Foreman with the words *Rumble in the Jungle*. When Morgan highlighted her with his flashlight, a black bra showed under the threadbare shirt.

"Damn it, Morgan," she snapped.

"I texted you, Joey."

Josephine Green shook her head and lifted a hand to protect her eyes from the flashlight.

"I even called you," he said. "Several times, but you never hollered back."

"I was working, Morgan. You know I gotta eat."

"That's not our deal," he said as he walked toward his car.

"Hey," Joey called. When the detective didn't respond, she picked up her purse and hurried behind him. "What's this about?"

When he got to his patrol car, Morgan opened the rear door and highlighted the backseat with the flashlight.

Joey stopped and stared at the seat. Morgan watched her until her shoulders slumped, and she unenthusiastically moved by him. She dropped her purse on the floorboard before sitting on the edge of the seat. Her feet remained outside the car. "What's this about?" she repeated.

Morgan pointed his flashlight to the ground, which gave them ambient light to talk by. He pushed his baseball cap slightly back on his head. "What do you know about The Eight?"

"The gang that folks are whispering about? Sounds like a bunch of bullshit."

"The California agencies say they're for real. Supposedly, they're moving a crew up here, but we can't find anyone that fits the bill."

"Why would they give a shit about this zip code?"

Morgan shrugged. "Territory probably, but we don't know for sure, and that bothers the brass."

"This affects me how? They don't run girls. Or do they? Do I have to be worried about them?"

"They don't mess with working girls. Even if they did, you wouldn't have to worry. You're one of my people, Joey. Just keep your eyes and ears open for them, understand? If you hear anything about new players doing anything, let me know. Okay?"

Joey smirked. "I'm not your people, Morgan."

Morgan leaned into her. "What's that?"

She looked away into the darkness.

He leaned in and tapped her sternum. "Because of what I did for *you*," he tapped harder, which caused her to lean back, "you belong to me. Never forget that."

Her eyes bore into him. "How can I ever forget? You won't let me."

The detective smiled as he straightened. "The Eight. Start poking around."

Joey clucked her tongue against the roof of her mouth. "Fine."

Morgan studied her for a moment. "Need anything?" His voice had softened.

Her shoulders relaxed, and she shook her head. "I'm good."

"Heard from Scrimmy?"

"She's back," Joey said.

"When?"

"Few weeks ago."

Morgan leaned on the car door and flicked his chin with a thumb. "Huh."

"I was sad to see her," Joey said. "I thought she escaped."

"Me too," Morgan muttered.

"She hasn't been the same since Rado got himself killed."

"How's her pimp going to take it?"

"Junior will smack her around for a few days, but she's an earner, so he won't take it too far."

They stayed silent for a few moments, each lost in their own thoughts.

"Hey, Morgan?" Joey whispered.

His eyes moved to her.

"You going to make me earn that extra four hundred?"

Morgan stiffened, his nostrils flaring.

"Shit," she said and shook her head. Joey then reached into her purse and pulled a condom out. "Come on, Detective. Let's get this over with."

Chapter 2

The next morning, Morgan arrived at the Monroe Court Building shortly before eight. He parked, got out, and lifted his face to the sun. Summer was his favorite season, and he recently found himself thinking about retirement to some place that remained warm all year long.

Technically, he could give up work any time. He'd put in more than his twenty years and could quit any day. He no longer had family in town since his parents had passed many years before. He didn't have siblings, and the only people he considered friends were in the department.

Was it the mission, he wondered, the forever battle between good and evil that kept him on the job? Or was it the thrill of the hunt, the occasional chase that sent his blood racing? He'd never get that jolt while sitting some place warm, drinking Mai-Tais until his heart exploded.

Morgan opened his eyes and closed the car door.

To the northwest stood the monolithic Spokane County Jail. To the west was the Public Safety Building (PSB), which housed not only the Spokane Police Department but also a portion of the Spokane County Sheriff's Office as well as the municipal court.

Over the years, as the police department grew, it expanded into neighboring properties, including a privately owned office structure known as the Monroe Court Building. Most of the early functions that left the PSB and landed at Monroe Court were "non-essential," such as Volunteer Services, Neighborhood Resources, and Extra Duty scheduling. Even the traffic unit was once located at Monroe Court. Now, most of those units had relocated to city-owned property on Gardner Street.

Morgan strode across the parking lot. He offered a small wave to a passing patrol car even though he wasn't sure who was behind the wheel.

It was a stroke of genius when the founder of the Criminal Task Force (CTF) first located the group in the Monroe Court Building. Since it was initially sold as a short-term solution, no one wanted to give up long-term space within the PSB. Government is about empire building, and relinquishing territory for something temporary meant sharing space was like waving a red flag that a department had too much room. It would soon be lost to a more aggressive, expanding entity. Therefore, when the founder of the CTF offered to station his team in the nearby office building, no one fought him, not even the budget hawks.

Morgan yanked open the door to the building, bypassed the elevator, and headed for the stairs.

The original mission of the CTF was to respond to the ever-increasing threat of crack cocaine and the gangs responsible for it. They were established in the early nineties before Morgan was ever in the department. They were a "kicker" to the department's already formed Special Investigations Unit (SIU), which focused primarily on the flow of narcotics through the city.

The unit faced certain disbandment when the crack epidemic waned. Luckily, there was always a new crisis to focus on. As crack declined, the team was pointed at the burgeoning meth problem. Later, when there was a sudden influx of automatic firearms on the streets, the CTF morphed into tracking illegal weapon shipments brought in by the Asian gangs. Whenever a new problem arrived in Spokane, one requiring a quick response, the CTF was assigned the task of reducing its impact.

What started as a surgical knife turned into a rubber mallet. The unit was no longer used to cut out a problem—they simply played "Whack-a-Mole."

It was a game James Morgan relished and played with a certain vigor.

The Criminal Task Force did not have a single, definable mission such as other units. It was a dangerous place for a team to reside. Since they were a small squad, they were agile and, therefore, easily pointed at a problem. That's how they proved their value. However, without a genuinely identifiable mission, they were continually on the chopping block during the department's annual budget review.

When Morgan stepped into the second-floor office, the team was already engaged in daily activities such as report writing, making follow-up telephone calls, or reviewing notes. He made his way to his desk and dropped his jacket over the back of his chair.

The whole office was a bullpen. There were no private spaces, nor was there a conference room or a confidential interview space. The team called it HQ, a term Morgan still appreciated from his time in the Marine Corps.

Sergeant Ken Bynum's desk sat next to Morgan's. With a red pen in his hand, the unit commander leaned forward over a report. At forty-one years old, Bynum was the only member out of the six on the team with a short, military haircut reminiscent of the rest of the officers on the department. Bynum's blue T-shirt was pulled tight across his thick chest, and his biceps bulged under its short sleeves even while the man remained in a resting position.

"You steal that shirt from your kid?" Morgan asked.

Bynum lifted his head to look at Morgan. "You're jealous because you're old and fat."

Morgan's eyes widened. "Fat?" He slapped his stomach. "This is hard as a rock."

"If rock was made from fat," Bynum said.

A loud guffaw erupted behind Morgan. He turned around to see Officer Courtney Earley.

Earley stood six foot six and weighed nearly two hundred forty pounds. Most of it was muscle, except for a recently softening midsection that pushed slightly at his faded *Black Label Society* T-shirt. A big man who had just turned thirty-two, Earley had once played defensive end for the University of Idaho. His long blond hair fell beyond his shoulders, and his scraggly beard hadn't been trimmed in weeks.

"What are you laughing at, big boy?" Morgan asked.

Amid his chuckling, Earley muttered, "If rock was made from fat."

Morgan stepped to the bigger man and patted him on the waist to call attention to his love handles.

Earley's grin faded.

"Careful, Morgan," Bynum said, "or he'll eat you."

The bigger man chomped his teeth.

"When's feeding time?" Morgan asked.

"It never ends," Earley growled.

Detective Nayla Senai walked over and leaned her hip against Bynum's desk. She was the only female member of the team. Originally from Ethiopia, she was tall, dark-skinned, and attractive. Her beauty hid a ferocity she carried due to her childhood. "Comparing sizes again?"

"Why?" Morgan asked, turning to her. "Want to judge the competition?"

"Not at all," she said with a cringe. "You already cry too much."

Morgan looked at the three of them and asked, "Is it pick-on-me day?"

"We pick on you because we love you," Bynum said.

"We love him?" Senai asked.

"Yeah?" Earley threw in. "When did that shit start?"

Sergeant Bynum held his arms wide. "There you go, Morgan. We're all hugs and kisses for you."

Morgan turned and looked at the last two members of the team huddled together at a computer—Officers Adrian Thorn and Jeremiah 'Doc' Strange.

"What about you two?" Morgan called.

Thorn looked his way. "What's that?"

"Got anything to say about me this morning?"

Thorn looked at Strange then back to Morgan. "You look pretty?"

The rest of the group laughed, and Morgan threw his hands in the air. "I hate you all," he said with a smile.

Bynum stood and said, "Addy and Doc, come here."

Thorn and Strange stole a final glance at their computer screen, stood, then walked over to the group.

Adrian Thorn was a tall, skinny man who wore a faded mechanic's shirt with the name Curt written in red cursive over the left breast. His well-worn Levis were covered in grease, much like his long dark hair. A pair of scuffed black boots completed the image. He had a slightly wild look in his eyes, as if he'd spent too long partying the previous night.

Jeremiah Strange ambled behind Thorn. He wore dirty jeans, a Los Angeles Lakers tank top, and red high-top basketball shoes that were scuffed and untied. His afro was large and unkempt. Strange had a wild look in his eyes as well, but it looked natural, like it would remain even after a good night's sleep.

When the team gathered around Bynum, he asked, "What's the latest on The Eight?"

Senai shook her head. "Rumor and innuendo. Everyone's heard of them, but nobody confirms they're coming."

Morgan said, "I've got nothing."

Bynum looked at the others who responded with mumbles and shrugs. "Jesus, people. We need to get something, *anything*, on these mopes."

"What about SIU?" Earley asked. "They getting anything?"

"They've got zilch," the sergeant said. "Same as you."

"Why is this so important?" Morgan asked. "It seems like some brass circle jerk."

"Circle jerk?" Senai asked.

Morgan made a quick pumping motion with his hand.

Senai's face pinched. "Gross."

"But it's done with a group of guys," Doc said. He and Thorn made the same hand motion Morgan had made and giggled as they did so.

Senai glared at them until their chuckling stopped.

Bynum continued with his briefing, "A couple more homicides occurred yesterday along the coast that local agencies believe to be attributed to members of The Eight. One in Santa Rosa, the other was in Eureka."

"Eureka!" Thorn yelled.

The entire team stared at him.

Thorn flipped his hair back, then shrugged. "Sorry. I have no idea where that town is."

"Anyway," Bynum said, bringing the team's focus back to him. "From what's being surmised, members of The Eight are leaving a trail of bodies as they move north. Here's the latest information on them." Bynum handed a folder to Morgan, who immediately skimmed the intelligence sheets.

An informant in Oakland had mentioned Spokane a couple of weeks ago. It made it into a report which made its way to the SPD administration. The brass had been up in arms ever since.

"Why not just ask the informant for some real-time intel?" Morgan asked. "That would clear things up faster than us running around with our heads cut off."

"They tried," Bynum said. "Oakland PD just discovered his body."

Morgan looked at the members of his team before speaking. "So, we're running around, afraid of the boogeymen, because of some rumor from a now-dead informant? It's not a full-scale invasion. We've handled gangs before."

Sergeant Bynum inhaled slowly, thought before speaking, then began. "It's their tactics. Even you can see that. It's next-generation stuff. They killed the family of one of their own who turned on them. They beheaded a rival gang member to send a message. They raped a girl and her mother because they suspected her of having helped hide someone they were looking for. This group isn't right. They're acting like terrorists."

When the sergeant said "terrorists," everyone's eyes moved to Nayla Senai. Terrorists had murdered her father before her mother fled to America when she was a toddler.

Senai shook her head. "They may *act* like terrorists, but is it because of their beliefs? If it is for money and power, they are not terrorists, they are criminals, and they can be broken. If their actions are because of religion… well, we'll have a different problem if it's because of that—one that won't be so easily solved."

Sergeant Bynum pulled his eyes from Senai to look at the rest of the group. "I don't need to remind you, but the current administration doesn't like this team. They tolerate it because we get results. When we stop showing them what we can do, they'll disband us, and we'll go back into regular rotation. How'd you like to handle property crimes, Morgan? Maybe run down some stolen bicycles?"

He didn't like that idea at all.

The sergeant focused on Thorn and Strange. "And you two. How would you like to go back to riding in a patrol car? Alone."

Thorn and Strange looked at each other and rolled their eyes.

"I'm *serious*," the sergeant said.

"We're on it, Ken," Morgan said, slapping the folder against Earley's chest.

"Please, people," the sergeant said, "get me something I can give to brass. Now."

The team broke up then and walked back to their respective desks.

"Morgan," Bynum said.

"Yeah?"

"Walk with me."

***

Outside the building, Sergeant Bynum scanned the parking lot before turning to Morgan. "What do you know about the Brown shooting?"

Tremaine Brown was a member of the Dead Boys, a gang that had migrated some of its members up from Los Angeles in the early nineties. Brown was the third generation of that migration, one that had occurred after the Great Recession when everyone was struggling to grow their businesses, even gangs.

A rookie police officer, Sean Thayer, recently shot Brown in the shoulder. The officer responded to a call of a rolling domestic dispute—a man and woman fighting in a car. Reportedly, when the officer stopped them, Tremaine was already out of the passenger seat and leaving the scene. Thayer hurriedly hopped out of his car, forgetting to activate his body camera. His in-car camera was on, but the vehicle was pointed in the wrong direction.

Whatever occurred leading up to the shooting was still up for speculation. What wasn't left for debate, though, was the officer shot an unarmed man. Tremaine Brown never had a gun. He wasn't even holding a cell phone that could have been argued to have looked like a gun.

After the shooting, the girlfriend stated Brown never assaulted her. Her claims were in direct contradiction to her broken nose and facial lacerations. She blamed those injuries on a rival woman who was after Brown's affections. Even though Brown had damage to his knuckles, they both claimed he had been in a fight with someone else. The girlfriend stated the officer got out of his car and shot Brown without warning.

A questionable shooting involving a rookie cop, an unarmed man of color, and an uncooperative girlfriend set the table for a settlement by the city.

"I know enough," Morgan said.

"The rookie's getting a raw deal," Bynum said, his jaw set. "You met him?"

"Not yet."

Bynum inhaled deeply before saying, "He's my nephew."

"Yeah?" Morgan said, studying his sergeant. "Why didn't you tell anyone?"

The sergeant ticked his head to the side, the way people do when they try to pop a crick in their necks. "He didn't want anyone to know so he could make his bones on his own. I don't blame him. I wouldn't want to think I got preferential treatment because of my uncle. I'd want to know I made it because of what I did, not because someone else called in a favor."

Morgan saw it then. Bynum was upset, even though he was trying to keep it locked down.

"The county detectives are up his ass," the sergeant said, "and they've got that idiot Parker shadowing their investigation." Major Crimes Detective Andrew Parker was one half of the newest team in Major Crimes. "Like that little pissant is going to stick his neck out to make sure Sean is getting a fair shake."

"He's the SPD shadow," Morgan said. "He'll see everything the county does."

"Yeah," Bynum said, "but that doesn't mean he'll do anything about it."

"Listen, I know he's a prima donna—"

"He's an arrogant prick, is what he is."

"I agree, but that doesn't mean he won't go to the mat for your nephew."

Bynum smirked. "I doubt it."

"I don't get what you're asking, Ken."

"Nothing," Bynum said, dismissively waving his hand. "I guess I'm not asking anything."

Morgan shook his head. "Then why invite me out here?"

"To blow off some steam. I can't talk with the others about this."

The detective watched him.

"I want to help my nephew, but he doesn't want to talk with me. He's closed off. I don't know why. We used to be close, especially when he was younger. Now, I can't get through to him, and my sister, his mother, is driving me crazy with her worry. She's calling and texting me non-stop."

Morgan shoved his hands into his jeans. "You've been in a shooting, and you've been around others who have been. It messes with everyone differently."

The sergeant's eyes softened as his thoughts drifted off.

Morgan said, "You want me to introduce myself, maybe? Give him a pep talk or something?"

"Maybe. Yeah. I'd appreciate that. If you could let him know people are pulling for him, that kind of thing, maybe that would help. What do you think?"

"I'll see what I can do."

The sergeant looked away for a second, then turned back to the detective. "Keep this between us."

"Of course."

"I don't want the guys to think I'm getting soft."

Morgan clapped Bynum on the shoulder. "Too late. They already know. It happened the moment you put on the extra stripes."

Chapter 3

Morgan spent the rest of the morning in West Central, a section of Spokane disparagingly referred to as "The Zone" for years. One of Spokane's earliest neighborhoods became rundown and blighted after decades of political apathy and economic migration. The remaining inhabitants of West Central were a mixture of blue-collar workers, felons, and drug users. The old money had long ago fled this area.

Nevertheless, the allure of underappreciated value finally brought some of the rich back. Through gentrification and redevelopment, they reclaimed a sliver of this territory that ran along the bluff overlooking the Spokane River. A planned community had been constructed along its ridge, giving the latest inhabitants of The Zone superior views of the city, the one thing the poor previously owned that the wealthy truly envied.

Called Kendall Yards, this new multi-use development featured not only beautiful homes and townhouses but contained trendy restaurants and modern office buildings. It was a picturesque enclave made up of hipsters and empty nesters. When the shiny community popped up, it blocked the original West Central residents from seeing the stunning view from their homes, once again reminding them of their place on the economic pecking order.

Morgan thought Kendall Yards was like brushing only the front of your teeth. It might look nice from the outside, but there was still rot occurring from behind. He hated the new development and its inhabitants. Instead of diluting The Zone with actual citizens, they should have stayed in their South Hill or far north neighborhoods where they belonged. With new, happy faces moving about the West Central neighborhood, it made it harder for him and the other cops to do their jobs.

The detective pulled his Charger to the side of Broadway Avenue and got out. Across the street was a small concrete building that housed the unimaginatively named convenience store, Broadway Foods. From where he stood, Morgan could see the back of the Kendall Yards development.

He entered a dilapidated, four-story apartment building and pulled the door quietly closed behind him. The detective ascended the uncarpeted steps two at a time. There was no elevator to take, and he likely would have skipped it, anyway. The hallways smelled like stale cigarette smoke and rotting food.

On the fourth floor, Morgan walked to the end of its hallway. The white paint on the walls was yellowed from age, and the ceiling showed signs of repeated roof leaks. He stopped in front of a red door with chipped paint that revealed a white layer underneath. A brass seven hung upside down.

With the flat of his hand, the detective banged on the door.

"What?" a man yelled from inside.

"It's Morgan."

"Shit," the voice muttered. Behind the door, there was a sudden movement.

Morgan cocked his head and listened. Then he grabbed the doorknob and wiggled it—locked. He jerked on it in frustration.

"Laszlo, open up," the detective ordered.

More rustling occurred in the apartment. "Inna minute."

Irritated, Morgan kicked the bottom of the door. "Now, goddamnit!"

The movement inside continued, and the detective began silently counting.

One thousand one.

One thousand two.

One thou—

The door burst opened to reveal Laszlo Nagy, a skinny man with long, stringy hair. He was naked except for a pair of gray basketball shorts that fell past his knees. Tattoos of twin dragons covered his slightly concave chest. Nagy's greasy skin shined, and a waft of odor from the man caused Morgan's nose to crinkle.

"What were you hiding?" Morgan asked.

"What?"

The detective glared at Nagy.

"I wasn't hidin' nothin'."

Morgan put his hand on the man's chest and pushed him back into the apartment. Nagy did not resist, and the detective slammed the door closed after he entered. "Show me."

"I wasn't hidin' nothin'. I swear!"

Morgan's push became a shove, and Nagy backpedaled until his legs hit the edge of his bed, and he unwillingly sat. It was a studio apartment, so there weren't many places to hide anything.

The detective began opening and closing the cabinet doors above the kitchen sink. He jostled the various contents as he went.

"The longer I look, Laszlo, the more pissed I'm going to get. You know this."

"C'mon, Morgan. I didn't do nothin'. I was just getting dressed."

Morgan stopped and angrily pointed at Nagy. The nearly naked man stared back at him—a scolded child. Finally, Nagy broke eye contact and looked down.

The detective returned his attention to the cabinets. He picked up various boxes, shaking them as he went. He stopped when he held a box of Lucky Charms. Morgan turned to Nagy, who watched him with wide eyes. The detective smiled as he shook the almost empty box. There was a slight swishing of something inside.

Morgan swiped his arm across the kitchen counter, pushing dirty plates, bowls, and silverware into the sink with an annoying clatter. He opened the cereal box and tipped it upside down. A handful of small white packages dropped onto the counter.

Morgan tossed the box into the sink on top of the dirty dishes.

"What is this?" he asked and pointed to the small packages of powder. It was the demanding voice a pet owner would use with a dog that had just dirtied the carpet.

Nagy muttered something Morgan couldn't hear.

"What?" the detective snapped.

"Heroin," Nagy said louder.

The detective studied the white packages. Stamped on each one of them was a black fist. "I've never seen this logo before. Where did it come from?"

"Some guys."

"*Guys?*"

"Uh-huh."

Morgan pulled one of the packages from the counter and tucked it into the pocket of his jeans.

"Hey!" Nagy yelled.

"Every time you lie, you pay a tax."

"Fuck me, Morgan!"

"I can take them all away, Laszlo, and then book you. How about that? Do you like those rules better?"

Nagy frowned and looked away.

The detective snapped his fingers several times. "Let's try this again. Where did you get the witch?"

The skinny man threw his hands up in defeat. "The Turk, man. The Turk."

Morgan tapped a finger next to the white packets. "The Turk gave you this?"

"Yeah, man, but don't rat me out. Please, Morgan."

"The Turk is letting you sell?" He didn't bother to hide his disbelief—Nagy wasn't worth it. "I thought you were done as an earner."

"I'm doin' better, Morgan. Really."

The detective studied Nagy. The man was as skinny as he remembered. He didn't see any new marks on his arms, but perhaps he was injecting between his toes or behind his knees. Maybe he was even smoking the drug. He scanned the apartment for a drug kit. Not seeing it, the detective said, "Doesn't look like you're doing better, Laszlo. How much are you using?"

"Hardly any. Just a taste now and then."

"Right."

"I swear, Morgan." He held up an open hand. "I'm better. Scout's honor."

The detective put a finger on one of the packages.

"I swear to God! I ain't usin' like I did. I got it under control. Jesus, man, not another one. I gotta earn."

Morgan removed his finger. He needed Nagy to continue to talk, and if he put the man behind the eight-ball by taking too many packages, he'd never keep him as an informant. One package was all he could take right now. There would be other times to add to his supply.

"Heard any rumors about The Eight?"

"The what?"

Morgan placed his finger back on one of the small white packages.

"Shit, man! Don't. I swear I don't know what you're talking about."

The detective pulled his hand back from the counter. "Okay, Laszlo, relax. Listen, if you hear the words 'the eight' or 'hard eight' or anything even close to that, I want you to call me. Even if you're at a craps table, and somebody says those words, I want you to tell me. Got it?"

"Yeah, man, I got it," Nagy said. "Hard eight."

Morgan moved toward the door.

"Hey, Morgan?"

The detective looked back toward Nagy.

"You really takin' that package?"

Morgan smiled. "When have you ever known me not to collect a tax?"

Nagy lowered his head.

Chapter 4

Yaban Karga rented several apartments in a building at the corner of Monroe Street and Maxwell Avenue. One of his apartments overlooked the busy intersection. Over the years, Karga had become well-known to the police department, especially the officers that worked in the regional narcotics task force.

Morgan didn't know if those officers were actively watching the man, but it wasn't worth taking chances. They might even be tapping his residence and phone since Yaban Karga was the rare breed that all agencies loved to monitor. He was neither a big fish nor a guppy. Instead, he was the quintessential middleman. Therefore, every agency wanted to know with whom he was talking.

While coming up in the drug trade, the Turk was always reliable to Morgan for intel, but over the last handful of years, he'd become less and less trustworthy. Partially because Karga had grown smarter and more experienced. He knew what he needed to give to continue to play the game and what he could keep secret. Karga's days of usefulness were probably in the rearview mirror.

Morgan wanted to know about this new supplier of heroin, and he needed to go to the source. It could mean a new player in town. If the CTF could jump on them first, it would again prove their usefulness to the department.

For a moment, he thought about calling the team and asking them to join him but doing so would alert them not only to his relationship with Laszlo Nagy but to how he grabbed the heroin from the dealer. That would lead to further questions.

Were there more drugs?

Why didn't he arrest Nagy?

Why didn't he put the package of heroin into evidence?

All were questions he needed to avoid, especially since his team would not like the answers. However, his results spoke for themselves and, in his mind, that's the only thing that mattered.

Besides, he already had a legitimate reason to talk with Karga if anyone saw him with the man and later questioned him. The Eight was the cause de jour, and he only had to mention the name of the gang, and he could talk with anyone he liked.

He sat off Karga's apartment building for thirty minutes, thinking about these things, when the man himself came out. Karga wore red sweatpants with bright white Adidas tennis shoes. His wife-beater tank top revealed arm-sleeve tattoos that covered his olive-colored skin.

With him was a dark-haired woman in a hot pink T-shirt, black shorts, and high heels. She was rail thin.

In his left hand, Karga held two leashes that led to two white Pomeranians. He passed the leashes to the woman before he made a call on his cell phone. The two of them strolled down the block.

Morgan's car slowly left its parking spot. He circled the neighborhood until he saw them walking toward him. He pulled to the curb again and watched.

The woman's free arm swung wildly as the two little dogs tugged and strained against their leashes.

Karga, a barrel of a man, gesticulated as he talked on the phone. His face contorted, and it was apparent he wasn't happy with whoever was on the other end of the call.

Morgan slipped out of his car and waited, watching the two of them as they approached.

When Karga recognized the detective, he stopped, and he reached for the woman, grabbing her by the arm she used for balance. She wobbled for a moment, then angrily turned back toward him. Karga hung up the phone and said something to her.

She glanced toward Morgan. Karga yanked her and spoke again. She looked once more at the detective, irritated now, before stalking toward the apartment building. Her thin legs wobbled on the high heels as the little dogs pulled on their leashes.

The Turk began walking again, but this time his arms swung wildly in a show of great confidence. A smile spread across his face. "Detective, what a pleasant surprise I am greeted with today."

"Turn it off," Morgan ordered.

Karga looked at the phone in his hand. "It is off."

The detective leaned into his ear and whispered, "Power it off. The DEA is watching you. They might be able to listen through the device if it is on."

The Turk leaned back and studied Morgan's face. Finally, he decided on a course of action and powered off the phone. It played a little chime as it went to sleep.

"The DEA is watching me?"

"For some time," Morgan said. It was a lie, of course. "So is the regional drug task force," he added. This part wasn't a lie, but he figured the revelation about the more prominent agency would get the Turk's attention and his trust.

Karga glanced around, searching for men with cameras and listening devices. Finding none, he turned back to the detective. "So that's why you haven't come to parlay in months?"

"You're hot."

Yaban Karga watched the passing traffic as he thought. Finally, he faced Morgan and asked, "If I'm so hot, then why are you here?"

Morgan reached into his pocket and pulled out the small white packet with the stamped fist. "Who's passing this?"

The Turk eyed the packet, then looked down the street. "Where did you get that?"

"Does it matter?"

Karga twisted his lips as he thought. "Me," the Turk said finally. "It's mine."

"I know that, but whose brand is it?"

Karga turned back to him and looked him directly in the eye. "It's mine."

Morgan slipped the packet back into his pocket. "I don't understand."

"I put the stamp on it. What's to understand?"

"Why?"

"Marketing."

Morgan stared at Karga until the man smiled the way a teacher does before they share a lesson.

"Different brands, Detective. People think if something is different, they will like it because it is so. I put a fist on some of the packets, a wildflower on others, even a monkey on some. Inside, it is the same product from the same source. But the customer, they think it is all different."

"So, it's nothing?"

"It is not nothing, Detective. It is heroin. The same as it has always been."

"But the fist?"

"It is advertising," Karga said. "I stamp them, and I upsell the product. Do you know this term? *Upsell.* I'm already in the middle. My cut of the pie is very thin. This makes it a little more. All the big companies do it. Why shouldn't I?"

Morgan shoved his hands in his pockets. He was disappointed the fist turned out to be nothing. Unfortunately, that was often how police work was. Turning over stones in hopes of discovering something valuable but often finding nothing except worthless dirt. Still, maybe there was an opportunity to get something worthwhile. "Ever hear of The Eight?"

"An eight?"

"*The* Eight?" the detective said. "Like hard eight?"

"The forty-four at the craps table?" Karga mimed throwing a set of dice.

"The Eight is a gang."

Karga shrugged. "Then, no. I have not heard of this."

"Seems no one has." Morgan headed toward his car.

"Hey, Detective."

He stopped. "Yeah?"

"The DEA? They are really watching me?"

Morgan's face flattened. "Have I ever lied to you?"

Yaban Karga considered his phone for a moment. He then dropped it to the sidewalk and repeatedly stomped on it. Without another word, the man spun and hurried toward his apartment building.

The detective smiled, knowing he had thoroughly spooked the man.

Chapter 5

Shortly after five, Morgan returned to his two-bedroom apartment in north Spokane. The complex was built in the early nineties and had, for the time, been wonderfully cutting edge. There was an indoor swimming pool for the winter months and one outdoors for the short summer period the area was known to experience. Both pools had attached hot tubs, which Morgan still referred to as Jacuzzis. The community's weight room was equipped with universal equipment and free weights, along with treadmills and elliptical machines.

He moved into the apartment community while he was a patrol officer. There was never a need to move again. Even as newer apartment communities were constructed in the area, the ownership group behind his complex continued maintaining all the amenities he enjoyed.

The door to his garage slowly rolled up, and he pulled in.

The police department had seized the late model Dodge Charger Daytona he drove following an arrest of a cocaine dealer. He loved the seizure law and how it helped fund his unit to go after the criminals that it stripped of their assets. It was a wonderfully ironic cycle.

A recent Supreme Court ruling would likely change how the department could apply seizure laws. Morgan might spend time reflecting on how the highest judges in the land always fucked up the system if the idea wasn't one he had made peace with long ago. Instead, he now took it as a fact that Supreme Court judges, regardless of their political affiliation, were working against the law enforcement community, so he no longer spent much time ruminating on it. That wasn't even taking into consideration his absolute loathing of the Ninth Circuit Court of Appeals. As far as he was concerned, those liberal bastards were downright handing the country to the criminals.

After he climbed out of the car and left the garage, Morgan started the door down.

He'd driven a series of cars the department had seized over the years. Many of them were fancy, tricked out rigs, but none of them held a candle to the Charger's Daytona series. Black exterior with black leather interior. Three hundred seventy horsepower HEMI V8 engine. The beast roared when it came to life. It practically jumped out of its glossy paint whenever he pressed the accelerator. He loved the car.

As he walked toward his apartment, Morgan eyed the civilian ride he parked in the lot in front of his building. It was what he was supposed to drive when he wasn't working. It was a 1987 4x4 Chevy pickup with a faded blue and white paint job. There was a new engine under the hood and a beefed-up suspension. She wasn't much to look at, but that was the point—he didn't want anyone looking at the truck. The damn thing ran like a champ when asked, and she never complained when he treated her roughly.

He lived on the third floor of Building B. After tossing his keys into a bowl near the front door, he took off his jacket and hung it in the closet. He continued into the kitchen, where he removed his gun and holster from his belt and placed them on the counter. With a tug, he pulled his badge free from the belt and tossed it on the countertop. It skittered until it hit the coffeemaker.

Morgan grabbed a beer from the refrigerator and walked onto his balcony. He looked down at the swimming pool, which was full of people trying to catch the last bit of evening sun. There was an eclectic mix of men and women, young and old, in and out of shape. For most, it only mattered that there was a pool, the sun, and some energetic pop music.

Three young women in tiny bikinis waved up at him. They looked like a Benetton advertisement, each carefully selected for this moment of friendship. The rainbow was black, white, and brown. Each had a red plastic cup in their hands.

"Hi, Jimmy!" the redhead called. She was pale and curvy, the type that was pleasing to the eye and, Morgan suspected, would be pleasant to the touch.

What was her name? He struggled to remember.

The women had recently moved into the complex and shared a three-bedroom unit. He had met them at a party thrown by his friend, Vivian. They weren't part of Viv's inner circle, and he suspected they would never be asked into that group. They were recent graduates from Eastern Washington University. He remembered that much. That type of girl wouldn't need what Vivian could offer, so they were only at her party as neighbors.

He waved back.

"Come and join us," the redhead called.

"In a bit," he said.

"Promise?" she hollered.

"No," Morgan said.

She laughed along with her friends.

The summer pool was one of the main reasons he loved his apartment. Although, he had to admit, he loved it less with each passing year.

Morgan stepped back into his unit and sipped his beer.

When he first moved in, he was in his late twenties. Now, he was fifty-one. He'd lived in the same apartment community for over twenty-two years.

He had moved a few times within the complex until he got the exact apartment he wanted, the one overlooking the pool. Several times, when his lease came up for renewal, he negotiated new paint or new carpet. Once he even got new kitchen cabinets. The owners knew he was a good renter. He always paid on time, and he rarely complained.

Over the years, he made friends with plenty of women who lived in the apartment community. Morgan wasn't the type to hang out in bars or go on dates. That wasn't his personality. He liked women, of course, but he enjoyed chasing criminals more. Women were a pleasant diversion, and the apartment community was a convenient place to meet them.

Initially, many of them wanted to make Morgan into something he never saw himself being—a boyfriend, or worse, a husband. He knew in his gut he would never be that guy.

Therefore, the pools, both outdoor and indoor, and the community weight room proved to be a good meeting place for Morgan. There was the occasional hook-up that sometimes grew into something less than boyfriend status but something more than casual. He liked those girls, but they were becoming fewer the older he became.

For a moment, he thought about grabbing his swimsuit and going down to chat up the redhead. Her pleasant paleness lingered in his memory. He was old enough to be her father, but that didn't seem to bother her.

His cell phone buzzed in his pocket. He pulled it free and looked at the screen. The phone number with the 509-

area code was one he hadn't seen before. Even so, he answered the call.

"Morgan," he said.

"Mr. Morgan?" The man's voice was timid.

"Who is this?"

"Mr. Morgan, my name is Desmond Ashdown. I've got a problem. I was told you could help."

Morgan pulled the phone away from his ear and looked at the number again. No one had given him advanced warning about sharing his number. He shook his head and returned the phone to his ear.

"How'd you get this number?"

"Michael Crocker, sir. He gave it to me. He said you helped him once."

Morgan closed his eyes and pinched his nose. *Crocker.*

"Are you still there, Mr. Morgan?"

"What do you want?"

"I… I'm being blackmailed, sir."

"File a police report."

"Well… Mr. Crocker, sir."

"What about Crocker?"

"He explained how you helped him. He said you could do the same for me."

Morgan opened his eyes. He would have to talk with Crocker about this.

"When can you meet?" Morgan asked.

"Tomorrow?" Ashdown suggested. "Lunch?"

Morgan thought about it for a moment. "Fine. Text me someplace. Make it downtown." As an afterthought, he added, "And expensive."

"Yes, sir, I understand," he said. His voice sounded small and gloomy.

"What's wrong, Ashdown?"

"It's nothing. It's just— I hoped I would feel better after talking with you."

"We haven't done anything."

"Well, no, we haven't, have we? It's silly to think I would feel better after a call."

"Yes," Morgan said. "That would be very *silly*." He hated the word silly.

Silence overtook the conversation until Ashdown said, "I will text you a location for lunch."

"Right," he said and hung up.

***

Morgan was startled awake when his phone buzzed. He'd fallen asleep in his chair.

After the phone call with Desmond Ashdown, he decided against grabbing his swimsuit and further making the acquaintance of the curvy redhead. Instead, he drank another beer and started a book about the Viet Nam war. He'd read it before, so it didn't take much for him to lose interest and drift into sleep. When he awoke, the book fell from his lap onto the floor.

He checked the screen before answering.

"Morgan," he groggily mumbled.

"Did I wake you?" she asked.

"No."

"Sounds like I woke you."

"I fell asleep in my chair."

"It's not even nine yet," she teased.

"I work weird hours."

"Who doesn't?"

Morgan grunted. "What can I do for you, Viv?"

"I need a favor."

Everyone was asking for favors lately, but Vivian wasn't the type to do that. She had asked Morgan to do various things, but she never asked for them as a favor. That was not her style. There was never the hint she would give anything in return. Morgan would have noticed that. Her asking for a favor immediately piqued his interest.

"There's someone I'd like you to meet, Jimmy. I'd like you to talk with her. Maybe give her some advice."

Morgan pushed down on the footrest and snapped his recliner into the upright position. "Gimme a few minutes. I'll be over."

He stumbled into the bathroom and splashed cold water onto his face. Then he combed his hair. His drill instructors would be disappointed in how long he'd let his hair grow, but it was part of the CTF job. It was now collar length and wavy.

If it wasn't for his face, he might resemble a character from a Hallmark movie or a romance book cover. It was thick and angled at the cheeks and chin. He bore more than a passing resemblance to several Russian statues, which was funny since he had no Eastern European blood in his veins.

A couple of women in his past had politely commented he was handsome, but most women said he looked strong. He liked that women saw him that way. One woman described his look as brutish, which surprised him since she seemed particularly fond of his face. They had a brief but complicated relationship.

He quickly brushed his teeth. Afterward, he ran his tongue over the front of them to feel that they were clean.

Morgan checked himself once more in the mirror. He was under no illusions about himself. Over the years, Morgan had lost a step and gained a couple of pounds. He tried to keep himself in shape, but time was the enemy. It was a game everyone eventually lost.

He flicked off the bathroom light as he left.

***

Vivian Basler lived across the apartment community in Building D, although she had a three-bedroom townhouse where her garage sat below her unit. Morgan first met Vivian several years before while swimming one evening in the indoor pool. They struck up an easy conversation that continued for a couple of hours.

She was in her late thirties when they first met and had recently celebrated her fortieth birthday. She still looked great in a swimsuit, and she was always put together no matter the time of day.

He knocked once, and the door opened.

Vivian wore a black blouse, white shorts, and white sandals. She was a tall woman, standing almost eye-to-eye with Morgan. Her long legs were perfectly tanned even though Morgan never once saw her at the outdoor pool. Vivian's blond hair, once long and flowing, had been cut short about six months ago.

Morgan's blood raced every time he saw her.

"Jimmy," she said and extended her manicured hand. She was the one who had started calling him 'Jimmy' around the complex, and it stuck. Nowhere else in the world would anyone else be allowed to call him that.

He touched her hand, and she pulled him in, kissing him lightly on the cheek.

That was the most affection he ever received from her. As much as he wanted, she had never gone further than a simple peck on the cheek. She would flirt, tease, and insinuate, but Vivian had never crossed a line with him. It killed Morgan that he hadn't been with her, but he never wanted it to change.

It was the perfect relationship—the never-ending chase—and he thought he might actually love Vivian for it. He often wondered if she knew what she did to him.

With her face near his, she sniffed him once. "You cleaned up before coming over."

"What?" he said, slightly embarrassed.

Her hand caressed his cheek. "Come inside. I want you to meet someone."

Morgan stepped into her apartment then. There was no television in her living room—only a couch and a couple of chairs. Plants of various sizes stood in the corners. Paintings hung on the wall. Soft jazz music played through a single wireless speaker. On the coffee table, a scented candle burned.

He couldn't place the aroma, but it smelled nice—the way a woman's place should.

Two glasses of red wine were on the table.

A smaller woman in her mid-twenties sat on the couch. Her long, light-brown hair cascaded over her left shoulder. She wore a white spaghetti-strap blouse and denim shorts. Her pale legs were tucked underneath her, and a pair of black flip-flops were on the floor.

"Jimmy," Vivian said, "this is Bambi."

"Bambi?" Morgan's eyes flicked back to Vivian, whose eyes remained on the younger girl. "Really?"

"Doesn't she look like a sweet little doe?"

"What's your real name?" Morgan asked.

"Leigh Gaston. Vivian thinks I should go by Bambi."

Vivian patted Leigh's leg. "She has some trouble, Jimmy. I'm hoping you can help her with it."

Morgan shoved his hands into his pockets and studied the girl. It was then he noticed the distinct darkness on the left side of her face. It had been lessened by make-up, but it was there. Morgan had seen the telltale signs of domestic abuse his entire career as a police officer, more than that if he counted what his father did to his mother.

"Who's your trouble?" Morgan asked.

"My boyfriend."

Morgan cocked his head. "Is he upset with you for wanting to work?"

Leigh glanced at Vivian, who said, "Tell him, honey. He knows."

When Leigh turned back to Morgan, she said, "I used to dance. That's how we met. He came into the club, worked his charms, and we went out. He made me stop dancing after that. I was good at it and supported myself. Now, I don't get to do that. He makes me sit around and wait on him. I don't like that. I want to do the webcams."

"With Vivian?" Morgan asked.

Leigh looked at Vivian again. "We met through a friend who told me about her. I figured I could get in on it, and it would be safer than dancing."

For years, Vivian had run a profitable internet business that started from her apartment. Initially, it was a single camera in one of her bedrooms. Then she rented another apartment in a nearby community and put a couple of girls in there, again with a room and dedicated cameras. Vivian was up to five units and fifteen girls. She was the online version of a madam. Her girls made virtual dates with men who paid by the minute.

When she first told him, Morgan thought Vivian was joking until she showed him one of the apartments. Vivian no longer performed on camera, preferring to set up her girls and work behind the scenes.

Morgan looked at Vivian. "She's outside your type."

"She's pretty, though."

Most of Vivian's girls had ethnic backgrounds—Eastern European, Eastern Asia, or Central American. They were girls who needed money and whose families weren't local or had trouble accessing the internet.

"I told him what I wanted to do, and he hit me," Leigh said. She carefully touched the side of her face. "I told him I would be by myself. Nobody would ever touch me, but he didn't care."

"I don't handle domestic disputes," Morgan said.

Vivian stood and moved toward him. "Would you intervene, Jimmy? For me?"

"And do what? Ask her boyfriend to back off so she can be on camera? Most guys wouldn't accept that." Morgan turned to Leigh. "Why not break-up and move on?"

"Because he's scary," Leigh said. "And he knows if I do this, I'm one step closer to getting free. Right now, I've got no job, no way to earn for myself. I'm dependent on him."

A new song started through the speaker. It was a low, moaning number filled with a saxophone player's angst. It irritated Morgan almost immediately since he generally disliked music.

"Listen," he said. "Get your shit together before you start doing this. It's not going to get better unless you leave. Go back to your family if you need help."

"I don't have family," she said.

"I'm not community outreach."

"Jimmy," Vivian said. He didn't know the last time somebody filled his name with so much disappointment.

"I'm sorry, Viv."

He turned and walked toward the front door.

"He's got a warrant," Leigh quickly added.

Morgan turned around. "Yeah?" Most dirtballs had warrants for chippy reasons, such as failing to appear in court following a traffic violation. The warrants weren't worth the paper they were written on. "For what?"

"Assaulting a cop."

Morgan frowned. "Your boyfriend assaulted an officer?"

"Uh-huh."

"What's his name?"

"Dontari Brown."

"Your boyfriend is Dontari Brown? He's with the Dead Boys, right?"

She nodded slowly.

And the brother of Tremaine Brown.

Morgan looked at Vivian. "The gang her boyfriend runs with is bad news. You'll find yourself in a mess of trouble if he gets wind of this. Dontari's not known for an ability to regulate his temper."

"I'm not worried," Vivian said. "I know a cop."

Morgan smirked. He turned to Leigh and said, "If he's got a warrant, I'll talk to him."

A look of relief spread across Leigh's face. Even Vivian looked reassured.

"I said *if* he's got a warrant. If he doesn't, I'm staying out of it, and you're on your own."

"He's got a warrant," Leigh said, her voice soft. "He's fully aware of it." Her eyes held no joy in revealing her boyfriend's trouble.

"Thank you, Jimmy," Vivian said. "I'll owe you one."

"Why's this so important that you'd ask for a favor?" Morgan asked.

Vivian slid her hand into Leigh's. "Can't you see this one is going to be special?"

Chapter 6

"What's wrong with you?" Nayla Senai asked.

Morgan and Senai walked along East Sprague Avenue. After breaking from that morning's debriefing, they decided to work this corridor to see if they could shake anything loose on The Eight. Even though he believed they were unlikely to find anything down here, Morgan didn't discount what could be learned in this corridor. Word had an odd way of traveling through the whisper stream.

There was an eight-block run from Helena Street to Altamont Street that, for decades, had been a mecca for pushers and prostitutes and a magnet for junkies and johns. Even though the same magnetic pull always drew cops, the black-market activity never entirely stopped. Even this morning—it was shortly after nine—the drug dealers and working girls were already out. They were in dramatically fewer numbers than yesteryear, though.

"Was I doing something?" Morgan asked.

"You were frowning."

Morgan grunted. "I was thinking about this neighborhood."

"It's turning around," Senai said. "Getting better."

"I guess," the detective said.

The East Sprague area had improved over the past decade after real estate investors and community reformers took an interest in it. Aging brick buildings were upgraded so trendy restaurants could invade the neighborhood. It was as if a parasite attached itself to a host, and the host had become better for it.

Several architecturally attractive apartment buildings sprouted up along Sprague Avenue. These modern structures housed a low-income population, a reminder of East Sprague's true lineation, and provided a shiny anchor that would hold the area back from genuinely improving.

That was fine with Morgan, as he hated progression toward the new. He wanted old and decrepit buildings to remain as they were. He liked this area being a haven for criminals and their ilk. If they didn't have a place to congregate and ply their trade, where would they go but into the neighborhoods of real citizens?

Politicians and developers didn't think that way, though. They spent their time in a fantasy world, in a dream of make-believe, where everyone could get along, and no one ever got hurt. Those people were foolish, and their choices only led to more stupidity and unfortunate incidents that some cop would eventually have to clean up.

Morgan kept his opinions to himself. Most people would think them the ramblings of an older man, a curmudgeon perhaps. He felt his musings were more than that, though. He thought he saw the world for what it should be—part beautiful, part ugly. Most people didn't want the ugly to co-exist with beauty. They hated ugliness and tried to hide it away, to extinguish it. Their fear of the ugly was a reminder of who they were or who they might be. Beauty was the mask the world put on for others to see.

Beauty was fake. Ugliness was real.

"There you go again," Senai said. "Another frown."

Morgan forced a smile. "Stop looking at me."

He saw her then, standing near a bus stop. She was a thin woman in tight jeans and a white sleeveless blouse.

"Damn it," Morgan muttered.

"What?" Senai asked, her voice low, and her eyes alert.

They approached the woman, who turned to face the detectives. By the look in her eyes, she was unafraid. "Aww, what, Morgan?" she said. "I ain't doing nothing."

Her hair was stringy and unwashed. She wore little make-up, not bothering to hide who she was to the world. When she spoke, it revealed a yellow tooth in the front of her mouth.

"Liliya Scrimshaw," Morgan said, "meet Detective Senai. Nayla, this is Scrimmy."

Scrimmy inhaled on her cigarette as she studied Senai, then turned her head and exhaled. "It's too early for this bullshit."

"I thought you made it out, Scrimmy. Moved to Montana and such."

"Clean is boring." Her eyes bounced as she spoke.

"Using again?" Morgan asked.

The woman quietly chuckled. "Did the sun come up this morning?"

"Got anything on you?" the detective asked.

Scrimmy tilted her head. "Why? You looking for a score?"

Morgan slowly glanced at Senai.

The prostitute continued. "No, I don't have anything on me. I'm not stupid. If you didn't take it, someone else would."

"Your pimp let you back in the fold?" Morgan asked.

"He took it out on me," she said, then inhaled on her cigarette. Smoke escaped from her mouth as she spoke. "But I could handle it. He's not the first man to lay a hand on me."

As Senai studied the surrounding area—presumably scanning for threats and opportunities—Morgan moved closer to Scrimmy. He could smell her then, that funk of someone who hadn't washed in several days. "What do you know about The Eight?"

She took a final inhale on her cigarette, dropped it to the sidewalk, and crushed it out with her shoe. "Why are you bothering me with this shit?"

"Because no one else is talking."

Scrimmy glanced at Senai, then to Morgan. The jerk of her head was barely perceptible.

Morgan turned to his partner, whose attention was focused on two men across the street. They were leaned in close as they spoke with each other. "Nayla."

"Hmm?"

Morgan lifted his chin toward the opposite end of the block. Senai's eyes shifted suspiciously to Scrimmy for a moment. When her gaze returned to Morgan, she nodded once before walking away.

The detective looked back at the woman. "It's just you and me now. What have you got?"

"You holding?" she whispered.

"For the right info."

Her eyes bounced uncontrollably, and she looked at the drivers of several passing cars before she spoke. "Over near Magnolia and Pacific. There's a house. The second one in. Got a flag hanging in the window."

"So?"

"It's not right," Scrimmy said.

"How do you mean?"

"New players have moved in. They're clearly in a gang, but they're not claiming. That's not normal, not in this neighborhood."

"No colors?"

"No colors, and they keep to themselves. Understand? They're driving old people's cars. Nothing flashy. They're not making themselves known, trying to fly under the radar. Sounds strange, doesn't it? I mean, real hinky."

Morgan thought about what she said. "Maybe it's a bunch of guys living together, working normal jobs, trying to get ahead."

Scrimmy smirked, rolled her eyes, then looked away. "Okay, Morgan. Sure. That's what it is. You're welcome for the information, by the way."

She returned to watching passing cars, trying to make eye contact with the drivers. If she was concerned about Morgan's presence, she was doing an excellent job of disguising it.

"Why are you talking to me, Scrimmy?"

She eyed him. "How do you mean?"

"We haven't gotten boo about them, but you... you come right out and tell me something like this."

The prostitute looked down at her feet. Her voice was barely audible. "I figure I owe you something for getting the man that did Rado."

Morgan nodded.

Scrimmy looked up. "Too bad you didn't kill him, though."

"He's serving life in Walla Walla."

"He got life. Rado got death. Doesn't seem fair."

"No," the detective said. "It doesn't."

Morgan shoved a hand into his pocket and glanced back toward Senai. She was on the opposite street corner, talking with a short Hispanic man. The detective pulled his hand free and shook Scrimmy's hand.

"You take care, sister. I'm glad you're okay, but I'm not happy you're back."

Scrimmy locked eyes with Morgan.

When he released her hand, she quickly made a fist around the little packet of white powder he'd taken from Laszlo Nagy.

Morgan turned and headed toward Senai.

***

The house was as Scrimmy described. Two houses in from the corner of Magnolia Street on Pacific Avenue. It was faded yellow with dirty white accents. The roof was in desperate need of replacement as many shingles were missing, and those that remained were curling at the edges in an attempt to escape from the house.

The railing had fallen from the porch, and a worn brown couch sat near the front door. Behind the outdoor sofa, in the front window, was a white flag. In its center was a black fist.

When he saw the flag, Morgan's pulse raced. He'd just given away the packet of heroin with the stamped fist. He wanted another look at the emblem on it.

Was it the same?

It looked similar, but he couldn't be sure. Maybe it was just his mind playing tricks on him, wanting to make a connection.

Maybe he could return to Sprague Avenue and find Scrimmy. He'd have to explain to Senai what he was doing.

Or he could talk with Karga again. After some consideration, he decided that's what he wanted to do. It wasn't like the man to lie to him. Once upon a time, they had a relationship built on trust, although Morgan knew one thing to be true—criminals lie. Even when you think they're dealing with you straight, they're still lying.

"You're frowning again," Senai said.

"Stop it," Morgan muttered.

With it settled that Karga had probably lied to him, Morgan pushed it to the rear of his brain and looked around.

It was almost ten in the morning, and the neighborhood was quiet. The two detectives were parked a couple of houses away in Morgan's car.

"The girl said this was an Eight house?" Senai asked.

"She only said it seemed suspicious."

Senai's head swiveled about. "What makes it any more suspicious than its neighbors? A flag with a black fist? Many houses in this neighborhood have flags in them."

It was then Morgan noticed the four houses around this one each had a flag hanging in its window. There was a blue Seahawks flag, a purple University of Washington flag, a black flag with the Chevy logo, and a red Tabasco flag. If it was a flag thing, the little yellow house didn't seem particularly suspicious.

"Could she have played you?" Senai asked.

"No," Morgan said, slowly shaking his head. "Not Scrimmy."

Senai studied Morgan. "If you say so."

Morgan's phone buzzed once. He pulled it out and read a text message.

CLINKERDAGGER'S AT NOON – DESMOND ASHDOWN.

He silenced the phone and returned his attention to the little yellow house. There were three cars associated with it. A 2002 white Buick LeSabre sat in the small driveway while a 2010 Chevy Impala and a 2008 Ford Taurus were parked in front.

"Not exactly gangster cars," he muttered.

"What does a gangster drive?" Senai asked.

"None of those," Morgan said. "Call radio and run the plates."

Senai reached for the in-car microphone, but Morgan held out his hand to stop her. "Do it on your phone, just in case someone's scanning."

She nodded and called dispatch on her cell phone.

Morgan's thoughts drifted while he listened to Senai recite the license plate numbers. It was a beautiful summer morning, and he was doing what he loved most—hunting bad guys. That's precisely how he thought about it, too. They were bad, and he was good. He also liked the term "hunting." His team hunted for the evil in society to cull it from the herd.

If the bleeding hearts didn't like that way of thinking, well… fuck them. They could live with the bad then, for him and his city would have clean streets if he had any say in the matter. Morgan realized he was going down a rabbit hole in his mind and needed to stop spiraling. He climbed back out and focused on the flag with the fist.

Did the black fist on a white background mean Black Lives Matter? Or was that the reverse? Didn't the white nationalists have a flag very similar to this? He would have to look that up.

When Senai quit speaking, Morgan turned his attention to her.

"All three cars were sold recently, within the last thirty days."

"And?" Morgan asked.

"None of them have been registered to the new owners."

"Figures."

Morgan knew it was a common tactic among criminals not to register the purchase of a car immediately. The state required a record of sale be fully completed and sent to the Department of Licensing within ten days. Had a criminal bought the vehicle at a car lot, then a salesperson would have walked them through the process, not letting them leave with the car until everything was properly signed and dated. Even the shady lots did that to cover their asses. However, in a private person-to-person transaction, the buyer and seller were only required to complete their side of the paperwork and send that to the state. Not doing so could result in a fine.

Whoop-de-doo, thought Morgan, a fine. How motivating is that to someone engaged in a felonious activity?

The detectives sat off the house for another twenty minutes, but there was still no movement. Morgan grabbed his cell phone, called up a contact, and sent a text message. He shoved the phone back into his pocket and started the engine.

"Giving up?" Senai asked.

"No," he said. "We've got other things to do."

Chapter 7

They headed toward a part of town known as East Central, which was just on the other side of the freeway. It was an area he once disparagingly referred to as Little Africa. That was before Nayla Senai was on his team. She helped clean up the last bit of lazy thinking on the subject.

He would never openly admit it, but Morgan knew exactly where those feelings about the area emanated. They weren't from his time in the department, and they weren't from his time in the Corps. They had been instilled courtesy of his father and his grandfather. Those two men practically preached to young James Morgan the idea that other races were stealing their country, their jobs, and their women. And women, well, they were supposed to be subservient as the bible had intended.

As an adult, Morgan no longer believed any of that nonsense, but he'd been indoctrinated into the hatred during childhood.

The Corps stripped away most of those beliefs by showing him that he was no better or worse than the man next to him. As long as everyone stood together, shoulder-to-shoulder, and worked as a unit, Marines could accomplish damn near anything. The Corps was made up of all races, and the color of your skin didn't matter for shit when bullets started flying from downrange. The enemy hoped to kill you for one simple truth—you were an American. If you wanted to get home standing up, Morgan knew you believed in each other, or you bled the same colored blood.

The Spokane Police Department was much less diversified than The Corps, but the same dynamic existed.

There were the cops and the bad guys, and when something jumped off, the only color that mattered was blue. The only real division was between the job's two pronounced personality types—the meat-eaters and the cake-eaters. Now, these groups demanded discrimination.

Meat-eaters were men and women who humped daily to catch those who did evil and tossed them into the cages where they belonged—cops like him.

Cake-eaters, on the other hand, were those officers who clicked off days until retirement, or the next promotion test, or vacation, or whatever excuse they could find to avoid doing real police work. And cake-eaters found a lot of reasons not to work.

Morgan had no problem discriminating against cake-eaters, regardless of race, gender, or sexual preference. For him, they were as bad as a criminal, for they stole money from the police department that could otherwise go to a good cop, a cop that could make a difference.

Like Detective Nayla Senai—she was a meat-eater.

"Where are we headed?" Senai asked.

"We're running an errand."

She glanced at him. "An errand? That's cryptic."

Morgan looked in the rearview mirror as he signaled a lane change.

"I don't like it when you take me on your errands. I never know if we're going to get into the shit, or if you're going to do something that I'll have to lie about later."

"I'll never put you in a position where you have to lie."

Her eyes slid to him.

"I'm serious, Nayla," he said. "Never lie. Always tell the truth."

She didn't respond but only looked out her window.

He headed northbound on Altamont Street for several blocks before turning eastbound on Hartson Avenue. He parked his car along the curb. He pointed to a brown California-split, where the entrance to the house immediately divided with stairs going up to an upper level and down to a lower level.

"Dontari Brown," Morgan said, "lives in that house."

"Tremaine Brown's brother?" Senai asked.

"He's got an open warrant. I confirmed it this morning."

Senai studied the house. "What's the warrant for?"

"Third Assault."

"He assaulted an officer? And it's just us going after him?"

Morgan checked his rearview mirror. "I'm more careful than that."

A 2001 GMC Yukon Denali pulled up behind them. Nayla looked over her shoulder. "The boys," she muttered, then spun in her seat and was out of the car. Morgan was quick to follow suit.

Courtney Earley's massive frame slid from behind the wheel of the dented burgundy SUV. When he stood upright, he ran a hand through his long hair, then stroked his beard. His black heavy metal T-shirt read *Disturbed*.

Exiting the passenger seat was Adrian Thorn. He wore another faded mechanic's shirt, discoloration showing where the missing nametag had previously been. His jeans appeared to be the same grease-covered pair he wore yesterday. Ray-Ban sunglasses covered his eyes.

From the back seat, Jeremiah Strange was the last to slip out. He was put together better than the previous day, wearing a black tracksuit and white Adidas shoes. Morgan knew from experience that Doc would have his gun in a shoulder rig tucked under his left arm. Strange appeared calm, so much so that Morgan looked at him twice.

Strange noticed the double-take and squinted at Morgan.

Earley asked, "What's the target, Hoss?"

"Over my shoulder. Brown California-split. Dontari Brown lives there."

"Dead Boy Don?" Thorn asked.

"The same."

Thorn continued, "You think it's wise to screw with Tremaine Brown's brother while we got one of ours being investigated for an officer-involved? Might be seen as payback, especially if something goes wrong."

"Yeah," Strange chimed in, "aren't we focused on The Eight?"

"Brown has a warrant for assaulting an officer," Morgan said. "It's been confirmed."

The members of the team looked at one another.

"I don't think he should get a pass just because of his brother," Morgan said. "I mean, if you pussies want to let him walk around free, then I'll—"

"Stop it," Senai said, shaking her head. "We're in."

The guys nodded in agreement.

"All right," Morgan said, "Nayla and I will take the front door. You three take the back."

"We're always in back," Strange stated.

Morgan studied the man. "You want to do it differently, Doc?"

"We'll take the front," Strange said. "We want the action."

"Fine. You guys quarterback the play."

Without further words, the trio started toward the front of the house, not waiting for a plan of action. Morgan reached out and grabbed Strange by the arm, stopping him as the other two continued.

"Hey, man," Morgan said, "You okay?"

"What?" Strange asked.

"Are you high?"

Strange's eyes focused then, and his face twisted in anger. "You fucking with me? It's called being in character." He yanked his arm free from the detective's grip. He then ran toward his teammates.

Morgan and Senai shared a glance, then trotted behind the three men. As they neared the house, the two of them broke off and moved to the rear of the house. Morgan quickly assessed the layout.

There was a sliding glass door onto an elevated deck. The stairs from the deck ran along the back of the house. There was no fence surrounding the yard. If Brown decided to run, he could either head directly toward the alley or run around the house to the front.

"Go to the other side," Morgan said.

Senai nodded and quietly moved across the rear of the house. Just as she took up her position, there was a loud knocking at the front door that sounded like several booms. Morgan mused Earley must have used the flat of his fist against the door since he was the one who hollered, "Spokane Police Department! Come to the door!"

In a moment, the sliding glass door quietly opened, and Dontari Brown appeared on the deck. He wore black jeans and white sneakers, but he was bare-chested. His head swiveled as he scanned the area. He quietly hurried down the stairs.

There was more banging at the front door.

Senai stepped out from behind her cover, her gun in hand. "Stop," she ordered. "Police."

When Brown landed on the ground, he ignored Senai's command and sprinted toward the alley. Since he was unarmed, Senai couldn't shoot.

The chase was on, and Morgan raced after the man.

From the front of the house, several more booms were heard, and Earley once again yelled, "Spokane Police! Come to the door!"

Brown made it to the alley and had several steps on Morgan, but the detective wasn't worried. He knew how to chase a man—keep the runner in sight and let them tire themselves out due to their lack of training and experience with adrenaline. However, Brown appeared to have the stamina to keep the pursuit on for some time. The man ran like he'd been trained to run at some point in his life, maybe in high school.

They soon exited the block, crossed the street, and entered another alley. Morgan's heart pounded in his chest, and he felt a sense of bliss rising.

The chase thrilled him. He didn't want it to be easy, and he didn't want it to be fast. Part of the joy in moments like this was pitting himself against another man and coming out the victor. The pain working its way through his body was oddly comforting now. He wanted to holler in joy. At this moment, Morgan was truly happy.

It occurred so fast he struggled to comprehend what had happened. He hadn't sensed her nor heard her. Suddenly, Senai was at his shoulder, with her eyes focused on Brown. She smoothly pulled by him. Her long legs strode in synchronization with her arms. It looked like perfect motion.

The joy Morgan felt was abruptly lost in the competition with a fellow officer. Instead of just keeping

Brown in view, he pushed himself harder than he needed so Senai would not beat him.

As they ran another block, Morgan's pace became erratic, and he struggled for breath. Abruptly, a stab of pain hit him in his side. He didn't stop running as he knew the pain wasn't fatal, but it hurt considerably and slowed him further.

Senai, though, remained a graceful leopard on the hunt. She continued to gain ground on Brown, who now struggled to keep his own pace. When she drew close to her quarry, Senai shoved the man in the back. The extra momentum caused Brown to stumble. His arms wildly wind-milled until he tripped and fell in the alley, his body rolling and tumbling to a stop. Senai leaped on him then, a big cat finally subduing her prey.

Morgan slowed to a jog and watched the woman control Brown, who no longer had any fight in him. All his energy had been exhausted during the chase. The man lay limp and panting as Senai put her knee onto his upper back as she handcuffed him.

The detective stopped and sucked deep breaths of air.

Senai grinned as she stood. "What happened to you? It was like you were standing still back there."

Morgan bent over at the hips. In between gulps of air, he rasped, "Careful, girly. Time is coming for you, too."

Chapter 8

Morgan entered the restaurant and waited for the hostess to acknowledge him.

After catching Dontari Brown, Morgan had called for a patrol car to transport the man to jail. Morgan told Senai to ride back to the station with the rest of the team.

"Why can't I go with you?" she asked.

"Because I've got a guy to meet."

"What guy?" she asked.

"A guy," he said, dropping into the Charger and driving away. He didn't wait for her to protest.

Located in a converted flour mill, Clinkerdagger's sits at the edge of downtown with a view of the Spokane River. The building had been shuttered in 1972 and redeveloped into a shopping center in preparation for 1974's International EXPO.

After identifying who he was meeting to the hostess, she escorted him to a table on the patio—outside afforded the patrons an unobstructed view of the river. After winter's runoff, it would roar with intensity. Now, in late summer, the river ran softly in the background.

Desmond Ashdown stood to greet Morgan. He was in his mid-forties and wore a tailored blue suit that hung nicely from broad shoulders. Its style and cut showed a man who was in shape and proud of how he looked. He had a banker's haircut and a salesman's smile. When he shook Morgan's hand, his grip was firm. The voice over the phone lied about his stature. "Desmond Ashdown," he said.

Morgan pulled back a chair and sat.

Ashdown, apparently still waiting for Morgan to introduce himself, seemed caught off guard. He looked around at the others on the patio, noticed none of them were looking at him, and sat.

"How do you know Crocker?" the detective asked.

"Michael?"

Not bothering to answer, Morgan simply stared at him.

"We belong to the club."

"The club?"

"The Spokane Club."

It figured Crocker would be a member of the private club for the area's wealthy and politically connected, but the way Ashdown said it irked Morgan. It was as if Ashdown thought him dense.

The detective frowned. His displeasure crept into his voice. "Crocker just came out and told you how I helped him?"

Ashdown blinked several times. "Well… no."

"What *did* he tell you?"

The man's confidence began to ebb. "He said you helped him."

"But he told you about *his* problem?"

Ashdown's face went slack, and he suddenly appeared sick. He glanced at the other tables before returning his attention to the detective. "Well, yes, but he only told me about it when I confided about my troubles."

"He's an idiot for talking," Morgan said. "I'm not sure I can help you. You're probably an idiot, too."

Ashdown's head jerked left and right. "I would *never* tell anyone."

"You told Crocker."

"I was scared. I didn't know who to turn to. We're old friends. I didn't know of his… situation until I revealed my problem."

Morgan lifted his eyes as a server approached the table.

"Are you gentlemen ready to order?" she asked.

Morgan ordered a steak salad, and Ashdown, suddenly looking ill, ordered a chicken Caesar salad. After she collected the menus, the server walked away.

Morgan leaned toward the other man and lowered his voice. "I'm here, so you might as well tell me your problem." He was irritated to be sitting with Ashdown, and he did little to hide it.

Ashdown closed his eyes for a moment, nodded a couple of times as he thought, then opened them again. "I made a mistake, Mr. Morgan."

"That's usually how problems start."

"I've been married for eighteen years to a great woman. I've got three children. Nice friends. A fulfilling career. The proverbial good life."

"For some people."

Ashdown blinked several times as he tried to comprehend what Morgan meant.

"Is there more to your story, or is that it?"

Desmond Ashdown swallowed with some difficulty, clearly not used to being talked to in this manner. When he got his emotions under control, he said, "My wife and kids went to visit her parents a couple months ago. Her mother has a heart condition, so she's worried about her. Anyway, some of the younger guys in the office were going out after work, and they asked me to join them. We had a drink in a bar, moved on, then another drink, and moved on again. It was obvious by how much they drank that they were in a different league than me. It's been a lot of years since I went at it like that. In all honesty, I don't know if I even drank like that in college."

Morgan twirled his finger, indicating for the man to speed his story along.

Ashdown glanced around to see if anyone had seen the detective's lack of respect for him. Not seeing anyone watching them, he continued. "I told them to leave me, and I'd catch a ride home, but what I really wanted was something to eat. I was sitting at the bar they left me in, waiting for the bartender to bring me a food menu, when a rather attractive girl sat next to me."

The man stopped then. He looked down and twisted the wedding ring on his finger.

Not caring much for Ashdown's regret, Morgan asked, "And?"

"She was nice. We chatted for a bit. She took an interest in me. I don't mean to make my marriage sound boring or that it's in a bad place, because it's not. It's very nice. But it's been some time since my wife has shown that kind of interest in me."

"She was setting you up," Morgan said.

Ashdown's gaze moved slowly and methodically around the patio. He seemed to study the patrons at the other tables. Morgan suspected he was looking for anyone he might know just in case he had to explain away this meeting. When he was satisfied there was no one he knew, he continued. "We talked for a bit. Then she bought me a drink."

"She bought *you* a drink?"

"Yes."

"Where were you at?"

"Flynn's. Over on Division. Do you know it?"

Morgan nodded.

"She seemed nice," Ashdown said.

"Of course she did."

"I don't know what happened then. My world seemed to slip out from underneath me. She drove me to a hotel somewhere."

"She drove?"

He nodded. "I was suddenly in no condition to drive. I mean, I probably shouldn't have driven before the drink she bought, but this seemed like something else. Like I lost total control. I don't even remember walking to her car. It's like a movie playing in my head with some scenes deleted. Does that make sense?"

"You were slipped something."

Ashdown shrugged slightly. "That's what I figured."

"Where did you go?"

"A motel."

"Do you know which one?"

"No."

"Then what happened?"

"I have visions from the movie in my head. They're spotty, broken, disconnected. Then I woke up on my front porch. I felt nauseous. I spent most of the next morning vomiting with a horrible headache."

"But your life returned to normal?"

"Not really, no. I mean, I felt like something had happened, but I couldn't place it. I lost a night of my life."

"When did the demand come?"

Ashdown's face whitened, and he bowed his head. He held onto the edge of the table like the man was experiencing a personal earthquake. A server and a young couple walked by on the way to their table. Morgan looked up and nodded. They noticed Ashdown's posture and quickly averted their eyes.

When the man finally regained some semblance of composure, he looked up and blinked several times. His eyes glistened as if he had fought back tears. "Two weeks," his voice cracked.

"Did they call?"

Ashdown reached into the inside pocket of his jacket. He pulled out a white envelope and discreetly handed it to Morgan. "She sent this with her demand. To my office." He leaned forward. "*My office*," he whispered harshly.

The envelope had already been torn open. On the front of the envelope, Ashdown's address had been printed by a computer. There was no return address. It was marked *private*. Inside were nine photos of Ashdown and a skinny blonde woman. They were raw and not posed. If what Ashdown said about the drugs was true, that he had indeed experienced a blackout moment, he appeared to be performing sexually throughout it. That, however, could have been a trick of the photographer.

Ashdown's eyes were closed in every picture, and at times his face scrunched. The woman always held his hands on her body, and her position blocked out any view of his groin. A lot of what Morgan was seeing was based on the perception of what a sexual experience should look like.

Her long blonde hair hid the woman's face. In one photo, where her face had not been hidden, that section had been slightly blurred. He looked at the pictures closer. The blurring appeared to be the only digital manipulation that occurred. In one photo, on her left shoulder, he could see a small tattoo of a butterfly. She had no other markings on her body.

Morgan tucked the photos back into the envelope and set it aside. "How much do they want?"

"They?" Ashdown asked.

"She didn't do this alone. Someone else was there taking pictures."

"Oh." Ashdown lowered his head. "That would make sense."

"And someone had to help get you into the car and drop you off on your porch. None of your neighbors saw anything?"

Ashdown's eyes widened. "Nobody has said anything, but I haven't gone around asking either."

"How much do they want?"

"I already paid them thirty thousand."

"And now they want more." It was a statement because he already knew the answer. Ashdown wouldn't have called him if the problem went away after the first payment.

"They want another ten thousand."

"If you do that," Morgan said, "pay them again, they'll ask for another. It won't stop until you're broke, and then they'll do what they want with the pictures. You understand that, right?"

Ashdown's eyes lowered.

"You understand."

"I didn't at first."

"But you do now?"

The man looked up. The fear in his eyes was unmistakable. "I do."

Morgan studied Ashdown. He seemed smaller and weaker after revealing his troubles—probably because of the proverbial good life he claimed to have teetered in the balance. "I'll help you."

Ashdown slowly perked up. His shoulders pulled back, and the color returned to his face.

"If I get the originals back, you give me the ten thousand that you were going to give them."

The man nodded.

"If I find they still have the thirty thousand, I keep it. It's lost money to you at this point."

Ashdown nodded once more, albeit slower.

"Who's the girl?" Morgan asked.

"Her name was Jenna."

"Jenna, what?"

Ashdown looked down at his hands.

The server arrived with their plates. As she put Morgan's salad in front of him, he said, "Put that in a to-go box."

A confused look crossed her face, but she said, "Okay." To Ashdown, she asked, "Are you staying, or would you like yours in a box, too?"

"I'll stay," he softly said.

She set his plate down and disappeared with the steak salad.

The detective leaned in and asked, "You don't know any more about Jenna than her first name?"

"That's all I remember. I don't know if she ever told me her full name."

"What about the bartender at Flynn's? The one that served you the drink. Do you remember him?"

Ashdown's eyebrows raised. "Him, I remember."

"Give me a description."

"He was in his late twenties and had an earring in both ears—the type that makes the big holes in them. Do you know what I'm talking about?"

"Yeah," Morgan said.

"He also had tattoos all over his neck and some on his face. He looked like a disaster, but he seemed nice enough, I guess."

"Did you ever hear his name?"

"She called him Paco."

"She knew him?"

Ashdown thought about it for a moment. "It seemed so, yes."

"Beyond the money, here's how this is going to work. If anybody ever asks about me, you've never heard of me. If anybody ever needs help, you never mention me."

"Like Crocker," Ashdown whispered.

"Like Crocker," Morgan repeated. "He broke our deal, and now he has to answer for that."

"He was only trying to help," Ashdown whispered.

"I don't care. Loose lips sink ships. They also end careers and send guys to jail. Got it?"

"Yes."

"If you call Crocker, text him, or alert him in any way that I'm coming to speak with him, our deal is off, and you can handle this problem on your own. Understand?"

"Yes, sir, I understand."

Morgan turned his attention to the pictures once more while he waited for his to-go box.

Chapter 9

The teenager fell awkwardly from his skateboard and collapsed into a heap. His helmet-protected head bounced once on the ground.

Morgan paused with a forkful of salad hovering in front of his mouth.

The teenager rolled onto his back, moaned once, and looked up with surprise at Morgan, who sat nearby on a bench eating his salad.

They were on an asphalted pathway in Riverfront Park, which sat next to the Flour Mill, where the detective had just been with Desmond Ashdown. Morgan had taken his to-go box and sat on the first quiet bench he could find.

He'd only gotten a couple of bites before the skateboarder hit a rut in the pathway and went down.

Morgan lowered his fork. "Need some help?"

"No," the teenager groaned. "I'm good."

"If you say so."

The teenager slowly got to his feet, grabbed his board, and limped away.

Morgan returned to eating and ruminating on the issue of Desmond Ashdown and Michael Crocker. He needed to focus on bigger, more important things—proving or denying the existence of The Eight being the top of that list—but Crocker's big mouth just created a new complication for him. Two of them, actually.

He needed to help Ashdown so the man would owe him one, and he needed to remind Crocker that secrets unkept are deadly.

Morgan stuffed another bite of salad into his mouth and chewed mechanically.

***

Morgan drove by the little yellow house near Magnolia Street and Pacific Avenue. There still seemed to be no activity. However, he noticed the flag with the fist had been reversed. It was now a black flag with a white fist in the middle of it.

He stared at the flag for a while, trying to understand the significance of the change. It must be a signal of some sort, but what were they indicating? If the fist did correspond to the mark on the package of heroin, were they signaling the arrival of dope? Or that they were out of the drug?

It could be a message to outsiders that it was safe to enter the house. Or maybe it meant the opposite—someone was watching. He was indeed watching, but someone had reversed the flag before he arrived.

For fifteen minutes, he sat in his car and surveilled the house. Nothing moved in or around it.

Perhaps the occupants reversed the flag when they left, Morgan thought.

Finally, he gave up observing the silent house, dropped his car into Drive, and left. He had other more important questions still left to answer.

***

Morgan still worried the regional drug task force might be monitoring Yaban Karga's apartment. Returning to the man so quickly after his recent contact might raise some suspicion.

However, he needed to talk with the Turk about the fist-stamped heroin package. It was too much of a coincidence that the little house on Pacific displayed a flag emblazoned with the same symbol. In his line of work, coincidence did not exist and, since there was no such thing as serendipity, that meant the Turk was lying to him.

Morgan parked his car, lifted his microphone, and hesitated. He considered checking out with dispatch and identifying who he was about to see. If he did, though, and the task force wasn't actively watching Karga, he just put it on the official record that he was speaking to the man. On the other hand, if he kept quiet and was observed going into the building where Karga lived, he would have some explaining to do.

Morgan placed the microphone back onto its holder. It would be easier to explain the latter problem than the former.

He exited his car, trotted to the front of the building, and entered. He climbed the steps to the third floor and silently walked until he was at the Turk's corner apartment, the one Morgan knew he spent most of his time in. He pounded on the door.

There was no answer.

The detective knocked again and followed it with several toe kicks to the bottom of the door. The racket he was making was hard to miss.

A door across the hall opened, and Morgan turned quickly around. A heavy-set woman in a muumuu stood in the opening.

"The hell you doing?" she grumbled.

For an answer, Morgan showed his badge.

Her lip curled to reveal several missing teeth. "I knew he was no good."

"Know where he is?"

"He's gone."

"Where'd he go?"

"He and his lady friend moved out in the middle of the night. Took them barky dogs, too. Thank God."

"They moved out?"

"That's what it looked like. They had a bunch of suitcases and boxes with them. The two of them looked like some sort of comedy the way they was rushing around, carrying things out."

Morgan's lie about the DEA was biting him in the ass now. If he couldn't find out about the fist-stamped heroin packets, he'd be left with a lingering question, and Morgan hated those. "Is there a manager in this building?"

The woman shook her head. "You can call the property management company, but it won't do no good. They hardly never answer my calls."

Morgan turned to the door. Maybe he should kick it open. If he did that, though, the woman could describe him.

"They made such a ruckus," the woman said, "I couldn't get no sleep. I was happy as hell when they finally left."

Kicking in Karga's door would be impossible to explain away, he thought.

"They drove off without even looking back. I watched them from my window." She thumbed back into her apartment. "I even had to pull their door closed after them. They was in such a hurry."

Morgan cocked his head. "You pulled the door closed?"

"Yes, sir, I did. I didn't go inside. I'm not that type—"

"Did you lock it?"

She shrugged. "I only pulled it closed. I'm not the manager. It's not my responsibility to—"

Morgan reached out and twisted the knob. The door opened. He turned back to the woman. "Thank you for your help."

"No problem, Officer. There are decent folks who live here like me. All we want is a quiet place for ourselves. We don't need no trouble."

The detective headed into the apartment and surveyed what was left. Couches, end tables, and a bed remained, but the closets were empty. The kitchen sink was full of dirty dishes. He walked by the small bathroom and into the bedroom. The bed was stripped of linen, and the closet door stood open, revealing its emptiness.

He returned to the living room.

Karga and his woman had made a hasty retreat. The detective let out a long, slow breath.

Because of his actions, Morgan had lost his chance to interview the Turk, but there was still someone else who might be able to answer his questions.

***

When Morgan arrived at the apartment building on Broadway, he yanked open the door and bounded the stairs two at a time, not bothering to be quiet this time. When he made it to the fourth floor, he hurried down the hallway until he was at Laszlo Nagy's apartment.

The door was opened, and he peered inside. Nagy sat on the edge of the bed. His forehead was wrapped in a bandage, and his hands gripped the mattress.

"Laszlo?"

Nagy lifted his head. Black and purple bruising surrounded his eyes. He looked like a raccoon.

"You okay?" Morgan asked as he entered the apartment.

"I've had better days." His voice sounded thick.

"What happened?"

Nagy lifted his eyebrows. "What do you think?"

Morgan crossed his arms over his chest. "I think you called the Turk to tell him we talked. He got pissed and repaid you with a beating."

"That's why you're the detective."

"You went to the hospital, I see."

"Yeah."

"Got a concussion?"

"No. My head must be harder than I think. I gashed it open pretty good when I fell into the counter. Got thirteen stitches."

Morgan's gaze went to the counter where he had poured out the packages of heroin. They were gone now. The Lucky Charms box was also gone from the pile of dishes. He opened the cabinet above the sink. The box wasn't there either.

"He took it," Nagy said.

"He reclaimed his drugs?"

"Not only a beatin', but now I'm startin' to jones, and I've got no way to earn. The double whammy." Nagy shook his head.

"The triple whammy," Morgan corrected.

"Right," Nagy said with a hollow chuckle. "The triple whammy."

"Tell me where he got the heroin, Laszlo."

Nagy shrugged, then winced. "I don't know, man. If I did, I would tell you. I promise. I would make that motherfucker pay for what he done to me."

Morgan nodded. "Yeah, I know, Laszlo. I know."

The skinny man gripped the bed and winced in pain.

"The Turk is in the wind," Morgan said.

Nagy stared at him.

"He isn't coming back, is he?"

The skinny man shrugged. "I don't know, man. I don't know."

"If you hear anything," Morgan said.

"Oh, I'll call you," Nagy said, his face twisting in a grimace. "You can fuckin' believe that."

Chapter 10

The disappearance of Yaban Karga soured Morgan's disposition. He drove aimlessly about, not wanting to return home at the end of the day. As he reconsidered his recent interactions with Nagy and Karga, he realized he had underestimated the situation.

He knew the Turk to be a man who could and would likely retaliate when provoked. That was the cost of business, Morgan rationalized, and Laszlo Nagy had to expect some pain from being in the game. But Morgan didn't think spooking Karga would produce this result.

The Turk's first instinct would be self-preservation, so fleeing made some sense. Running to Nagy's apartment, assaulting the man, and then collecting the outstanding heroin seemed like an unnecessary risk if he genuinely believed the DEA was after him.

Why do that?

Why was the heroin so important?

Was it the money he would gain from selling it?

Or was it that the Turk feared who he initially received it from?

Morgan then wondered if the Turk had beaten Nagy before or after he fled from his apartment. It had to be before, he surmised. It would have taken time for Karga to get his things together. The empty apartment spoke to that fact.

Did he also end the connections to his other dealers or just this one?

He would have to determine who Turk's other dealers were now. He used to know them all, but as they left the scene, Karga became more compartmentalized, and

Morgan stopped pressing to know who the players were. There always seemed more significant and more immediate problems in need of a whacking, and he knew the Turk would always be there if needed—as he had just proved.

Besides, the regional drug task force would be keeping some tabs on the man so Morgan would be wasting his most valuable resource—his time—by following his network.

Which meant he had a choice now. He could either shake down a bunch of lowlifes or approach the drug task force. Neither of those seemed appealing.

As he continued to drive and think, Morgan soon found himself in Hillyard, another economically lagging neighborhood of Spokane. Impulsively, he yanked the steering wheel and pulled into the parking lot of The Quick-E Mart, a convenience store at the corner of Bridgeport Avenue and Nevada Street. An electronic bell dinged as he walked through the doorway. The clerk behind the counter lowered his head.

As he approached the wraparound counter, Morgan said, "Long time, no talk."

The clerk was tall and skinny, with blemish-free olive skin. He glanced around the store to ensure no one else was inside before softly saying, "Detective."

"I need some information."

"I don't do that anymore."

"You don't do *what* anymore?"

"Everything is cool now."

"Everything is not cool, Marvin."

"But my brother is out of jail. He's in a halfway house. He's doing good."

"Oh, I see," the detective said in an unnecessarily loud voice. "Now that your brother is on the path of the righteous, he can never know about our arrangement."

Marvin had trouble swallowing.

The detective leaned over the counter and lowered his voice into a menacing tone. "Because if I told him it was you who ratted him, ratted his dealer out, well, that would ruin Christmas dinner, wouldn't it?"

"I did it for him," Marvin said.

Morgan stared at him. "It won't matter. You ratted on family. That's the only thing that matters."

The clerk put his hands on the counter and lowered his head. "What do you want, Detective?"

"There's a new gang in town. The Eight. Ever hear of them?"

Marvin lifted his gaze to meet the detective's. "You're coming to me. Why?"

"I'm scraping the bottom of the barrel."

The cashier glanced around. "What do you think I can do for you? I run a store."

"Ask around. Keep your eyes open. This place is ground zero. You know it, and I know it."

The store's entry bell chimed, and Morgan looked over his shoulder. Two black men entered the store. One was considerably taller than the other, but both dressed in low-slung jeans and baggy tank tops. Both wore blue baseball caps emblazoned with the word GIANTS. The hats sat cockeyed on their heads. They were engaged in a joking conversation and hadn't paid any attention to the detective.

Morgan had contacted the shorter one previously, but he couldn't immediately place the man's name. He knew, however, because of their hats that they were members of

The Emerald City Giants, the gang from whom Marvin's brother had previously bought his dope.

He turned back to the cashier, whose eyes were now wide with fear. Morgan grabbed two packs of gum and tossed them on the counter. "Gimme a couple Powerball tickets," he said.

The cashier looked toward the rear of the store, then turned to the Powerball machine. He pushed a couple of buttons, and the machine produced a ticket. He laid the strip of paper next to the gum.

The detective watched the two males as they worked the soda machine. The name of the short one finally clicked—DeShaun 'Bilbo' Harmon. Morgan was now confident he'd never seen the tall man before.

The detective turned back to the clerk and muttered, "Nothing else."

Marvin quickly added the selected items into the cash register and announced a total.

Morgan paid with cash, collected the gum and Powerball ticket, and stepped outside. He tucked the items into his jacket before leaning against the hood of his car.

From his position outside, he watched the two gang members approach the cashier and put their sodas on the counter. Bilbo made a comment that caused the clerk to laugh. He waved them on without ever taking any money.

The two men stepped outside, both sipping from the straws of their sodas.

"Hey, Bilbo," Morgan said. "Who's your friend?"

The two stopped and stared at the detective. Neither bothered to say anything.

"I've got a question," the detective said.

The tall man said, "We don't talk with the pigs, uh-huh."

Morgan shook his head, then looked at the shorter, older man who still had his straw in his mouth. "What's his problem?"

Bilbo lowered his drink and said, "He doesn't like cops."

Morgan studied the tall man. "I've never seen you around."

"No, shit."

"What's your name?" Morgan asked.

The tall man leaned toward the detective and sneered. "I don't have to legally give you that, uh-huh."

Morgan pulled out his phone while he spoke. "You don't?"

"That's right. I don't have to tell—"

He took the tall man's picture.

"The fuck? You can't do that."

The detective turned his attention to the shorter man. "Tell your friend to take a hike, Bilbo."

"You can't tell me what to do, uh-huh," the tall man said.

Morgan ignored him. Instead, he stared directly at the shorter man.

Finally, Bilbo said to his partner, "Walk."

The taller man glared at Bilbo with disdain. He made a sucking sound through his teeth before he turned and sauntered toward a blue Impala lowrider.

Bilbo watched his friend amble off. When the other man was out of earshot, he said, "You got a question, Morgan, or we just going to stand out here with our dicks in our hands?"

"Who's your partner?"

"He's my cousin."

"What's his name?"

Bilbo shrugged. "I don't know. You'll have to ask him."

Morgan chuckled. "You don't know your cousin's name?"

"We have a big family," Bilbo said. "It's easy to forget."

"Right."

The man sipped his soda before saying, "You know the game."

Morgan did, and it was one he loved.

"Ever hear of The Eight?" the detective asked.

Bilbo eyed him.

"Need me to repeat the question?"

The shorter man sucked on his straw again before answering. "Why are you asking about them?"

"They're moving into town."

"Let 'em move. It's a free country."

"No, it's not," Morgan said. "This is *my* country."

Bilbo smiled. "That don't make a difference, Morgan. If they wanna come, they'll come. Besides, we're already here. Nothing you do is gonna stop it or turn back the tide. It's like trying to push back an ocean's wave."

"You're a fucking philosopher now?"

Bilbo's grin didn't fade.

Morgan tried a different angle. "Don't you want them to stay out? Tell me what I need to know, and we'll keep them out."

The shorter man shook his head. "That's not how it works. We do our own dirty work. Let 'em come, and we'll chase 'em out by ourselves."

"They're already here, then."

Bilbo shook his head. "Did I say that? I didn't say that."

"You're not going to give me anything?"

"You know the rules, Morgan. I'm not sure why you're pretending you don't."

Morgan thumbed toward the other man's car. "Take off, man. I'll catch you later."

"No," Bilbo said, "you most definitely won't."

Chapter 11

That evening, Morgan returned to his apartment. He grabbed a can of beer and walked out onto the balcony. Once again, the pool was surrounded by bodies tanning themselves before the evening sun fell past its useful apex and dipped below the horizon.

The young women from the Benetton ad were there. They were in the same bikinis and sunglasses from the previous evening. Was it too farfetched to imagine they had remained in the same position for the past twenty-four hours? Could he pretend for a moment they had stayed there so he could walk onto his balcony and admire their youthful beauty?

The redhead with the pleasant paleness waved up at him. Morgan raised his beer in a toast.

"Coming down tonight, Jimmy?" she hollered.

"Not tonight," he said. "Going back to work."

"Aww," she said in playful disappointment. Even from where he stood, Morgan could see her pouty face.

He turned and went inside. He undressed and stepped into the shower with his beer. The hot water pelted his body while he slowly drank the cold amber liquid. His thoughts drifted to the problems currently surrounding his life.

Desmond Ashdown had asked for his help, and there was an opportunity to make some quick money. That was the problem he would work on later tonight.

That prospect came courtesy of Michael Crocker's loose lips. If Crocker was talking about how Morgan had helped him, then the man was a liability. Morgan would have to deal with him soon. How to do so was the question.

Would a simple scare convince Crocker to be quiet, or would force need to be applied? And if force didn't work, would Morgan be willing to go further than that to keep Crocker silent? What he had done for the man would cost him his career and might land him in jail.

Yes, Morgan finally decided. He could go further than merely scaring the man.

Once he decided on a course of action for that problem, Morgan sipped his beer again and turned his mind to The Eight. The California street gang had originated in Oakland, California, in some neighborhood where 44th Street was prominent. The founding members took their name from a dice game term for rolling two fours, which the craps dealers called a "hard eight."

Morgan supposed it was a decent enough name for a gang. Gang members often chose silly names for their tribes and gave each other goofy monikers like Pac-Man, T-Bone, and Cheese, but they were straight killers who were not to be underestimated. Doing so could and would get a man killed. The Oakland Police Department had picked up credible information that The Eight intended to move north into Spokane. Since reading that intel, Morgan had gleaned no further details on The Eight except that everyone on the street was staying oddly quiet about it. Everyone else was coming up equally empty on any meaningful information.

In the late eighties and throughout the nineties, Spokane was a growing market for gangs and crack cocaine. Morgan had come on the job in the middle of that terrible season in the fight for law and order and made his bones in the long war. It had seemed overwhelming at times. As the war leveled out, the battles were more frequently won by the cops. The gangs were still there, of course, but they had retreated further into the shadows.

So why was there now so much interest in this area from The Eight?

Morgan finished his beer and tossed it over the shower door. The empty can clinked on the floor. He quickly washed his hair and his body. After getting out and toweling off, he dressed in clean jeans and a blue T-shirt. He then brushed his teeth and combed his hair. He clipped his gun and badge to his belt.

After slipping into a lightweight jacket, he opened the front door.

The redhead from the pool stood there with her right hand raised, ready for a knock. She wore a faded green cover-up that hid most of her pale skin but still managed to highlight her curves. In her left hand, a nearly empty bottle of Corona was hooked between two fingers. A smile spread across her face.

"Going somewhere?" she asked. Her voice was soft and full of promise.

"Back to work."

Her smile faded into the familiar pout. "But the sun is going down."

"That's when the bad guys come out."

She sipped her beer, but her eyes never left Morgan. He didn't bother to look away. Instead, he focused on her soft, puffy lips as she swallowed.

"What time will you be back?" She left her mouth partially open after she finished her question. Her tongue peeked out between her teeth.

"I don't know."

She clicked her tongue once against the roof of her mouth. "Well," was all she said before she turned to walk down the stairs slowly.

He moved to the railing and watched as she stepped off onto the sidewalk. Only then did she look up at him. When she saw Morgan, she turned and sauntered away. Her hips swayed only slightly, as if she were holding them in check.

Morgan chuckled to himself and locked his front door.

Chapter 12

Flynn's stood in the middle of what the patrol officers call the Bar-muda Triangle, a two-block strip along Division Street of nothing but thriving liquor establishments. Though most of the locations had been bars for more than fifty years, they'd recently been turned over, renovated, upgraded or, to use the words of the real estate jackals, gentrified.

No more than ten years ago, the bars were dirty and seedy. Morgan remembered those days well. The establishments might have had a series of different owners for decades, but the bars had remained dives loved by loyal customers—the 211, Ugly Betty's, and Fast Eddies back when Eddies was still sketchy. Those were the bars that Morgan liked.

He didn't appreciate the slick and updated nature of the new bars that invaded this area. Borracho's Tequileria, Boom Box Pizza, The Globe Bar & Grille, and The Blind Buck catered to the hipsters and the posers. New owners had acquired even Fast Eddies. It might look and smell the same, but it was now a destination for college kids looking to "spin the wheel" on their birthday in hopes of winning a free drink.

Ridiculous.

Around the corner on Main Street, the area's trend toward the new continued. The soul of downtown had been sucked out and replaced by whiskey dens, wine bars, and tap houses for the modern yuppies.

Morgan hated all these establishments that had shown up in the name of progress.

Only Flynn's remained which gave Morgan hope that someday the new establishments would suffer the effects of time just like people did. He wondered how long Flynn's could push back against the parade of redevelopment as its landlord must no doubt want to see someone update his building.

Flynn's sat north of The Blind Buck and stuck out like a sore thumb. Its peeling yellow façade and painted bike advertisements were a long-ago remnant of its time as a purveyor of two-wheeled transport during the '40s and '50s. For those hipsters who barhopped along the two-block stretch, Flynn's allowed them to say they hit a dive bar. For anyone older than forty, it was a respite, a place to take refuge from the endless thumping of modern hip-hop and the hopeless whining of current pop music.

When he opened the door, the smell of fried food and stale beer greeted Morgan. It was warm inside, as if the establishment's air conditioning had failed to do its job.

AC/DC's "Have a Drink on Me" pounded through the speakers. He knew the song due to his time in the military, but it didn't make him happy. In fact, it did nothing for him. Morgan disliked music in all its forms.

He scanned the establishment. It was too early for the college crowd to invade the joint, and there were only a handful of people in the bar.

The bartender was in his early thirties and wore a wife-beater tank top. Tattoo sleeves ran from the back of his hands up over his shoulders and around his neck.

For a moment, the detective thought about Ray Bradbury's *The Illustrated Man,* a science fiction novel he'd read many years ago.

Morgan walked to the end of the bar, away from customers, and nearest the kitchen entrance.

The bartender eyed the detective as he went by.

Morgan paused when he noticed someone he recognized.

In the booth nearest the back was Tremaine Brown, his left arm in a sling. Sitting next to him was a younger white woman, her nose bandaged, and her eyes blackened. Brown was whispering to her and didn't seem to notice him.

"I make it as Liquor Control Board," a voice behind him said. Morgan turned around. The bartender leaned on the counter. His hair was cut short on the side, but long on top, causing it to fall foppishly to the left. In both of his ears were black gauges about the size of a dime. "No one is overserved, and our permits are in order. Feel free to look around."

Smiling as genially as he could, Morgan said, "Yeah? How'd you ping me as Liquor Control?"

"The jacket, man. Only the LCB walks in with a jacket when it's eighty degrees out. Hiding your badge, right?"

Morgan opened his jacket, exposing both his gun and badge. "Police."

The bartender's air of confidence slipped, and he straightened. His eyes flicked to the back booth. "You looking for someone, Officer?"

"You."

The bartender blinked. "Me?"

"Let me see your driver's license."

"What did I do?"

Morgan snapped his fingers, then waved two of them impatiently toward himself. The bartender pulled his wallet from his back pocket and tossed it on the counter.

The detective pointed at the wallet. "What's that?"

"My wallet."

"Did I ask for your *fucking* wallet?"

"What?"

"Did I stutter?" Morgan asked.

"No, sir."

"Then, pull out your license and hand it to me—*politely*."

The bartender's eyes flicked over Morgan's shoulder and then back to the detective. "Am I in trouble for something?"

"Yeah, Morgan," a voice behind him asked. "Is he in trouble for something?"

In a low and threatening tone, Morgan said to the bartender. "Don't move." Then he slowly faced Tremaine Brown and the dark-haired woman standing next to him. To Brown, Morgan asked, "The bartender a friend of yours? Maybe you want to step in and take his place?"

Brown shook his head. "No, man, I'm good."

"Besides, you cops already did enough," the woman said. She motioned to the sling on Brown's arm. "He was shot and then his brother got arrested today. The cops is out for our family."

"Your family?" Morgan's eyes slid from the woman to Tremaine. "She belongs to you?"

"You think I'm his property?" the woman snapped. Her voice rose to an almost shrill level.

Morgan grinned. "Honey, I *know* you're his property."

Her eyes widened, but she lowered her voice. "Motherfucker."

Morgan studied the woman's injuries. "The smacking you gave her didn't take, Tremaine."

"He didn't hit me, you sonofabitch."

Brown said, "I wouldn't hit a woman, Morgan."

Morgan leaned into the woman to study the bruising around her eye. "Maybe he should have. Might have taught you some manners."

The woman opened her mouth to say something, but it was cut off with a grunt when Brown pulled her into him, silencing her.

Morgan smiled. The pecking order had been established.

"What are you doing in my joint, Morgan?"

"This is where you hang, Tremaine?"

"Depends."

"On what?"

"On what you're doing here."

"Health inspection."

Brown laughed. "Health inspection, huh?"

"I'm taking an interest in the welfare of the community," the detective said. "You know how it is,"

"Yeah, Morgan, I know how it is. We're gone."

As the two turned to leave, Morgan asked, "Hey, Tremaine, what do you know about The Eight?"

"He ain't telling you—" the woman started, but Brown glared at her until she fell quiet.

"Maybe that smacking did some good after all," Morgan said.

Brown shook his head. "Jesus, man, you never stop. You know we shouldn't be speaking to you, what with our recent problems with your department and all. It might be seen as interfering with an investigation."

"Am I bothering you?"

Brown thought about it for a moment. "Nah, man, you and me, we're cool."

"See, man? You're not my problem. As I said, I'm here for a health inspection."

"All right. I get you."

"About The Eight. Ever hear the enemy of my enemy is my friend?"

Brown considered the words. "I haven't, but I like it. I'm going to remember that. I'm going to let you in on a secret, Morgan. The Eight, it's all chatter. They don't have the infrastructure to get up here."

"Infrastructure? Use more words like that, and I won't forget you went to college."

Brown flashed him a brief smile. "The Eight don't have a pipeline up here. If they suddenly showed up, they'd be on an island. It doesn't make sense." Brown looked over Morgan's shoulder to the bartender and lifted two fingers in a victory sign. "Peace, Paco." He then walked out with his woman in tow.

The detective turned back to the bartender, who had remained stuck in place. "Paco? Your driver's license says your name is Wallace Blair."

He shrugged. "People used to call me Wally, but I hated that."

"But Paco? How'd that come about?"

"One of the regulars at a previous joint gave it to me. Slang for Ps & Qs. Pints and Quarts. He rolled Paco from it."

Morgan laid the driver's license on the bar and took a picture of it with his phone. He pushed it back to him.

"Tell me about Jenna."

Paco's shoulders slumped, and he lowered his eyes. He muttered, "Aw, shit."

"I'll take that as confirmation that you're acquainted."

"She's just a girl I know."

"Just a girl who told you to drug an unsuspecting customer. How many of those have you done?"

"Don't you have to read me my rights?"

Morgan jumped over the bar top and grabbed Paco by the front of his tank top. He pulled him across the counter toward him, twisting the shirt as he did. "This isn't about your rights, Paco. That guy you drugged? He is my friend. Understand?"

Paco's stomach was on the bar, and he raised his hands in surrender. It appeared as if he were bodysurfing on the mahogany counter. Morgan let go of his shirt and glanced back at the two patrons still in the bar. Both made a concerted effort to be looking elsewhere at that moment.

The bartender smoothed his shirt. "Listen, man. I don't know what you're talking about."

"Let's go outside," Morgan said and motioned toward the rear of the bar.

"For what?"

"To finish this conversation."

"Why?" Paco asked.

"Let's go," Morgan said, snapping his fingers. "Now."

"I'm sorry about your friend," Paco quickly said.

"Yeah? Really? Then prove it. Either you help me now, or we go out back where people can't see what I'm about to do to you."

Paco glanced around the bar before leaning slightly in. "She pays me."

"To do what?"

"Drop some shit in their drinks," the bartender whispered.

"What *shit*?"

"I don't know. It's in a little bottle." Paco looked around again before continuing. He kept his voice low. "That's all I know. What happens after that? That's on her."

"You don't know what she does?"

"She walks out with them, and they never return."

Morgan folded his arms over his chest. "How did you meet her?"

"Here."

"Not where. How?"

"Oh," Paco said. "She approached me."

"While you were working?"

"Well, no. After we hooked up."

"You hooked up?"

"Yeah. She came in one night. She drank, and we talked. Then we hooked up."

"Where does she live?"

"I don't know."

"You took her back to your place?"

"My place?"

"Where did you hook up?"

"The bathroom." The bartender thumbed toward the end of the bar.

Morgan's gaze floated toward the end hallway. "Classy. So, you know nothing about her except she screws in restrooms and pays you to drop something into a drink now and then."

The bartender stared at him.

"All right. We're getting nowhere, so here's what's going to happen. You're under arrest."

"For what?"

"Mopery."

"The fuck is mopery?"

"It's what you're doing now."

Paco's face scrunched. "You can't do this."

"I can do anything I want. And when we get to the station, I'll bring in my friend to identify you."

Paco waved his hands in a calming motion. "Hey, now. Slow down."

"I'll build my case around you. You're the mastermind of this scheme."

"You didn't read me my rights," Paco whined.

"Yeah, I did."

"No, you didn't."

Morgan moved beyond the end of the counter and now stood in the opening to the back bar. "Are you calling me a liar?"

Paco swallowed, then opened his mouth to say something, but nothing came out. He was a cornered rat that knew the cat had him in its sights.

"That's what I thought," Morgan said. "After my friend identifies you, I'll upgrade your charge to extortion."

"Extortion?"

"That's right. Jenna is extorting my friend, and you helped. Except, when I tell the story, you're going to be the architect of this plan. The big cheese, if you will."

"Come on, man, I don't want any part of this."

Morgan shrugged. "Too late. You either point me to her or take her fall. At this point, someone's going to jail. You get to choose who—"

"She's a dancer," Paco blurted.

"A dancer?"

"At The Red Light District."

"That so? Why didn't you tell me that sooner?"

"Because we hook up."

"It's happened more than once."

The bartender only blinked his admission.

"How many times?"

"Twice so far."

"Twice?"

"Well, three times if you count the first."

"I am. And after you hook up, you drop something in a drink, and she pays you?"

"Not in that order, but yeah."

"And that's why you didn't want to tell me?"

"I thought maybe you would give up and go away."

Morgan leaned his hip against the counter. "Listen, Wally. I'm not going away. And if you call Jenna, text her, send a smoke signal, that I'm sniffing around, I will come back here and put my foot so far up your ass you won't walk straight for the rest of your life."

"What?"

"What?" Morgan repeated.

"You can't say that."

"How come?"

"Because you're a cop."

Morgan stepped fully behind the bar now and approached Paco. He clenched his fists and held them at his sides. "Do you understand what I said, or do I have to make it clearer?"

The bartender lifted his hands in surrender. "I'm good, man."

"You going to lie to me again?"

Paco's arms slowly lowered. "No, sir."

"Now, you're learning."

Morgan slugged the bartender in the stomach. Paco fell to his knees and coughed.

The two remaining patrons averted their eyes as the detective walked by them on the way to the exit.

***

Morgan knew The Red Light District on East Sprague was only one of over a hundred locations the club has scattered across the country. There weren't many strip clubs in Spokane County, but it was by far the nicest.

Saying that, though, was like saying McDonald's was the classiest fast-food restaurant in the nation. It didn't mean much.

Morgan approached the front door. A slender man in his late twenties stood nearby as a bouncer. His black T-shirt was printed with *The Red Light District*. The man muttered automatically, "Ten bucks."

For a moment, the detective thought about badging him. However, flashing the piece of metal clipped to his belt would tell everyone there was a cop in the house. If Jenna was worried someone was looking for her, she'd be wary of getting near him.

He reached for his wallet.

"You a cop?" the bouncer asked.

Morgan raised an eyebrow.

"The bulge under your jacket. And the jacket. Who wears a jacket on a night like tonight?"

Morgan shoved his wallet back into a pocket, then opened his windbreaker.

"Health inspection, huh?" the bouncer asked with a smile.

They stared at each other for a moment before the bouncer waved Morgan inside. The detective entered the club where the thumping music rendered any other sound obsolete.

A light-brown girl from some Central American country was on stage. Morgan took a moment to appreciate her as she gyrated around a pole. She had tossed her shoes and bikini to the side and was now wholly naked. The woman grabbed onto the bar and flipped upside down. She hung there for a moment, hands-free, with her legs wrapped like a python around the chrome pole.

The detective's focus moved away from the dancer. No girls were walking the floor that resembled the woman from Desmond Ashdown's pictures. Morgan didn't want to approach one of them and ask for Jenna. That would be like sending a flare into the night, and his target would rabbit. If that happened, he might never find her.

Morgan took a seat in the back of the club.

A waitress approached him then. "Can I get you something?"

"No, thanks," he said politely.

"There's a two-drink minimum," she said.

"Bring me anything," he said. "I don't care."

She shrugged before wandering off into the darkness.

The annoying music changed to something with guitars that sounded like chainsaws. Morgan grimaced. He'd quit paying attention to music after he left the Marines. He knew a few songs from that time, but his musical awareness depended entirely on his friends. Truth be told, Morgan preferred silence to noise. He'd often sit in his apartment with nothing on but the hum of the building. It allowed him to be alone with himself. He wasn't in a hurry to escape who he was by falling into the fantasy that music presented to others.

He did his best to block out the noise and let his gaze drift from girl to girl as they moved about the club. While many were attractive, he wasn't interested in them for anything more than a lead to Jenna. If he thought asking one of them would get him closer to her, he would do so. But he had a sneaking suspicion these girls wouldn't take too kindly to a cop bracing them, especially here. It had long been rumored the dancers at this club engaged in opportunistic prostitution, whether it be the occasional hand job in a dark corner or a quickie in the parking lot.

It took roughly an hour for all the girls to work through their rotation on stage. When the cute brown girl from some Central American country returned and grabbed the chrome pole, Morgan stood and left the club.

Chapter 13

When he got home, Morgan changed into a pair of shorts and T-shirt and immediately went to the community's gym.

Even though the sun was down, he could still hear some people at the outdoor pool, enjoying a night swim. He didn't bother to see if the girls from the Benetton ad were there. He didn't need to encourage the redhead with the pleasant paleness any further. There would be time for that later. He had things on his mind tonight, and rolling around with a young woman, as distractingly enjoyable as it might be, would not further his interests.

The gym the apartment community provided had been state of the art when he moved in twenty years ago. Luckily for him, the owners continued to maintain it as so. It was nearly ten o'clock when he arrived, and he immediately began pushing, curling, and pulling weights.

His mind drifted over the events of the day and the problems he currently faced. The one that bothered him now was the stripper only known as Jenna. If he approached her straight ahead, he ran the risk of her disappearing to somewhere he couldn't find her. There was no way of knowing how many extortion jobs she already ran or continued to operate. It was probably far more lucrative than stripping, so she wouldn't hesitate to bail on The Red Light District to protect her racket.

Could he run it as a legitimate police operation and use some of the department's resources?

Doing so would alert others to Ashdown's problem and would jeopardize the payout he expected to get from the man. It could also lead back to his work with Michael

Crocker, and neither man needed that exposure. No, he needed to handle this problem on his own.

Perhaps he could sit outside the club, surveilling it, and wait for Jenna to show up, but that would require more of his personal time, which he currently didn't have available. Getting a solid ID on her might be difficult in the brief time it took her to walk from her car to the front door.

What Morgan needed was someone who could get inside the club without suspicion and get close to the woman. He only needed the most fundamental piece of information—her real name. He could do the rest from there.

He stopped mid-curl and put down the weights. He picked up his cell phone and called Vivian, who answered on the second ring.

"Hi Jimmy," she said, her voice filled with happiness.

"Hey, Viv, how are things?"

"Leigh said her boyfriend was arrested today. Was that your handiwork?"

"She asked for my help. That's the best I could do. If she wants him to stay gone, she's going to have to get involved and file for an order of protection."

"Regardless, she's grateful."

"How grateful?"

"Excuse me?"

"I need a favor from her."

Vivian was silent for a moment before saying, "I'll have her stop by in an hour." Her voice was flat, the sense of playfulness gone.

"It's not that type of favor, Viv."

"It better not be," she said.

Vivian hung up without waiting for Morgan to respond.

***

After Morgan finished his workout, he returned to his apartment and showered. It was almost eleven when there was a knock on his door. Leigh Gaston stood in the doorway, wearing white sandals, tight blue shorts, and a white T-shirt that read *Princess*. Leigh clasped her hands in front of her and clutched the strap of her small white purse.

He stepped out of the way and let her in.

She continued walking until she was in the middle of his apartment. Leigh turned around and faced Morgan. Her eyes never scanned the apartment. Instead, they remained on the detective. Concern filled her gaze. She thrust her chin out in a rebellious nature as if she was standing up to an unknown fear—a child bravely facing the darkness.

"Viv said I had to come and see you. She said I owe you for what you did."

Leigh lowered her hands to her sides and pulled her shoulders back, which thrust her breasts out. She kept her chin boldly up and didn't say another word. She waited for Morgan to ask his favor.

"You were a dancer, right?"

Leigh squinted and slowly said, "In Post Falls. Yeah."

"Ever dance in Spokane?"

"No," she said, her brow furrowing. Her shoulders relaxed, and her breasts settled to their normal position. Her fear diminished and was replaced by curiosity.

Morgan stepped to the kitchen counter and picked up an envelope. He removed several pictures and thumbed through them until he found one that showed Jenna's blurred face. She was in a dominant sexual position with Desmond Ashdown.

He stepped back to Leigh and handed her the photo. "Do you know this man?"

Leigh studied the photo. "No."

The detective tapped the photo near the blurred face. "What about her?"

"No."

"I need to know who she is."

"It's blurry," Leigh muttered.

"She dances at The Red Light District and goes by the name Jenna. It may be her real name, it may be a stage name, but the butterfly tattoo on her arm, that's real." He tapped the photo again. "Focus on that."

Leigh looked up at Morgan. "Are you asking me to dance there? If Dontari gets out and finds me there…"

"I'm not asking you to dance. I only need to know who she is. Get her real name. Or the license plate of her car. Anything that gets me closer to her."

Leigh examined the photo again. "Can I ask why?"

"That girl is blackmailing that guy," Morgan said. "He's my friend, and I'm doing him a favor, but I can't get any closer to stopping it until I know who she is."

"And if I get you that information, we're square on getting Dontari out of my house?"

"Even if you don't do it, we're square. He had a warrant, and I got to arrest him."

"I owe you, and Viv expects me to repay you. Whatever you want—that's what she said." She pulled her shoulders back, which brought her breasts up again.

"You don't owe me," Morgan said, "especially not that way."

Leigh blinked several times as she tried to comprehend the detective's refusal. When she did, she relaxed her shoulders.

"And you shouldn't be with him either," Morgan said. "He's a road that leads to nowhere good."

"I'm done with him, Jimmy. I got an attorney today, and he's filing a request for a no-contact order."

"That's good," Morgan said.

Leigh tucked the photograph into her purse. "I'll get you something on this woman."

She walked by him then and let herself out of the apartment.

Chapter 14

Morgan looked up from his report when Major Crimes Detective Andrew Parker walked into the Criminal Task Force office. Parker wore an ill-fitting black suit, white shirt, and black tie.

"You look like a junior FBI agent," Morgan said.

"Is that a crack about my height?"

Parker stood several inches under six feet but was built like a Mack truck. Due to his bodybuilder physique, he would look awkward in a suit, no matter how nicely cut.

Along with his partner, they were the newest team in Major Crimes. They had earned the nickname the Hot Heads because the brass and other detectives could easily provoke them. Morgan, like most in the department, was surprised when those two promoted up from property crimes following the departure of two senior detectives. Initially, he didn't think they would last beyond ninety days. It had been almost a year now.

"No, Parker, it's a crack about your suit."

Parker ran his hand down his tie. "At least I look like a detective. You? You look like a bum."

Sergeant Bynum spoke up then. "Be nice. That bum is my bum."

Parker shook his head. "Sarge, why do you protect this jagoff?"

Morgan leaned back in his chair and crossed his arms over his chest. "What exactly do I need protecting from, Parker?"

"Did you contact Tremaine Brown last night?"

Morgan glanced at Bynum, then refocused on Parker. "I didn't *contact* him. I saw him at a bar. He said hello on his way out. That was all."

"That's not what I heard. Brown's lawyer contacted the detectives investigating his shooting—the shooting I'm the shadow on. He made a stink about you talking to Tremaine. That's why I'm here now—to do damage assessment."

Morgan's grin was without mirth. "Shit rolls downhill."

"Like I said, Morgan, that's why I'm here. You're the bottom of that hill, and the turd is landing on you."

James Morgan leaned forward in his chair and put his elbows on his desk. "I was in a bar downtown. Tremaine Brown was also there. I did nothing wrong."

"Which bar?"

"Flynn's."

"Uh-huh. Did you threaten him?"

"Not at all."

"That's not what Regina Baird said."

"Who?"

"Regina Baird," Parker repeated. "Tremaine's girlfriend."

"See? I didn't even know her name. Ask him about our talk. I would say it was pleasant."

"Then why would she contact the lawyer?"

Morgan understood then. This wasn't about Tremaine. It was about the girlfriend. He had nothing to worry about. "She and I had words. Tremaine and me, we're good."

"Why weren't you nice to her?"

"She was mouthy. She needed to be brought down a peg."

Parker lifted his hands in frustration. "C'mon, man. We're investigating an officer-involved shooting. Why would you mess with the guy's girlfriend?"

Morgan shrugged. "I didn't mess with her. She was chirping at me while I was chatting with Brown, so I shut her down. Simple. Brown knew she was out of line as well."

"And did you *really* arrest his brother, Dontari?"

"That was a coincidence."

"Coincidence? You're kidding me. Only idiots and scumbags believe in coincidence."

Morgan fought back a smile. Maybe Parker had more on the ball than he gave him credit for.

"Listen, Parker, Dontari was a Dead Boy with an outstanding warrant for third assault. You can't expect us to ignore something like that."

"Why not? SIU knew about the warrant, and they were letting it sit until we finished with this investigation."

"You're telling me SIU ignored a lawful order from a judge?"

Parker shook his head. "No, that's not what I'm saying. What I'm telling you is they were going to arrest him *after* we finished our investigation. That's called being a team."

"Dontari assaulted an officer," Morgan said. "He deserved to get grabbed."

"Who did he assault?" Parker asked.

"What?"

"Who did Dontari Brown assault that made it so damn important for you to grab him?"

"He assaulted *an officer*," Morgan said. "Period. That should be enough for you, but I can see where your loyalty lies."

Parker pointed at Morgan. "It's bad enough for the rookie as it is. It's not going to look any better with you sticking your nose into it. Keep yourself clear of this. Got it?"

"Pound sand."

"What?"

Morgan leaned back in his chair. "If you were doing your job, you'd have already cleared the kid. He's got a uniform. That already puts him a mile ahead of Brown."

"You're not investigating the shooting, Morgan. Maybe you should shut the fuck up."

"You're only worried about the optics of the shooting, Parker. How about you worry about the officer involved in it?"

Parker glanced at Bynum. "He's your problem, Sergeant. I can't help the stupid." The smaller detective turned to leave.

Morgan jumped up behind his desk. "Parker!"

The door to the CTF office closed, leaving the detective standing behind his desk, his face warming. Bynum moved next to him.

"Relax, Morgan."

"That little shit."

"*Relax.*"

Morgan dropped into his chair.

"Did you arrest Dontari Brown?"

"What about it?"

"Nothing," Bynum said, walking back to his desk.

"He had a warrant," Morgan said, "and we arrested him cleanly. That's it. He might even have bonded out already. Who knows?"

"You never told me about it."

"Because there was nothing to tell."

Bynum gave a sideways glance to Morgan. "On this one, pal, I think this was something you should have passed up the chain of command."

Morgan stared at his desk for a few minutes, lost in thought. He checked his watch, stood, and left the office without saying goodbye to Bynum.

Chapter 15

Morgan knew the man jogged during his lunch hour. He was a creature of habit. That's how he first wound up in trouble—blindly following his habits, not believing he could or would ever befall misfortune. It's the same thing with most rich men. They think they're untouchable until someone reaches out and puts the finger on them. Then their world falls apart since they've never had to scrape and claw for what they own.

When Morgan helped Michael Crocker out of his predicament, he explained the danger of following the same routine and of setting himself up as a mark. Yet the man continued to do the same things—a robot stuck in a logic loop. Crocker was a smart man with a brilliant legal mind who just couldn't get out of his own way.

Shortly before noon every day, the man would leave his office, walk several blocks to The Spokane Club, change into his work-out clothes and leave for a jog along the Centennial Trail. He would pass over the Monroe Street Bridge on the west side of the structure, which was closest to the club. He would also return along this route. His three-mile run, the same distance every day, fell between twenty-nine to thirty-two minutes depending on his pace, which was the only thing Morgan ever noticed that varied in the man's running schedule.

At 11:50 a.m., Morgan left the Monroe Court Building and walked southbound toward the bridge. The sun was bright and almost directly overhead. To the east, the purple carriages of the Riverfront Park gondola ride glided down its path above the Spokane River. The gondolas disappeared underneath the bridge and would finish the first half of their journey further to the west before circling back to return to the park.

There were two points on the bridge where the sidewalks' paths were covered, a brief respite from the weather or the sun. Morgan checked his watch and decided to stop at the first covering.

Traffic continued to pass by while the river below provided a low ambient rumble. Along both sides of the bridge, ugly chain-link fencing had been raised above the concrete railings to protect would-be jumpers from themselves. Instead of leaving the bridge as it was so most of society could enjoy the view, the city decided to stop that small minority who wanted to use the bridge to exit this world.

Morgan dismissively shook his head and looked away from the fence. It was yet another stupid decision made to protect people who shouldn't be saved. If they wanted to kill themselves, let them, he thought. The world would be better off without them.

The detective leaned against one of the support columns, hiding from passersby. He had several minutes before he expected Crocker to be on the bridge, so he busied himself reading the various graffiti markings. It was mostly the musings of kids and not gang graffiti.

He was reading a poem about an old man from Nantucket when an elderly woman walked through the south side of the covering.

"Oh!" she exclaimed when she saw him.

The detective nodded and forced a smile, but it did little to ease her fears. She clutched her small bag of groceries to her chest and hurried on her way.

Morgan peeked in the direction of The Spokane Club and began to question himself. Perhaps he should have just gone to the man's house, but then he might have had to deal with his family. He could have gone to his office, but it would have been the same thing, except he would have dealt with assistants and security guards. He couldn't have raised his voice there, and he would have been in a subordinate position.

No, this was a solid play. He decided the worst that would come from this small excursion from his office was a walk in the sun. The detective bet Crocker's habits hadn't changed in the almost two years since he helped the man. Morgan frequently saw the man on the bridge running to or from the club, and it was always around this time.

He glanced north to where the Public Safety Building and the Monroe Court Building stood, but he couldn't see either of them. He could see the top of the county courthouse, its spire reaching high above everything else. His eyes flicked down to the sidewalk path. No one was walking across the bridge from that direction.

Most Americans, Morgan mused, avoided walking anywhere anymore unless it was under the guise of exercise. Why did he care since he didn't walk anywhere daily, either? Deciding his thoughts were hypocritical, he shrugged and turned to look south again.

A man now jogged across the bridge toward him. He wore shorts and a white T-shirt. It looked like he had sunglasses on, but it was hard to be sure from this distance. He appeared to be Michael Crocker, but Morgan wasn't entirely confident.

He leaned back into the covering and relaxed, trying his best to listen for the oncoming runner. The detective hoped he would hear Crocker's footsteps. With the noise of the passing traffic and the river below, he wasn't sure he could hear anything that soft.

He breathed in and out, counting several seconds on each inhale and then on the exhale.

Suddenly, the runner was at the entry of the covering. It took only a split second for Morgan to realize it was indeed Michael Crocker. The detective's hand shot out to grab the man's T-shirt, but he missed it. Instead, he hit him on the shoulder.

The force was enough to knock Crocker off balance, spinning him around, which caused him to collide into the opposite corner of the covering. His feet slipped out from underneath him, and he fell onto his buttocks. With his back leaning against the wall, Crocker looked up at the detective.

Morgan hadn't intended to start that rough, but he knew how to work with what opportunity gave him.

He stepped to Crocker, grabbed a fistful of the man's T-shirt, and lifted him to his feet. The detective then leaned into his fist and pinned the man to the wall.

"Morgan?" Michael Crocker croaked. His hands wrapped instinctively around Morgan's wrist.

The detective punched the man in the stomach.

Crocker tried to bend over, but Morgan's grasp stopped him. He brought up a leg in reflex to ease the pain and almost kneed Morgan in the groin. The detective punched down onto the top of Crocker's bare leg. The man howled in pain.

"Listen!" Morgan yelled over Crocker's wails and the noise of the passing traffic.

Crocker stopped hollering.

Morgan couldn't see his eyes, and it pissed him off. He snatched the sunglasses from Crocker's face, then put them on his own. He pointed an accusatory finger at the man. "You were supposed to keep your mouth shut, Michael."

"What did I do? *What did I do!*"

"You talked."

"No, I didn't."

Morgan slugged Crocker in the stomach again.

Crocker squealed. He was a not man built for physical confrontation.

"You told Desmond Ashdown about what I did—about what we did—to protect you."

Crocker sucked for air as he looked left and right. There was nowhere to go. His hands gripped Morgan's wrist tighter, but he didn't fight back.

"Tell me you didn't tell him," Morgan said.

When Crocker didn't answer, Morgan hit him a third time.

Crocker sucked for air, but none came. Tears filled his eyes as he struggled to breathe.

An elderly, homeless man entered the concrete covering then and stopped. "Hey! What are you doin' to him?" he yelled.

Morgan looked over his shoulder. "Police business."

The homeless man wore tan polyester pants and ratty tennis shoes. His dirty white T-shirt featured Spuds McKenzie, a Bud Light spokesman of yesteryear. The bum pointed at Crocker and said, "That don't look like no police bidness."

Morgan released Crocker, who slumped in the corner. He turned to the older man and pointed at the badge on his hip. "You wanna be a part of this discussion?"

The homeless man ran his fingers through his thinning gray hair. "No, sir. Looks like you got it unner control."

"Then move your ass along."

Crocker tried to move by Morgan then, but the detective grabbed him by the shoulder and shoved him back into the corner. Morgan's eyes remained on the homeless man.

"Yeah, okay," the old man said. He turned and shuffled out of the covering.

Morgan had to make it quick now. There would be others who might walk by. Others who weren't on the fringes of society and might be intimidated so easily.

He pointed at Crocker. "We had a deal."

"Deal?" Crocker rasped as his breath came back to him.

"You were supposed to keep your mouth shut."

Crocker swallowed before speaking, "He's the only person I've told."

Morgan studied Crocker, trying to determine his level of truth.

"I swear, Morgan. I swear!"

"Why'd you talk?"

Crocker righted himself and pulled his shoulders back. "He's my friend, and he was in a bad way. I thought maybe you could help him."

"Do I look like the Salvation Army? If anybody is ever in trouble again, you tell them to call the cops. Not me. Got it?"

Crocker nodded.

"And if I hear you ever mentioned how I helped you again, I swear to God, I'll put you in the ground."

Crocker's eyes widened.

"Tell me you understand what I'm saying."

"I understand what you're saying, Morgan."

"What we did can land us both in jail, and I'm not going for you. You should understand that better than anyone."

Crocker nodded. "I understand. I'm sorry."

Morgan shoved the man, bouncing him once off the concrete wall. He took off Crocker's glasses and handed them to him. When the detective stepped back, he waved north and said, "Feel free to finish your run, your honor."

Superior Court Judge Michael Crocker carefully put his sunglasses on. "I think I'm good," he said and started an amble back toward The Spokane Club, rubbing his stomach as he went.

Chapter 16

The white flag with the black fist was displayed again. The Buick, Chevy, and Ford were still parked in front of the little yellow house.

"Have the cars moved since yesterday?" Nayla Senai asked.

Morgan studied the vehicles. "I'm not sure. Take a picture of how they're situated."

"What do you think the flag means?" she asked as she lifted her phone for a picture.

"It's a signal. They've switched it out twice now. White, black, now white again. What that signal means, I've got no clue."

A late '70s Cadillac Eldorado drove down the street. The shiny black car had been lowered so its body almost touched the ground. Most would consider it a silly-looking ride, but to many who lived life on the street, it was a symbol of success. Behind the wheel was a younger black man, his head bouncing to the music emanating from inside.

Further down the street was a new white BMW 3 series headed in the same direction.

As the Cadillac went by, Morgan didn't bother to look at its driver.

"I got the plate," Senai said. "Want to follow him?"

Morgan shook his head. "That car and its driver belong here. The car up there, though..."

The BMW drove toward them. It slowed considerably in front of the house they had been watching. The driver, a white male, glanced at the home, then looked forward and drove away.

"Did he check out the flag?" Morgan asked.

"Maybe," Senai said, "but he was definitely checking out the house."

Morgan slipped his car into Drive and watched in his rearview mirror as the BMW turned southbound. The detective pulled from his parking spot and accelerated to the end of the block. He ran through the Stop sign at Napa Street and turned southbound.

Without being told, Senai's head swiveled back and forth as she searched for the white car.

The BMW had a head start, but Morgan had acquired a scent and wasn't about to let the BMW get away from him. He accelerated to Second Avenue and raced through another Stop sign before turning westbound.

"Ahead," Senai said. "Hamilton onramp."

The two-door coupe was entering the onramp to the Hamilton Street Bridge. The Dodge Charger's engine whined in excitement as Morgan accelerated. As his speed climbed to seventy miles per hour on a road whose limit was thirty-five, the detective reached down to activate his emergency lights.

When the Charger crested the onramp, he could see the BMW stopped at the Trent Avenue traffic light. Another car was in front of the white BMW while others boxed it in. Morgan deactivated his emergency lights and slowed.

He could see the driver of the BMW glancing into his rearview mirror several times until the light changed. When it did, the BMW drove northbound on Hamilton, changing lanes several times. Each time he did, Morgan switched lanes with him.

"He's panicking," Senai said.

The car changed lanes to pass a stopped city bus.

Morgan grabbed the microphone for the police radio that was hidden under the dash. "Ida seventy-seven."

"Ida seventy-seven," dispatch responded.

"Run a plate," Morgan said and then called out the numbers on the Washington license plate.

A moment later, dispatch called, "Ida seventy-seven, that plate returns to a 2018 BMW Series 3. Registered to Timothy Dalrymple. Driving status is clear."

"Copy," Morgan said, placing the microphone back into position.

"Does that name mean anything to you?" Senai asked.

"No."

Morgan activated the car's emergency lights again.

"Why are we stopping him?"

"Because we can."

Senai glanced at the microphone. "Are you going to call in the stop?"

Morgan smirked. "Not yet. Let's see what we find first."

She turned forward, and her face hardened.

"Call it in," Morgan said, "if you want."

Senai reached for the microphone but hesitated. "It's your stop," she said and slowly lowered her hand.

Half a block later, the BMW pulled into the parking lot of a 7-11. The Charger stopped behind the BMW. Morgan dropped the vehicle into Park and quickly left the car. From the corner of his eye, he could see Senai was out, also.

He watched the BMW for a moment. The driver didn't make any furtive movements, and this wasn't a high-risk stop. There was no reason to call the man out. Morgan stepped from behind the safety of his car door and walked along the side of the BMW. The driver's window was up, and his hands remained on the steering wheel.

The man spoke with someone over a hands-free connection in his car. Morgan couldn't hear what was being said as the voices were muted through the window, but he could see the driver talking and nodding.

Morgan tapped the window with his finger.

The man glanced in his direction but failed to lower the window. Instead, he turned forward and continued talking.

Morgan looked across the hood of the car to Senai. "You believe this guy?"

Senai didn't bother to make eye contact with him. She appeared to be visibly searching the interior of the car. "Does he realize he's buying himself a ticket for pissing off the police?"

Morgan slapped his hand against the window.

The man didn't look at him, but instead held up a finger and continued talking.

Morgan had enough now. He put his hands on the top of the car, watched the man for another moment, then kneed the driver's door. He stepped back to study the dent he'd created.

The sound of Morgan's knee against the side of the car put the driver into action. He quickly ended his call and climbed out.

"The fuck, man?"

Morgan shrugged. "You're probably wondering why we stopped you."

"No, man." He pointed to his car. "I'm wondering why you dented my car."

"What are you talking about?" Morgan asked.

The driver pointed to the dent in his door. "My car! You did that."

"That was there when we pulled you over."

As Senai walked around the car, the upset man turned to her. "You saw him do it, right?"

Senai's eyebrows raised.

The driver pointed again to the dent. "He hit my door."

Morgan shook his head. "No, I didn't do that. He's trying to avoid a ticket."

"Oh my God!" the man said. He threw his hands in the air and turned in a circle.

"Let me see your driver's license," Morgan said.

"For what?"

"Not signaling properly."

"Not signaling? Are you kidding? You dented my car."

Morgan thumbed in the direction they'd come. "You didn't properly signal your lane changes."

The man calmed then, and his eyes narrowed. "I signaled."

"Not properly," Morgan said.

"Yes, I did. Every time I changed lanes, I signaled. I knew you were back there."

"You're required to signal one hundred feet before a lane change. You signaled while you changed lanes. By definition, that's not proper."

"Are you kidding me?"

"Why would I do that?"

The driver bent down and touched the dent in the car door.

"Your license," Morgan repeated. "If you don't present it, that's another ticket."

The man straightened and stared at Morgan. Finally, he dug into his back pocket and removed his wallet. He pulled out his driver's license and handed it to the detective.

Timothy Dalrymple. Thirty-four years of age with an address on the South Hill. Morgan was familiar with the area, and it was likely an apartment.

The driver smirked. "You're stopping me for failure to signal lane changes?"

"He stopped you because you were white," Senai said.

"What?"

Morgan fought back a smile. Even though Senai was a rule follower, she occasionally enjoyed playing around. They were rare moments but ones that Morgan enjoyed.

"Wait. He stopped me for being white?"

Senai shrugged. "You're white, aren't you?"

"Timothy," Morgan said.

Dalrymple's eyes snapped to Morgan.

"What do you do for employment?"

"What?"

"Your job? What do you do?"

The man's face was now beet red, and he glanced several times between Senai and Morgan. "I'm between jobs."

"What did you do before?" Morgan asked.

"I was a loan processor."

Morgan thought about asking him why he was looking at the little house on Pacific but didn't want to bring further attention to it.

Dalrymple shrugged. "You got a problem with that?"

"How do you pay for this car without a job?"

"I paid cash for it," Dalrymple said with a satisfied smirk. "When I was working, of course."

"Of course," Morgan said.

"Do you stop everybody and ask them how they pay for their cars?"

"Only the white people," Senai said.

Dalrymple stared at her. "Are you serious?"

"He has white guilt."

The driver looked at Morgan. "What's your problem, man? Did I do something to you?"

The detective reread the driver's license. "Do you still live on the South Hill?"

"Yeah, sure."

"Mind if we search your car?"

"What?"

"Mind if we—"

"Are you kidding? You stop me for no reason—"

"I told you," Senai interrupted. "He stopped you because you were white."

Dalrymple shook his head. "That's not a reason."

"Can we search your car?" Morgan asked.

"No, you cannot search my car. You need a warrant for that."

Morgan rolled the driver's license through his fingers. "Who were you talking to on the phone?"

"What?"

"Who," Morgan repeated, "were you talking to on the phone when we stopped you?"

Dalrymple thought for a moment before saying, "My pastor."

"Your pastor?"

"That's right."

"You wouldn't get off the phone when we stopped you because you were talking with a man of God?"

"That's right. Got a problem with my religion, too?"

Morgan laid the driver's license on the hood of the BMW and took a picture of it with his cell phone. He put his phone away but left the license where it was.

"You're free to go," Morgan said flatly.

"What?" Dalrymple asked, confusion evident on his face.

Morgan turned to Senai. "This guy. Every time I say something, he responds with what. Am I stuttering or something?"

"What?" Senai said.

Morgan rolled his eyes.

"I'm not getting a ticket?" Dalrymple asked.

"We can give you one if you want. Or we can search your car if that will make you feel better."

Dalrymple raised his hands. "I'm good."

Morgan and Senai turned to walk back to their car.

"Hey," Dalrymple called. "Who's going to pay for this?" he asked, pointing at the dent in his door.

"Call your insurance company," Morgan asked.

When they climbed into the car, they watched Dalrymple study the dent in the driver's door.

Senai said, "Did you hit his car?"

"The dent was always there."

Senai stared at Morgan.

"Seriously," he said.

"It was always there? I don't remember seeing it when he drove by."

"I don't know what to tell you."

She shook her head. "You're pushing your luck, Morgan."

"If we're not pushing, we're not working."

The Charger backed out of the lot and headed southbound on Hamilton.

Chapter 17

He was made-to-order for a recruiting poster—tall, broad-shouldered, and handsome with a dimpled chin. His deep blue uniform fit as if it was tailored, and his boots were shined to a high gloss. Rookie Sean Thayer was everything the department would want in a poster boy.

If it was 1950, Morgan mused silently.

Unfortunately, today, the fact that he was white with blonde hair and blue eyes was a hindrance in how the public perceived the shooting of Tremaine Brown.

Thayer stood near his patrol car in the parking lot of the Monroe Court Building.

After Morgan parked and exited his car, he lifted his hand in acknowledgment of the rookie.

"Who's that?" Senai asked.

"The kid who shot Tremaine Brown."

"What are you doing, Morgan?

He shrugged. "He needs a pep talk."

"From you?"

"Why not?" he said and headed toward the rookie. "I'll meet you upstairs."

Thayer walked toward Morgan, and he extended his hand just before they met. "Sean Thayer," he said.

"Jim Morgan."

"What can I do for you, Detective?"

Morgan and Thayer had traded emails to set a meeting time, but Morgan was elusive in why he wanted to meet.

"Back in uniform."

"Another day answering phones. They said they'd put me back in the rotation in a day or two."

"That's good."

"What's this about?"

"I wanted to hear how you're doing."

"I'm not supposed to talk about the shooting," Thayer flatly said.

"I didn't ask about it, and I don't want to know."

Thayer's brow furrowed.

"Listen, kid. Everyone's second-guessing why you shot Brown. Frankly, I don't care. Brown is a turd, and he got shot. That's how life goes."

The rookie's brow remained crinkled, but now he tilted his head.

"Your Bynum's nephew, and that means something, especially to me. I want to make sure you're okay."

His expression relaxed slightly. "I'm fine."

"Have you heard anything about me?"

Thayer shrugged. "Most of the guys say you're stand-up."

"And the others?"

"They say you're an asshole."

"Then they're all right. But know this—I'm here if you need me. I'll help you out any way I can. Understand?"

"You don't know me."

Morgan tapped the rookie's badge. "I know that, and that's what counts. It's the only thing that counts. Those animals on the street," he said, thumbing behind his shoulder, "they don't matter in this equation."

A smirk began to form at the edge of the rookie's mouth.

"I'm not joking around. This is serious. This is life or death. That badge separates you from everyone. Got it?"

Thayer's smirk faded.

"The idiots who run city hall have no idea what we face. Therefore, they don't matter. The jackals in the press?

Those self-righteous pricks set us up to knock us down. They also don't matter."

The rookie watched Morgan intently now.

"And the citizens? Those sheep are helpless without us. They call the moment something is uncomfortable in their lives, but they turn their backs on us if we don't do our job with a smile. So they can pound sand." Morgan tapped the rookie's badge again. "That piece of tin makes us brothers. It makes us special. Do you understand?"

Thayer nodded.

"Anyone, and I mean *anyone*, gives you shit, then push back hard and stand your ground. Believe in that badge. Believe in the brothers who will stand with you. I'm one. Your uncle is one. In thirty minutes, I could have half the department standing in this parking lot with you."

"What about the other half?"

"That half," Morgan said, disdain creeping into his voice, "that half are the cake-eaters. You can eat meat, or you can eat cake, but you can't eat both. The cake-eaters, they die alone. Those who eat meat, we always stand together. Are you hearing what I'm saying?"

"Yeah," Thayer said. "I hear you."

The detective pulled a business card and pen from his jacket and wrote his cell phone number on the back of the card. "That's my cell number. Anytime you want to talk, you call me. Doesn't matter the time of day, I'll be there."

He handed the card to the rookie, who took it and examined it.

"We stand together," Morgan said, "or they break every one of us."

Thayer tucked the business card into his pocket. "You've been through what I'm going through?"

"If you've asked around about me, then you know I have."

He turned and walked toward his office.

Chapter 18

Shortly after five, the Dodge Charger crept around the corner of the warehouse building, its tires crunching gravel as it went.

A Lincoln Navigator was pulled into the same spot the Subaru had been several nights before. It was one of Joey's usual haunts. He couldn't always be sure, but he would bet a couple of bucks she was inside this vehicle.

Even though it remained light out, one of the oldest transactions of humanity still took place. Nothing stopped the sex trade—not the puritanical leanings of society, the redevelopment of a neighborhood, nor police efforts. It would always find somewhere to go down.

Morgan stopped his car and climbed out. To avoid making a noise, he didn't close his door.

Activity erupted inside the Lincoln. The driver jumped on top of the passenger. Through the windows, the detective could see an arm lifted high and brought down fast—*repeatedly*. Someone threw punches inside the SUV as the big rig rocked side-to-side.

Morgan ran to the side of the vehicle and peered in. A heavyset man was on top of Joey. She covered her head with her hands, but it didn't stop the man from hitting her.

The detective opened the driver's door, reached in, and grabbed the man by the back of his slacks. Morgan yanked, and the pants came down around the man's buttocks—they were unzipped.

The man glanced over his shoulder. "What the—"

Morgan snatched the driver by the feet and yanked him from his seat. The man's face hit the center console, then dragged across the seat. As the detective pulled the man from the SUV, his forehead clipped the running board before he fell to the earth. The driver rolled over then, his pants around his ankles and his manhood exposed. He lifted his hands to his head, hollering in pain.

The detective kicked him in the ribs once, which caused the driver to squeal and reflexively rollover to his hands and knees. The heavyset man wheezed for breath.

Morgan watched him then. He could arrest the man for assault, but what good would that do? He had an expensive truck. He'd no doubt get away with the crime. His type always did. At least, they always *seemed* to get away with it. Morgan glanced at Joey, who was upright now in the Lincoln, collecting her things. He'd promised her long ago he would protect her if she took care of him.

That settled it. He needed no further internal argument. He kicked the heavyset man once more, this time in the face. The man collapsed to the ground, unconscious.

Joey was out of the SUV by then with her purse clutched in her hand. She walked away from Morgan.

"Joey," he yelled. "Get it in the car."

"No, Morgan. Not now."

"I'll take you someplace safe."

She stopped but didn't turn to him.

"Sit in the front seat. Let's go."

Joey looked over her shoulder. He had never let her ride upfront before. Doing so could imply something inappropriate if another officer saw them. Whenever she had been in his car, and it had only been a few times, it was always in the back seat.

He hurried to her and grabbed her by the elbow. He escorted her to his car and helped her into the passenger seat. Morgan climbed behind the driver's seat.

The Charger continued around the building, leaving the unconscious man lying in the darkness.

***

Josephine Green lived in a one-bedroom house she rented on Sharp Avenue near Helena Street. It was two blocks from the Spokane River. In another era, it may have been a nice place and in a cute neighborhood. Today, the area was inhabited by the working poor or those, like Joey, who earned their living through criminal enterprise.

Morgan had never been inside her house before. He knew where she lived, of course, but there had never been a reason to be inside her home.

Nothing she owned appeared to be new. Everything had the feeling of having been used by someone else before as if it were purchased from thrift stores or the items were given to her through some charity.

Regardless, the small house was tidy. Morgan detected the lingering odor of marijuana, perhaps having embedded itself into the fabric of the furniture and carpet.

As soon as they arrived at her house, Joey walked straight into the bathroom to clean herself up. Her nose had been bloodied and her lip cut. At the minimum, she would end up with a blackened right eye as it was already swollen closed. He hoped there was no permanent damage.

When the shower turned on, Morgan searched through the refrigerator, hoping to find a beer. There wasn't much inside. Mostly fixings for sandwiches. On the kitchen counter were a small marijuana pipe and a baggie of weed. He knew she used heroin, but he didn't see her rig—the brown leather bag that would no doubt have a needle, spoon, and cotton balls in it.

There were a few out-of-date magazines on the couch. They were gossip rags like *People* and *Us*. Morgan flipped through them, looking for celebrities he might know. He saw a couple, read the captions that went along with their pictures, then tossed the magazines to the side.

After some time, the shower turned off. Joey remained in the restroom for a while longer, then came out with a towel wrapped around her. The brown skin of her shoulders glistened. Her face looked considerably better, but her right eye remained swollen shut. She looked worn and tired.

"Thanks for getting me home," she said.

Morgan stood. "I'm sorry that happened."

She shrugged. "It's the life."

Joey untied the towel and let it fall to the floor. He'd never seen her fully naked before. She was frail, made so through street life and the drug use she'd embraced. She remained attractive, though it wasn't like Vivian nor the redhead with the pleasant paleness. Instead, it was the muted beauty of a woman who had been mistreated by men and the unfortunate choices she had made for herself.

"Come on," she said softly. Resignation filled her voice. "Let's do this. I'm tired."

"Joey," Morgan whispered. He bent to pick up the towel.

With her hands at her sides, she stared ahead, unashamed to be naked in front of him. "You don't want to? I'm saying thank you."

He handed her the towel.

"I want you to do something else."

She grabbed the towel and frowned. As she wrapped it around her torso, she said, "If that's what you want, then sit down."

"Not that. I want you to keep an eye on a house."

Her single eye blinked a couple of times before she walked into her bedroom. She sat on her bed. "What do you mean?"

Morgan explained the house on Pacific Avenue with the intermittent flag changes. He told her he suspected it might be connected to The Eight somehow. "Something is going on," he said, "and I think we're getting made every time we're nearby. I'm not sure, but it's a gut feeling."

"How'd you find out about it?"

"Scrimmy."

"Why'd she tell you about it?"

"Because of her old man."

Joey slowly nodded. She already knew that story.

"It's a few blocks from your beat. Take a walk by it now and then. Tell me if you see anything."

"Okay," she whispered.

They remained silent for a couple of moments. Morgan finally asked, "Before I go, is there anything you need?"

She met his eyes. "I'm out, and I'm going to hurt tonight. The weed's not going to cut it."

"Give me a minute," he said.

Outside, he popped the trunk on his car. In a far corner was a crumbled Jack in the Box bag. Morgan grabbed the sack, straightened it, and stuck his hand inside. He removed a small package of heroin, leaving only two left. None of these packages were stamped with any logos. For a moment, he thought of Yaban Karga and wondered where he might have fled.

Morgan crumpled the hamburger bag and tossed it back into the corner of the trunk, then closed the lid.

He'd read and listened to the news stories of cops in other jurisdictions who stole drugs to sell. He would never do that. The drugs were his stock in trade. If he kept his informers happy, they kept him happy. He knew it was illegal, but it was how the street worked. The politicians and the lawyers—the ones who created the laws—had no clue what the life was really like, and they hamstrung working cops with their unrealistic rules. If he had to bend a law for the greater good occasionally, then Detective James Morgan was more than willing to do so.

When he walked back into the house, Joey was asleep on top of her bed.

He pulled the covers back slightly, then scooped her up. She was lighter than he expected. He placed her under the covers. Carefully, he unhooked the damp towel, pulled it from her, and draped it over a dresser knob. Then he laid the blankets over her. He pulled the small packet from his pocket, carefully wiped his prints from it, and placed it on the nightstand next to her bed.

Morgan locked up her house as he left.

Chapter 19

When he returned home, he immediately took off his badge and gun before removing a beer from the fridge. He felt a certain level of frustration growing in him. The mystery around The Eight bothered him. No gang had ever arrived in town with this level of hype and yet remained so invisible.

They all had their reputations, of course. MS-13, the infamous Mexican gang that caught the attention of politicians, was the flavor de jour. Everyone seemed afraid of them now.

In the nineties, it was the Bloods and the Crips. For a while, fear swirled around the Asian gangs because they barely spoke English, and officers had trouble identifying their names. Even with all that built-in hype, none of those gangs ever arrived in town with all the hoopla The Eight was getting.

It just didn't make sense to move into a locale with so much heat.

He stepped onto his balcony and looked down at the pool. It was full again as the evening sun was setting. Two of the girls from the Benetton ad were there. The black girl wriggled her fingers at him, and the Asian girl giggled.

A knock at Morgan's door took his attention from them. When he opened the door, the redhead was there, wearing only a black bikini and flip-flops. In the crook of her finger was a half-empty bottle of Corona.

"Hey there," Morgan said.

"Are you coming down to the pool?" she asked.

"Not tonight. Maybe tomorrow."

"I'll believe it when I see it," she said. Her eyes locked onto the beer in Morgan's hand. "Got another one of those?"

"You already have one."

She lifted hers to check how much remained, then she tilted the bottle to her lips, quickly draining it. "I'm out," she said, handing him the empty bottle.

Morgan knew if she crossed the threshold into his apartment, there would be no turning back with this one. It was in her eyes.

He stepped back and let her inside.

She strolled by him like she knew it was only a matter of time.

Her eyes took in his apartment—the living room with its two recliners and a big-screen television. On one wall was a large black-and-white photograph of Mickey Mantle hitting a home run. On the connecting wall was an equally large color photo of Ken Griffey Jr. catching a ball over the outfield wall, robbing its hitter from going yard.

Morgan struggled to remember her name.

Studying the pictures, she said, "I take it you like baseball."

"I like excellence."

She turned around and placed her hands on her hips. "Yet you've been playing hard to get?"

"I have?"

"Don't you find me excellent?"

"I do," he said, and he wasn't lying. Standing in his apartment, in her bikini, her pale soft skin within reach as she flirted with him, Morgan physically reacted as any man would. His pulse quickened, and a tingling sensation traveled throughout his body, but something wasn't right.

Mentally, he hadn't engaged with her, and he wasn't sure why.

She moved toward him.

He struggled to remember her name.

She slid her arms around his neck and looked up into his eyes. "I've only got one question for you, Jimmy."

"What's that?"

"Are you going to give me that beer, or are we going straight to bed?"

"Why don't I get you that beer?"

Disappointment filled her eyes, and her arms slipped from him.

Morgan couldn't understand why he didn't want to grab this woman and have her immediately. She was young, attractive, and willing. What more could he want?

He went to the kitchen and threw away her empty bottle. Then he grabbed a can of beer from the refrigerator and turned around. She was there next to him.

"Here," he said, handing it to her.

Something felt wrong in the whole scenario, and it bothered him.

She placed the beer on the counter, then rested her hands on Morgan's chest. "What's it going to take to get you?"

The tingling he initially felt was gone.

"Don't you want me?" she asked and forced her lower lip into a pout.

And there it was—the desperation. She was throwing herself at him, and Morgan hated that. Just like the street, he wanted the chase. He didn't want it to be easy. Victory without challenge was nothing to revel in. It's one of the reasons that he longed for Vivian Basler, the never-ending chase she had forced him into running.

Morgan grabbed the redhead's hands, slowly pulled them from his chest, and lowered them to her sides.

"It's not that," he said.

"Then what is it?" she asked, her eyes pleading.

He wanted her to stop, to make her go away, but he didn't want to be overly mean about it. Finally, he said, "I don't remember your name."

Her eyes quickly refocused. "What?"

Morgan shrugged.

"How can you not remember my name? We talked for like thirty minutes at Vivian's party. I've been flirting with you for a couple weeks now. I've been throwing myself at you."

"I guess it wasn't important."

She yanked her hands from his.

"Fuck you," she said and extended her middle finger. She turned and headed to the front door. "Asshole!"

Her butt wriggled while she hurriedly walked away, and Morgan suddenly felt a jolt of excitement. He jumped and grabbed her by the elbow, which spun her around. She pulled her arm free.

"Don't touch me!"

"Wait," he said.

Her chest heaved as she took large, angry breaths. Her fists were balled, and her feet stood shoulder-width apart. Even in a bikini, the redhead looked ready for a fight. "I can't believe I offered to go to bed with you."

"Please don't go," Morgan said, his voice low and calm. He couldn't believe he just said please. He never said that.

"You're too old for me, anyway," she said. Her fists shook with anger. "What was I thinking?"

"I want you to stay," he said. The tingling sensation had returned. He reached out for her hand, but she swatted him away.

"No! God! You're as old as my dad."

"Tell me your name, *please*." Again, with the please, Morgan thought. He now sounded like a pussy. "I won't forget. I promise." *Promise* was almost as bad as *please*. What was wrong with him?

She shook her head. "Maybe you could be as old as my grandfather."

"I'm sorry," he said. "I'm an idiot. I should have paid more attention to you."

The redhead stared at him. The anger in her face was in full bloom. He held her gaze until she looked away.

Morgan thoroughly enjoyed this moment. The chase was on, and it was beautiful. He even said so. "This is beautiful," he mumbled.

"What?" she said, her lip curling.

He covered his verbal slip by saying, "You're beautiful."

She studied his face, then smirked. "You're sort of ugly."

He grabbed her and jerked her to him. She didn't fight it, but her eyes widened in surprise. She pulled her head back from him, waiting and watching. Morgan leaned slowly down and kissed her. She relaxed in his arms and kissed him back.

When they broke their embrace, she looked at him and said, "Alyssa. My name is Alyssa. You better not forget it again."

Chapter 20

When Morgan walked into HQ, all eyes turned his way. The entire team was gathered around Sergeant Bynum's desk.

"What's going on?" Morgan asked.

"There was a shooting last night," Bynum said. The look on his face confused Morgan. He couldn't tell if the sergeant was suspicious or disappointed.

"Who?"

"A drive-by," Senai said.

"Yeah. Okay," Morgan said. "It was a drive-by. So, who was shot?"

"Regina Baird."

"Tremaine Brown's girlfriend?"

"That's correct," Bynum said. "Brown's girlfriend."

"She caught one in the ten-ring," Courtney Earley said, tapping the middle of his chest.

"She's dead?" Morgan asked. "Who was assigned the case?"

"Delaney and Burkett."

Holding up a yellow sticky note, the sergeant said, "They called for you."

"Me?" Morgan asked. "Why?"

Each team member watched him with some form of curiosity.

"They didn't say," Bynum said. "They just asked that you call them after you got in."

Morgan snatched the note from the sergeant's fingers and stared at it. Nobody said anything at that moment. His eyes met theirs, and he knew what each was thinking.

Could he have somehow been involved with Regina Baird's shooting?

Protesting would have made him look weak.

And guilty.

Morgan turned and left the office. It took only a few minutes to walk from the Monroe Court Building to the Public Safety Building. He waved to the county deputy assigned security and passed by the metal detectors. He proceeded toward the locked doors that permitted entrance to the hallowed halls of the Spokane Police Department.

Fluorescent light bounced off freshly waxed linoleum floors. The older he grew, the less he enjoyed being in this building. There was a time he loved it, almost rejoicing in the history of the men and women who previously worked there. That was when he was naïve.

Now he knew what these halls truly represented.

They were a gauntlet filled with brass-collared toadies and other ladder-climbers who would sacrifice a junior officer like a pawn if it allowed them to reach their own goals. Morgan believed that the real cops in the department were the ones who spent as much time away from these hallways as possible.

The detectives' offices were at the far end of the hall. He knew they all had a tough job, every cop did, but due to the proximity to chiefs and captains, these detectives eventually would become tarnished.

Some detectives became outspoken union rabble-rousers who spent too much time worrying about the politics of the job and not enough *doing* the job. Those types were no longer cops in his mind. They were hacks, marking time until retirement.

He carried the yellow sticky note between two fingers as if it were covered in mold. When he walked into the

Major Crimes office, he stopped at the cubicles of Quinn Delaney and Marci Burkett. They were huddled over some paperwork.

Delaney and Burkett were passable as detectives, but to Morgan, they were members of the department's attaboys.

Throughout his career, he'd come to realize that the administration recognized three types of officers—"the attaboys," "the gotta-gets," and the "can't-waits."

The attaboys were the officers that the administration loved to pat on the head whenever they did something right—no matter how small. That was Quinn Delaney and Marci Burkett—they could do no wrong. If anything in their careers seemed like it might be hinky, it was brushed to the side as they continued along their golden, protected path.

The gotta-gets were the officers who hadn't quite figured things out yet. "He's gotta get his officer-initiated stops up," "She's gotta get better at defensive tactics," or "He's gotta get out of his car more," were all examples of things the administration might say as things to encourage this type. Those officers were on the bubble. In the eyes of the brass, they were able to move up or down, and the administration didn't really care which occurred. That's where most of the department toiled.

Then there were the can't-waits. Those were the officers that the brass couldn't wait for them to quit, retire, or fuck up. They just wanted these officers gone and off the department's roster so they could free up space for some recruit that would hopefully grow into an attaboy or at the very least, grind away as a gotta-get. Morgan knew he was a can't-wait in the eyes of the administration and that pissed him off. He had done plenty of good work over the years, but no matter how hard he worked or what he accomplished, he would never rise to an attaboy.

Morgan coughed.

Both Delaney and Burkett looked over their shoulders.

He held up the yellow sticky note. "You rang?"

Delaney spun in his chair to face him while Marci stood and crossed her arms.

"Yeah," Delaney said. "Thanks for coming over."

Burkett studied him with barely disguised disdain. Morgan reflected the same to her. She was a piece of work.

"You want to know where I was last night?" Morgan asked.

"That would be nice," Delaney said.

Morgan crumpled the little note and tossed it on Delaney's desk. "Why?"

"There was a homicide," Delaney said.

"Tremaine Brown's girlfriend. I heard. How does that impact me?"

"We heard you had a verbal confrontation with her a couple days ago."

"How you'd hear that?"

"So, it's true," Delaney said.

Morgan sneered. "Parker talks too much."

Delaney glanced at Burkett, whose disgust had transformed into a stony façade. The woman was trying to throw off an intimidating vibe. It didn't have the desired effect. Instead, it had the opposite. Morgan wanted to mess with her now.

"We'd like to know where you were last night," Delaney said. "Just to clear you off our list of possibles."

Morgan raised his brow and gave Delaney an incredulous look. "You're serious? A stat-five maggot takes one in the chest, and you immediately assume a fellow officer might have done it?"

Delaney shook his head. "It's not like that. We're trying to clear everyone who might be suspect."

"Right. So, you look inside the department first. Attaboy, Delaney. Excellent work."

Burkett jumped to the defense of her partner. "We heard about your run-in with Tremaine and his girlfriend. We didn't cause this problem. You did."

"It wasn't a run-in, sweetheart. Get your story straight."

"Then tell us about it," Burkett said.

Morgan was disappointed she hadn't bitten on the sweetheart comment. He was confident she would have. He turned his attention fully to Delaney. Maybe snubbing her would tweak the female detective.

"Unless we clear you," Delaney began, "that confrontation could be a thread for a defense attorney to use. Understand? I don't believe you did it, Morgan."

"Gee, thanks," Morgan said dryly.

Delaney continued without missing a beat. "Do I like you? No, not even close, but—."

"I don't like you," Morgan said, "since we're being honest."

"I don't like you either," Burkett added. "So, we're three for three."

Delaney sighed and shook his head. "What I was going to say was I don't need to like you do to my job and do it properly."

Morgan pressed his lips together. "Then ask away so we can get on with our lives."

"Where were you last night?" Delaney asked.

"I was with a girl."

Delaney grabbed his notepad and a pen. "What's her name?"

"Alyssa."

"Last name?"

Morgan shrugged. "I don't know."

Delaney glanced at his partner before asking, "Where did you meet this girl?"

"She lives in my apartment complex. The Alexandria Apartments, up north. Cute redhead, mid-twenties."

Burkett's face scrunched. "Mid-*twenties*?"

"I don't know." Morgan cocked his head. "Maybe early twenties."

"Oh God, gross," Burkett said. "You could be her dad."

"Hey, I don't judge your sex life, Missy."

Burkett rolled her eyes.

"Listen," Delaney said, "We'll follow up on this. If it is as you say it is, everything will be copacetic."

Copacetic, Morgan thought. *What an idiot.*

***

He was still in the hallway of the Public Safety Building, almost to an exit when Internal Affairs Lieutenant Neil Culkin saw him.

"Morgan!"

The detective paused, fighting the urge to continue and leave the building. He turned to see Culkin hurrying toward him.

The lieutenant grinned as he approached. Culkin was a good-looking man who wore Dockers and a red button-up shirt. His gun and badge were clipped to his belt. To Morgan, both items looked more like props than tools on him. The lieutenant's dark hair belied his years as he had recently passed his fiftieth birthday. His mustache danced as he spoke.

"I heard you spoke with Sean Thayer yesterday."

"And?" Morgan said.

"I'm wondering why a rookie would be meeting with you?"

"I was offering words of encouragement. That's all."

Culkin's smile was easy but disingenuous. "Listen, Jim. The shooting already doesn't smell right. We don't need your stink around it as well by giving the kid some bad advice."

"My stink?"

The lieutenant's smile faded. "You know what I mean. Keep away from the rookie until this is done. Okay?"

Morgan opened his mouth to say something, but closed it, realizing nothing he said would help this moment.

Sometimes less is more, Morgan thought.

He nodded.

Culkin's smile returned, and he patted Morgan on the shoulder. "Thanks for being a team player."

***

Outside the Public Safety building, Morgan's cell phone buzzed once, indicating he'd received a text message. He pulled it out to read.

SHE IS DEMANDING THE 10K. DO I PAY IT? HAVE YOU GOTTEN ANYWHERE?

Morgan stopped and thought about the text. If he caught Jenna in the transaction, he could arrest her and be done with this problem. Extortion was a felony.

He could then get a search warrant following the arrest. However, if he found where she stored the pictures, he would need to book them into evidence to make her charges stick.

That meant a lot of eyes would be on the photographs. The more people who knew about them, the more likely the story would get out. The press would eat a tale like this up, which meant they'd go after everything they could get through the Freedom of Information Act.

All for a charge that likely might not stick in the long run and a hunt for photographs he didn't know he could actually locate.

And there was no guarantee he would discover who her partners were.

So, there was only one guarantee Morgan could make—arresting Jenna wouldn't solve Desmond Ashdown's problem.

AGREE TO PAY HER, Morgan texted. LET ME KNOW WHERE/WHEN PAYMENT IS TO BE MADE.

***

Morgan drove to Pacific Avenue and sat off the little yellow house with the flag. The white version with the black fist was out again. Morgan scanned the other places. Their flags were a blue Seattle Seahawks helmet, a red flag with the Eastern Eagles logo, and a flag for the Boilermaker's Union.

He froze.

All the flags were now different. He hadn't noticed it before, as he was so focused on the switch between black and white fists. There were four other houses with flags in them.

Morgan pulled his cell phone from his pants pocket and took photos of the houses he was nearby. He started his car, pulled up to the house with the black fist in the window, and took a picture.

The flag moved slightly, as if someone from behind watched him.

The detective lowered his camera and drove slowly out of the neighborhood.

Chapter 21

When Morgan returned to the department, only Nayla Senai and Courtney Earley were in the office. Senai spoke on her telephone while Earley concentrated intently on his computer screen.

"Big man, what are you doing?"

Earley leaned back. "Research, but it can hold if you've got something hot."

"I'm sending you four pictures," Morgan said as he worked on his phone. He called up the photos, attached them to an email, and sent them to Earley. "They're all on East Pacific. You can see the street numbers on the houses."

"Okay."

"Run the houses and find the listed owners. I'm going to bet the taxpayer address is different than the house address."

"Rental houses?" Earley said.

"Exactly. Contact the various owners. Find out who's living there."

Earley nodded.

Senai hung up the phone and joined them. "What's going on?"

"You know the house on Pacific?"

She nodded.

"The other houses around it," Morgan said, "the ones that also had flags. Well, they're switching them as well."

"What?"

Morgan showed her the pictures he'd taken with his phone.

"You didn't have any luck finding the legal owner of the house, right?"

Senai shook her head.

Morgan swiped to the picture of the black fist flag and showed Earley. "Nayla's worked this one. Make the others a priority. If you find the owners and get somewhere with them, circle back to this one, okay?"

Earley nodded.

"I can do it," Senai said.

"No, you're coming with me," Morgan said. To Earley, he continued, "Also, get Doc and Adrian on those houses. We need eyes on them."

"You got it, Hoss." Earley spun to his computer.

"What are we going to do?" Senai asked as she followed Morgan to the door.

"We're going to chat with someone."

"Damn it," she said. "You know I hate it when you're cryptic."

***

Tremaine Brown lived in an apartment community off Hartson Avenue and Arthur Street.

Morgan knew precisely which apartment as he'd contacted Brown there before. He parked his Dodge at the edge of the complex and got out. When Senai followed suit, she asked, "We're contacting Brown?"

"Yeah."

"Aren't Delaney and Burkett working his girlfriend's killing?"

Morgan walked toward the apartment buildings. "They are."

Senai hurried up to him. "Then why are we doing this?"

"I want to offer my condolences."

Senai suddenly stopped. "What?"

Morgan halted and turned to her. "I may not have liked the woman, but that doesn't mean she needed to catch a round. If you don't feel comfortable coming with me…"

He didn't bother to wait for her to accept. He turned and continued toward Brown's apartment.

Senai fell silent as she walked behind him.

Morgan knew other gang members lived in these apartments. He'd been here alone before and was okay with it, but he appreciated Senai being with him—especially today.

They walked up to the second floor of the second building and knocked. On the outside of the door was a wireless camera. Morgan knew if Brown was inside, he would see it was him.

A moment passed, and the door opened. Brown stood there in low-slung black jeans and an open club shirt. He was barefoot. The sling he wore at the bar the previous night was gone. The apartment smelled of marijuana.

"Hey, man," Morgan said. "I'm sorry to hear about your girl."

"What kind of bullshit is this, Morgan?"

"No bullshit. I heard about your girl and came to pay my respects."

Brown's face scrunched in disbelief.

"We may be on opposite sides of the fence but, you and me, we've always played the game a certain way. Or am I wrong?"

Brown rubbed his chin and glanced at Senai. "We play the game straight, you and me, yeah."

"I'm sorry for your loss," Morgan said.

"What do you want, detective?"

"Nothing." Morgan stuck his hand out.

Brown studied it for a moment, then tentatively shook it.

"If you know anything about the shooting, work with the detectives assigned to the case, okay? They're good at what they do. They'll find who did it."

The man's brow further corrugated.

"Take care, Tremaine."

He was down a couple of stairs before Brown said, "Hey, Morgan."

The detective stopped and looked up. Nayla was by his side.

"Thank you. I appreciate it."

Morgan nodded once and then continued down the stairs.

When they were back in the car, Senai muttered, "Wow. That was almost… human."

Morgan softly chuckled as he started the car. The engine roared to life.

"I'm serious, Morgan. That was kind."

"That's called playing it forward."

"Don't you mean *paying* it forward?"

"No. I meant playing."

"I don't understand."

"I just showed the kid some kindness, and what did it cost me? Nothing. A couple minutes of lowering myself. Now, when I need something from him, really need something, he might just remember this moment. If that happens, then it will have been worth it."

"So, this whole thing was a lie?"

Morgan glanced at Senai. "Do you *really* think I care if his woman bought it? She was sleeping with the enemy. Fuck her. She got what she got."

Senai turned forward and stared out the windshield.

His phone buzzed once. He pulled it out and read a text from Desmond Ashdown.

She wants me to drop it off now—The Red Light District.

Morgan couldn't go there with Senai and watch the transfer without alerting his partner that he was working something off the books. He closed his phone and shoved it into his pocket.

***

When they returned to HQ, Courtney Earley was still behind his computer, but now he was on the telephone with a pencil in his hand. No one else had returned.

Senai walked woodenly back to her desk.

Morgan dropped into his chair, and he slid some papers toward himself. Outside agencies had flagged several reports for him to review. He had just begun to read one of them when Earley hung up the phone and spun around.

"That's the last of them," he said.

"What?"

"I tracked down the owners of the five houses. All of them are rented to the same person. Can you believe that?"

Morgan stood and walked over to Earley. "Who's the renter?"

"Some chick name Stephanie Zentgraf."

"Ever heard of her?" Morgan asked.

"No," Earley said. "She doesn't have a record either."

Morgan turned to Senai. "Hey, Nayla, ever hear of a Stephanie Zentgraf?"

"Isn't she a tennis player?"

He waved her off and turned back to the big man. "Good work, buddy. Let's find this woman and figure out what's going on."

Earley nodded and turned back to his computer.

The door to the office opened, and Sergeant Bynum walked in.

"Morgan," Bynum said, while settling into his chair. "Didn't you work Yaban Karga as an informant?"

Morgan felt a tingling sensation at the back of his neck—the thrill of the chase had returned. "You mean the Turk?"

"That's right. The Turk. I thought his name seemed familiar."

Morgan approached the sergeant's desk. "What about him?"

"His body was found a couple hours ago along the river. Detectives are out with it now."

The tingling sensation Morgan felt turned into a cold chill running along his spine. "You sure it's Karga?"

Bynum shrugged. "How would I know? I'm only passing along some scuttlebutt. Check for yourself."

Chapter 22

Morgan pulled off Downriver Drive and parked. He made his way toward the crime scene via a freshly worn footpath of crumpled grass. As he hurried, he could see several police officers talking with a group of people in swimsuits. Two yellow rafts were pulled ashore. Inside both inflatable boats were coolers Morgan suspected would be full of beer.

The crime scene was already marked off with yellow POLICE LINE—DO NOT CROSS tape to form both an inner and outer perimeter. The inner was closest to the body, and two men in suits were in there now. The other perimeter was wider, and members of the forensic unit assembled there.

Near the outer perimeter tape stood Officer Leya Navarro, a clipboard in her hand. Morgan walked up to her. "Log me in," he said.

"For what purpose?" Navarro asked.

"That's Yaban Karga, right?"

"He's one of them, yeah."

"One of them?"

Navarro looked toward the crime scene. "There's a woman with him."

"His girlfriend?"

"I don't know," Navarro said. "Maybe."

Morgan ducked under the nearest line of yellow tape.

"Detective!" Navarro yelled.

"What?" Morgan asked from the opposite side of the DO NOT CROSS line.

"You can't go in there," Navarro said.

"That's my informant. Log me in."

Morgan stared at Navarro until she relented. "Fine."

He spun and walked toward the edge of the inner perimeter tape. Major Crimes Detectives Dallas Nash and Glenn Higgins bent over the bodies of Yaban Karga and the woman that Morgan suspected was his girlfriend.

Morgan wasn't a fan of either detective. They were about the same age as he, but Morgan figured both to be cake-eaters. He could never really determine where their loyalties fell, either to the men on the department or to the brass. Because of that, he distrusted them.

"Nash," Morgan called.

Dallas Nash looked up from the body and glanced around until he made eye contact with Morgan.

"Yeah?"

Morgan waved Nash over to the inner perimeter tape line. Morgan was smart enough not to enter the inner perimeter. Doing so would require an additional report from him and would also raise all sorts of red flags. Morgan knew when to hit a hornet's nest and how hard, but also when to let it be.

Nash sighed and ambled over to Morgan.

"That's Yaban Karga, right?"

"Why are you here, Jim?"

"If that's Karga, he's been my informant over the years."

Nash frowned. "Is that so? Maybe you have some insight into what got him killed?"

"Not really. I just heard he bought it and wanted to see how. Figured maybe I could help or something."

"Unless you can point to someone who wanted to do him harm, there's not much you can do."

"How was he killed?"

Nash pursed his lips while he thought. When his face relaxed, he said, "They were both shot in the back of the head. Execution style."

Morgan looked back up to the road where a multitude of police vehicles was parked. "Where's his vehicle?"

"There was no vehicle here when we arrived. Someone drove them here and killed them. Tire tracks were destroyed by arriving patrol vehicles. Know anyone who would want to kill either of them?" Nash asked.

Morgan looked back to Nash. "Karga—no. And the girl I never met. I only saw her once. A real pretty thing."

"You can't tell that now. The bullet blew her face away. Him, it took the top of his head off."

"How did you ID them?"

"He had his wallet. Her ID was in her pocket."

"What was her name?" Morgan asked.

Nash paused, as if considering whether to share the information. Finally, he said, "Stephanie Zentgraf."

"What?"

"Zentgraf," he said. "Stephanie. Why does that name mean something to you?"

Morgan had trouble swallowing before speaking. "I thought you said it was the tennis player."

Nash rolled his eyes, then moved back toward his partner. The Major Crimes detectives lurked over the dead like two vultures appraising something they were about to eat.

Morgan watched them for a few minutes before heading back to his car.

***

He returned immediately to HQ, ran up the stairs to the office, and burst in. Only Bynum remained at his desk.

"Where's Nayla and the big man?" Morgan asked.

"They went out to relieve Thorn and Strange on the Pacific House. Did you confirm the body was Karga?"

"Yeah," Morgan said.

He wondered if he should tell Bynum about Stephanie Zentgraf's murder and her connection to the homes on Pacific?

Since Earley had already run her name through the system, it was unlikely anyone would hear about it for at least a few days. Morgan was concerned if he shared the information now, someone would suggest they involve the regional drug task force, or worse, the Major Crimes detectives. He wanted to crack whatever was going on at the houses and not hand it over to someone else in the department.

For a fleeting moment, he worried he might be putting his team at risk by not sharing the information about Karga and Zentgraf's murder. No, he decided, they were professionals. This holdback of intel would not negatively affect them as such. Besides, he would share the information in the morning.

"Everything okay?" Bynum asked.

Morgan nodded. "Everything's fine."

Chapter 23

When Morgan arrived home from work shortly after five, Alyssa stood outside his apartment. She wore skimpy jean shorts and a black bikini top. She had stepped out of her sandals and was standing barefoot on the concrete. She leaned her back against the building and held a bottle of Tecate in her hand.

Morgan raised a questioning eyebrow as he stepped onto the third-floor landing.

"How much do you work?" she asked with a slightly accusatory tone.

"A lot."

"No kidding." She lifted the bottle and took a sip. "Some cops came by asking about you."

"What did they want?"

"They wanted to know where you were last night."

"What did you tell them?"

"What do you think I said? The lady cop. She doesn't like you, does she?"

Morgan slipped his key into the door's lock and turned it. "Is that why you came by? To tell me that?"

"I'm horny," she said, her voice low and throaty. She stepped behind him and slid her arm around his stomach.

He pushed the front door open and stepped inside, breaking her grasp. He heard her tsk, but she still followed him inside, shutting the door behind her. He tossed his keys on the kitchen counter and turned around.

She was immediately upon him, a tangle of arms and legs. He pushed her back as her mouth struggled to find his. To him, it was awkward. It was as if he was her first boyfriend, and she couldn't get to him fast enough.

Alyssa opened her eyes and was confused. "The hell, Jimmy?"

"Not tonight," he said.

Her brow furrowed, and her lower lip pushed out. "How come?"

Morgan shrugged, but he knew why. It was the game of push and pull. If she pushed forward, he would pull back. If she pulled back, he would push forward. If he kept a lover off balance, if he never let them know where they stood, he believed he could be in control of any relationship. And if they decided they no longer wanted to play the game, that was okay with him. Relationships were messes he didn't want in his life.

Alyssa stared at him.

"It wasn't that good," Morgan said.

Her eyes briefly widened before her hand whipped out. The hard crack across his cheek was loud. A hint of a smile appeared at the corners of his mouth.

Her brow furrowed again, but the pout was now gone. "You think that's funny?"

"Not necessarily."

She shook her hand as it obviously stung from the slap. "Then what is it? Why is it so hard for you to just go to bed with me?"

"Because you throw it at me like you don't respect it."

Her mouth opened and closed several times like a fish out of water. She finally said, "I respect it."

"No," Morgan said, "you don't."

Her hands balled into fists as she struggled with what was occurring. The tingle of excitement made itself known in Morgan. Her anger excited him, and he wondered how much he could push and pull this girl.

"I'm sorry for saying it wasn't good," he said, "because it was."

She looked away, but her eyes remained hard, and her hands stayed curled.

"It was great."

Alyssa blinked a couple of times, and her eyes softened. Her hands stayed balled, though.

"But you make it too easy and too cheap, like it's some sort of handshake you share with every guy you meet."

Her eyes hardened again, and her mouth twisted.

Morgan fought to control a smile.

Alyssa's fists shook as she spoke. "You're calling me a *whore*."

"That's how you're acting."

She opened her hand to slap him, but he didn't flinch. She threateningly held it up in the air, then dropped it. "Maybe I won't see you anymore."

"I understand."

Alyssa sighed. "I don't get you, Jimmy. All I want to do is be with you, and you're awful."

Morgan watched her.

"You're a mean man," she said. "No one has ever treated me like that."

The tingle was at full buzz now. He slowly stepped toward her, but she didn't move. When he lightly grabbed her chin, she looked up at him with doe eyes. The buzzing in his chest had grown to a full rumble. He kissed her on the lips, and she relaxed. Morgan pulled her into him and kissed her further.

When they parted, her eyes remained closed, but her mouth opened slightly.

He led her into the bedroom then.

It was the push and pull.

***

Morgan awoke to a knock at his door. Alyssa softly snored next to him and didn't move at the sound. When he slid out of bed, she rolled over and tugged the sheet with her. It was too warm to have much more than that.

He slipped on his jeans and grabbed his T-shirt before leaving the bedroom. There was a second knock as he pulled the shirt over his head. He looked through the peephole before opening the front door.

Leigh Gaston stepped in without being invited. "Were you sleeping?" she asked as she passed him in the hallway to the living room.

"What time is it?" Morgan asked.

"Nine-thirty. I got the information you wanted."

"Yeah?" he said. With the deaths of Yaban Karga and Stephanie Zentgraf, he'd forgotten about Desmond Ashdown and his blackmail problem.

"Jenna is a stage name. Her real name is Ellen Simpson, and she drives a yellow Honda. Here's the license plate." She handed him a torn piece of paper with six digits written on it in pink ink.

Morgan glanced at the numbers before tucking the piece of paper into a pocket. "Thank you."

"I followed her, too."

"You didn't have to do that."

"I know, but I did. I was sort of having fun watching her. Is that what police work feels like?"

"Sometimes."

"So cool. Anyway, after her shift ended, about midnight, she went straight to The Better Kitty Adult Bookstore. Do you know the one? On Second?"

Morgan waited to say anything, as it felt like Leigh had more to tell.

"I followed her inside."

"That could have been dangerous."

Leigh ignored his admonishment. "When she was inside, she didn't bother looking around. She went straight to the back and had a conversation with the manager, maybe the owner. I don't know what he is."

"How could you tell?"

"The office has a big window in it. You can see everything inside. Probably so whoever's working can see people inside the store. It works in reverse, too."

"What happened then?"

Leigh smiled. "Pushy much? Anyway, I pretended to shop while she talked with the manager guy, but she left pretty quick. I'll tell you what—he didn't look happy. Then the guy came out and asked if I was looking for anything specific."

Morgan was about to ask a follow-up question when a voice behind asked, "Who is she?"

Leigh's eyes widened as she looked over Morgan's shoulder. He looked back to see her.

Standing in the middle of the hallway, naked and unashamed, was Alyssa. Her feet were shoulder-width apart, and her hands were on her hips.

Morgan turned his attention back to Leigh. "Go back to bed," he said flatly.

"I want to know who *she* is," Alyssa said, her voice rising. "Is she your girlfriend?"

"Go back to bed or go home." Morgan did not bother turning to face her.

The apartment was silent for several beats. Finally, Alyssa stomped her foot once, then retreated to the bedroom, where she slammed the door.

"She seems nice," Leigh said.

"What happened with the guy?" Morgan asked.

"The manager? Nothing. He asked some questions about what I liked, made some small talk, that was it."

"What's he look like?"

"Medium height. Fat. Five o'clock shadow. Kind of sweaty. The greasy kind."

"Did you get his name?"

"He answered the phone as I was walking out. Said his name was Ricky. That's all I know."

"Ricky," he repeated.

"Yeah, like a little kid. So, we're good?"

"Yeah," Morgan said. "We're good."

Leigh started for the door, then stopped, turning back to Morgan. "Good luck with your… friend," she said, a hint of a smile playing at her lips.

Morgan remained in the living room as Leigh let herself out. When the front door closed, he faced the bedroom. He didn't know what was occurring in there. Alyssa could be dressed for all he knew, ready to storm out and head home. He shook his head.

Women problems—just what he did not want in his life.

When he entered the room, she was in bed, propped up with the pillows behind her, a sheet wrapped around her, hiding her breasts. Her arms were crossed over her chest, and hatred burned in her eyes.

"Who is *she*?" Alyssa asked. Her lips pressed tightly together when she finished speaking.

"It was work."

"Police work comes to your house at nine-thirty at night? That's bullshit, Jimmy."

"I'm helping a friend. She's helping me."

"Is she a girlfriend? You need to tell me. I'm not batting clean-up to another woman."

"I didn't know you liked baseball."

"Shut up. I mean it."

"She's not my girlfriend." Morgan shrugged and continued, "But if she was, would it matter?"

Alyssa's mouth dropped open.

He thumbed toward the door. "Are you staying, or are you going? Make your choice." It was the push and pull, and he was giving it to her in spades.

She stared at him, still thinking about his last question.

"Because I'd like you to stay," Morgan said.

He took off his shirt and pants then slid into bed. He pulled her down from her sitting position and climbed on top of her.

"Who was she?" Alyssa asked, her voice soft.

"I already told you. She was work, and that's all that matters." It was the most truthful thing he had ever said to a woman.

Morgan kissed her then, and she stopped asking questions.

Chapter 24

When Morgan arrived the next morning, Internal Affairs Lieutenant Neil Culkin was at the front of the Monroe Court Building. He tracked Morgan as he parked his car a couple of rows away and slowly climbed out.

Even though he noticed the IA lieutenant as he pulled into the parking lot, Morgan still closed his eyes and lifted his face to the sun after exiting his car. He was going to enjoy the small summer ritual, regardless of who was watching.

"Morgan," Culkin hollered.

The detective ignored the lieutenant's call and instead focused on the warmth spreading across his forehead and cheeks.

Now closer, Culkin said, "Detective."

Morgan dropped his chin and opened his eyes. He blinked a couple of times before saying, "Good morning, Lieutenant."

"Not for you."

"Why is that?"

"There's a man in intensive care at Sacred Heart. Brought in yesterday. He was found behind an industrial building, badly beaten. He had an interesting story."

Morgan wanted to make a wisecrack but knew now was not the time.

"He said he was with a prostitute when someone pulled him out and beat him."

"And this affects me how?"

Culkin pointed at Morgan. "He described the man as looking like you."

"There are a lot of guys that look like me."

"Not with a gun and badge. He said the guy who did this was a cop."

"That's all you got," Morgan said, "and yet you still come over to accuse me?"

"I showed him your picture. He said it was you."

"Of course he did."

"Mind showing me your hands?"

Morgan pulled his hands from pockets and held them defiantly up to Culkin.

The lieutenant smirked. "You know as well as I do you didn't hit him. You kicked him."

"C'mon, Neil—"

"Lieutenant."

"—you're fishing, and I've got work to do."

"He described the prostitute. Black. Short afro. Late twenties. Not hard to pull a list of all known prostitutes who fit that description. Guess what name came up?"

Morgan shrugged.

"Josephine Green."

The detective remained silent.

"She's marked as a confidential informant. Want to know by who?"

"By me," Morgan said.

"That's right, by you." Culkin grinned. "I've got you, Morgan. I've finally got you."

"You've got shit, Neil. That's called a coincidence."

"I don't believe in coincidence, Morgan. Neither do you, I suspect."

Morgan stepped by the lieutenant then.

"We're not done," Culkin said and grabbed Morgan's arm.

The detective stopped and stared at the hand wrapped around his bicep. For a moment, Culkin considered the action he had taken. Then he slowly let go.

Morgan said, "If you want to continue threatening me, I want my union rep. This is harassment." He turned toward the Monroe Court Building and kept walking.

Culkin laughed. "I've got you, Morgan."

***

Only Nayla Senai and Courtney Earley were in the office, reviewing something together when he walked in.

Morgan stood at his desk until they turned his way. "Anything new on the neighborhood of flags?"

Earley shrugged. "No change since yesterday. Both Thorn and Strange are out there now. We'll go out in an hour. We'll bring a couple different cars with us, keep switching up as much as we can, and as much as the motor pool can support."

Senai asked, "Do you want us to involve anyone yet? Patrol maybe? SIU? We have a hole in coverage at night unless you can get the authorized overtime."

Morgan shook his head. "Won't happen. We don't know what we're dealing with yet."

"Something is going on with the flags," Senai said. "We should be able to get some help. Could we apply for a warrant?"

"We haven't even identified anyone coming or going yet. What kind of warrant are we going to get based on the information we have?"

Earley suggested, "Bad home decorating choices?"

"We wait until we get better intel," Morgan said and stepped behind his desk. He dropped into his chair.

Morgan then ran through the hot sheet, a daily update provided by the team in Crime Analysis. It was a synopsis of the major crimes of the previous day and trends that were appearing in the city. The hot sheet was supposed to keep every officer up to date with the latest incidents and intelligence that could make them more effective. Morgan skimmed the report to learn the murders of Yaban Karga and Stephanie Zentgraf were not mentioned. He wondered why they hadn't made the sheet. It seemed counterproductive to solving that crime.

His eyes drifted to the members of his team as he thought about revealing the information on Karga and Zentgraf. One of them may hear about it soon enough and come to him with it. Regardless, as soon as the team did, he was sure it would be Senai or Bynum who would suggest—no, insist—they alert Major Crimes and the regional drug task force about the link to the houses on Pacific. Then the CTF would lose control of the investigation.

One more day, he decided. Just one more day, he'd keep the information to himself, and then he would tell the team. He would let them determine the course of action at that point. If they wanted to move beyond the houses since they could not get into them, so be it. He was hoping they would find something today to get them inside.

From his pocket, he pulled the piece of paper Leigh Gaston had given him last night. On it was the name Ellen Simpson. He ran it through the system. Locally, there were three Ellen Simpsons, but only one fit her age bracket.

Ellen Mae Simpson. Twenty-nine years old. Last known address was in the neighboring city of Spokane Valley.

She had a lengthy record, mostly for petty crimes such as underage drinking, Third Degree Theft, which he suspected was shoplifting, a malicious mischief charge, and public intoxication. Simpson also had multiple traffic infractions.

Nothing in her criminal history pointed to her being a ringleader in an extortion case, but everyone starts somewhere.

The next step would be to talk with her, but he needed to meet with someone else first.

Chapter 25

Morgan's Dodge Charger crept into the area behind the industrial building. There was no car behind there. He continued around the back of the structure, coming around the other side. He re-entered Sprague Avenue and continued eastbound. He surveyed the street.

With the recent improvements along this corridor, the level of open prostitution and drug dealing had decreased, but he could still easily spot its participants.

It was the lone woman walking casually down the street. Or perhaps she stood near a bus sign. Regardless, the woman made frequent eye contact with the drivers of passing cars. If she behaved in that manner, she was a prostitute. She could try to lie her way out of it, but normal women—those with families and homes—did not do that.

Occasionally, there would be a man nearby whose attention was solely focused on the actions of the woman. When she walked, he followed. When she turned and headed in the opposite direction, he would do the same. He was her pimp, and he was keeping her on a short leash.

There would often be a kid who stood in the doorway of an abandoned building, not moving. He was a waypoint. People could walk up to him, trade a few words, and he would direct them to where either a drug transaction could take place, or the interested party could locate a prostitute.

On the roof of the same abandoned building was another kid. This one was a spotter. He would call out whenever the police or a potential rival came into the neighborhood.

More participants were in the street game, but Morgan's thoughts were interrupted when he saw her.

She stood near the bus stop, waiting for a ride she would never take. If a bus approached, Morgan knew she would step back, allowing it to pass. If an officer approached, she would say she was waiting for the bus, a perfectly acceptable reason to be on the street corner. And if she knew a cop was still watching her, she could always choose to step on the bus, ride for a few blocks, then get off and start the game all over again.

Morgan pulled his car to the curb and got out. She didn't bother turning and running. Liliya Scrimshaw had no reason to fear Detective James Morgan.

She continued to scan the passing cars, more out of habit than an expectation to pick up a john in front of the detective.

"Scrimmy," Morgan said as he approached.

She reluctantly stopped eyeing the traffic and turned to him. "Morgan, we need to stop meeting like this."

"Where's Joey?"

"How would I know?"

"When's the last time you saw her?"

Scrimmy shoved her hand into her purse, then pulled out a cigarette and lighter. "Been a day or so, I guess. She in trouble or something?" She lit the cigarette.

He shook his head and turned to survey the streets. "I'm looking for her."

She chuckled. "Of course you are."

Morgan slowly turned to face her. "What's that mean?"

"Everyone knows you got a thing for her."

Morgan's skin went cold, and a scowl formed.

Scrimmy pulled the cigarette from her mouth. "Not everyone. I mean, just me and her, I guess. We talk sometimes."

Not hiding the menace in his voice, he said, "That's dangerous."

She blinked a couple of times before saying, "I haven't told no one about it."

"Best keep your imagination to yourself, Scrimmy."

The woman smoked as she warily watching the detective.

"And I don't have a thing for her. Got it?"

"Sure, Morgan. I got it."

"She's a…" Morgan started to utter the word, but he paused. He didn't want to say it about Joey.

"Whore," Scrimmy said. "We all are."

"Right," the detective muttered.

Scrimmy sucked on her cigarette and blew out the smoke. Her tongue pushed the underside of her lower lip as she studied Morgan. Finally, she said, "I ain't seen her, Detective."

"If you do, let her know I'm looking for her."

"Of course."

Morgan lowered his head and walked toward his car.

***

He drove to Joey's house and banged on the door. When there was no answer, he pulled a small pouch from the inside of his jacket. He removed a ball rake and a pick from inside and set about unlocking her door. Morgan had learned the lock picking skill from a burglar he'd grabbed several years ago. The guy was a peripheral suspect in a case. Realizing he wasn't necessary, Morgan decided to release him in exchange for some lessons. It was one of the better trades he'd made over the years.

It took less than two minutes, and he was inside her house. He moved quickly through, checking each room. She wasn't there.

Standing in her living room, he called her cell phone. He listened for a ring or buzz, wondering if her phone might have been left behind. When the call went straight to voicemail, he hung up.

Morgan stood alone and wondered where in the hell Josephine 'Joey' Greene was.

***

He returned to East Sprague for one last attempt to find her. She was nowhere along the street. Even Scrimmy had now vanished, presumably into someone's car for the oldest exchange known to man.

As Morgan continued eastward, his attention settled on the Better Kitty Adult Bookstore. He slammed on his brakes, yanked the steering wheel to the side, and parked.

He walked in and looked around.

In the middle of the store was a small counter with a skinny woman standing behind the register. At the rear of the store was an office with a window in it. No one was inside.

Sex toys of all sizes and types lined the walls. Several circular stands displayed lingerie. There were multiple shelves of DVDs.

On a large screen TV hanging on the west wall, a pornographic movie played. A woman was having sex with several men. The sound was off. Instead of the audio track, music with screechy guitars and a singer who yelled the words played through the speakers hanging in the store.

The woman behind the counter leaned on her elbows and earnestly watched the film. She was in her early twenties, with raven black hair shaved along the sides. The remaining hair ran down to the middle of her back. Large red plugs stretched her earlobes to well beyond anything he'd seen before. A nose piercing that looked like a bone hung below her nostrils.

He approached the counter, but she didn't bother facing him. Instead, her eyes stayed locked on the screen. In a bored, detached manner, she muttered, "Looking for somethin'?"

"Is Ricky in?"

She blinked a couple of times, but her attention never left the screen. "He'll be in later," she murmured.

"What time is he normally in?"

The clerk's eyes slowly widened, and she licked her lower lip. Her focus remained on the television. Morgan didn't bother to glance back to see what was occurring on the screen.

He was about to repeat his question when she finally blinked and said, "He works the late shift."

"What time will he be in?"

With an irritated smirk, she said, "Three."

"What's his last name?"

"Huh?" She leaned slightly toward him, pushing an ear in his direction. The pounding and screechy music had risen to a crescendo.

"Ricky's last name?"

She nodded but didn't answer right away. She grimaced as she watched the screen. Finally, she muttered, "Gaspari."

"Thank you," he said. "You've been very helpful."

"For customers only," she mumbled as she tugged at one of the red plugs in her ear.

Chapter 26

Morgan was antsy.

He couldn't find Joey, and the pressure from Internal Affairs Lieutenant Neil Culkin lingered at the back of his mind.

Then there was the problem of The Eight. His team couldn't confirm nor deny their existence. Maybe the team had gotten close with the discovery of the neighborhood of flags, but he couldn't be sure. Anytime they were in the neighborhood, no one entered or left the houses. For all he knew, it might only be some weird neighbors with a flag fetish, or they were engaged in some bizarre game they'd learned from the Internet.

Then there was the murder of Yaban Karga and Stephanie Zentgraf to consider. She had rented these houses, and he was selling heroin marked with a fist. Morgan was hiding these various connections not only from his team but the homicide investigators as well.

Sure, he wanted to get the bust, but he felt like he owed Karga to discover what happened to the man. Morgan started this whole thing in motion by taking the packet of heroin from Laszlo Nagy, then lying to Karga about the DEA watching him.

His team was already sitting off the neighborhood of flags, so there was no reason for him to go there now. Doing so might send another warning to whoever was inside the house.

To distract himself, Morgan decided to work on Desmond Ashdown's problem. He considered a stop by HQ to run Ricky Gaspari's name through the system, but he figured he could do that later. He didn't want to run it over the radio. He drove by The Red Light District and searched the parking lot for the little yellow Honda registered to Ellen Simpson—the stripper known as Jenna.

When he didn't find the car in the parking lot, he headed toward Spokane Valley and her last known address.

It was an apartment community north of the river in a part of town known as Millwood. They were newer apartments built on a hill with a view overlooking the valley. It took a moment for him to understand the layout and which building she lived in. He slowly ascended the steps to her second-floor unit. He listened for a few moments, then knocked.

No one came to the door.

He was about to reach into his jacket and pull out his burglar's tools when he considered the other apartment behind him. If someone were inside there, they could be watching him through the peephole. Hell, they could record him illegally entering her residence. A healthy dose of paranoia had kept Morgan out of trouble for most of his career.

He removed his hand from his jacket, turned around, and knocked on the opposite door. A small dog barked from inside. He listened to the yapping for several moments, then knocked again. The barking intensified, but no one came to the door.

Morgan spun quickly then and pulled the leather pouch from his jacket. It took some time, but he finally opened both locks. He slipped into the apartment and locked the door behind him.

Even though it was in the afternoon and still sunny outside, the apartment was utterly dark. Blackout curtains hung over the windows—a requirement for a career spent working late hours.

He found a light switch and illuminated the room. As he moved through the apartment, he continued to turn on the lights.

The first order of business was to confirm this was, in fact, Ellen Simpson's apartment. The apartment was in disarray. Clothes were scattered about, and empty takeout food containers were left in the kitchen.

Morgan scanned through various items of mail left on the breakfast island. Unfortunately, he found only advertisements or letters addressed to Occupant. He tossed the mail back on the counter and continued his search.

The bedroom was in a similar state as the living room and kitchen. The bed was unmade, and no sheet covered the mattress. There weren't any pictures on the walls. A baseball bat stood in the corner. On the nightstand, he found a crumpled speeding ticket issued to Ellen M. Simpson. She had been cited for driving 43 miles per hour in a 35 MPH zone.

He put the speeding ticket back where he found it and returned to the living room.

****

It was after six when a key slid into the lock, and a woman casually stepped inside the apartment. The early evening sunlight illuminated her. She wore a hoodie, yoga pants, and tennis shoes.

Morgan stood in the far darkened corner, his gun in his hand.

The woman dropped an overly large purse on the floor and shut the door behind her. The apartment darkened again.

She flicked on the hallway light switch as she moved into the kitchen. Morgan was reasonably sure it was Ellen Simpson. He'd seen her Department of Licensing picture, and she was in an apartment rented to her. Two plus two equals four, he thought. But this wasn't mathematics, and sometimes things weren't always what they seemed.

She unzipped her hooded sweatshirt and dropped it to the floor. She wore a sports bra, and her skin was sweaty. She kicked off her slip-on tennis shoes and walked into the bathroom. The shower turned on, and she was gone for a moment. When she walked back out into the living room, she had the baseball bat cocked high above her shoulder and stared into the dark corner where he was seated.

"Don't scream," Morgan said.

"I'm not going to scream," she said. "If you come toward me, you'll never walk again."

They remained that way for a moment until he lifted the gun from the side of his leg so she could see it. If she seemed surprised by the addition of the firearm, she hid it well.

"How'd you get into my apartment?" Ellen asked.

"Put the bat down."

Ellen lowered the metal bat to her shoulder, like a ballplayer waiting for the pitcher to step back to the mound. "You've got another thing coming if you think you're going to rape me."

"I'm not here for that."

She shifted her weight from one leg to the other. "What are you here for?"

"Do I need to keep this out?" Morgan asked, wiggling the gun. "Or can I put it away?"

"I think you made your point."

He tucked it into the holster on his belt. His badge had been removed earlier and hidden in his pocket.

"What's this about?" Ellen asked, letting the bat dangle by her leg.

"The blackmailing. You had to figure this would come back to haunt you at some point."

She shrugged. "I never thought about it."

"Then it's time to start. Everything stops tonight."

Simpson shook her head. "I don't control it."

"Gaspari runs the show."

Her head cocked at the mention of Gaspari's name, and she slowly stepped toward the kitchen counter. Morgan wasn't sure if she was getting ready to make a run for the door, so he placed his hand on his gun. She made an exaggerated show of gently setting the baseball bat on top of the kitchen island.

"Ricky's the lead dog," she said. "I follow."

"Not true. You find the mark, Ellen. You set them up. I'd say that puts you on point."

She ran her tongue under her lip but remained silent.

"Do you feel any guilt about this?"

She shrugged. "They bring it on themselves."

"How's that? You drug them."

Ellen glanced away for a moment before saying, "Listen. I've only done it a few times. Why are you busting my balls?"

"Because it's blackmail."

"Not for me. After the photographs are done, I get paid, and I'm out."

"How much do you get paid for this?"

Pride flashed through her eyes. "Two grand."

"Two thousand?" Morgan said. "Really?"

The satisfaction Simpson felt faded from her eyes. "What about it?"

"And you've said you did this a few times, so that's three. Is that right? Three times?" Morgan didn't believe it was only three, but he went with it. "So, you're saying you've made six grand for your part in this scheme?"

Anger filled Simpson's eyes, and she placed her hand over the bat.

"Not a lot of money for the risk you're taking."

"It's not that much risk."

Morgan chuckled. "Girlie, you're taking as much risk as Ricky, but you're not sharing in the profit. You'll get just as much jail time as he does when this thing goes bad."

Her hand slid off the bat like a snake retreating into a hole. She crossed her arms and said, "How do you know so much?"

Morgan tapped the side of his head. "I'm smart like that. Do you know how much Ricky is blackmailing these guys for?"

Ellen glanced away for a second, then turned back to Morgan. "It doesn't matter."

"You bet it does matter. You do the hard work, the dirty work. He's pimping you out. You're his whore."

"We just make it look that way." Her lip curled. "I'm not a whore. I don't fuck any of those guys."

"He's using your body, Ellen, and taking the profit. You're getting scraps. Tell me what that sounds likes."

She scrunched her lips together and stared at him.

"Sounds like you're a whore."

Her face reddened. When she spoke, her voice was low and husky. "How much is he taking?"

"Tens of thousands."

She smacked the island. "Are you fucking kidding?"

Morgan stood now. "And that's from just one guy."

"One guy?"

"My friend—the reason I'm here. And Ricky is sending text messages that make it look like the demands are coming from you. The victims only know about you."

The red slowly drained from her face, and she looked as if she was about to be ill.

Morgan put his hand on his gun. "It ends tonight. Is that clear?"

She nodded.

"I'm going to see Ricky now," Morgan said. He drew the gun from its holster and pointed it at her.

She inhaled and brought up her hands in a defensive manner. "Wait!" she cried.

"If you warn him—"

"I won't," she said.

"—I'll come back. We won't talk. You won't see me."

She stared at him.

"Do I have to prove I can hurt you before I leave?"

"No," she whispered and pushed her hands further toward him. "You don't have to do that."

"Tell me you understand."

"I understand."

Morgan holstered his gun. "Then we have an agreement."

"We have an agreement."

Chapter 27

The first thing Morgan noticed when he stepped into the Better Kitty Adult Bookstore was that the annoyingly loud guitar music had been replaced by rap music. It was still loud and annoying, but the screech was gone. There was now loud bass thumping. It wasn't better, and it wasn't worse. It was a different kind of unpleasant.

Morgan examined the front door. It had an old-fashioned spin lock on it. He turned it and secured the door. He pulled the cord on the *Open* sign to click it off.

A heavyset man sat in the office and looked up when Morgan neared the store's sales counter. He left the office then and forced what he probably thought was a reassuring smile. He wore faded blue jeans and a white T-shirt emblazoned with a *Vivid* logo. Sweat beaded on the man's forehead. "What's your flavor?"

Morgan stared at him.

"What do you like? I can help you find it. Are you looking for some movies? Maybe some toys? We've got all sorts of—"

"Ricky Gaspari?"

He wiped a meaty hand across his forehead. "Yeah."

Morgan wished he knew a little more about the fat man. If he had stopped by the department, he could have run him through the system to see what kind of record he had. Was he a career criminal? Was he wanted for a previous offense? Or was he one of those rare breeds who was able to conduct his criminal enterprise below the radar?

"Let's step into the office," Morgan said.

Ricky Gaspari blinked a couple of times. "For?"

Morgan reached under his jacket and removed his gun.

When Gaspari saw it, he immediately raised his arms. "Whatever you want."

"Lower your hands and step into the office."

The big man put his hands by his sides and backpedaled into his office until he dropped into his chair. Morgan scanned the desk, looking for a gun. Not seeing any, he said, "Open the desk drawers. Slowly."

Gaspari put his hand on the handle of the top drawer but hesitated. "There's a gun in here."

"Then open it slowly."

The man did as he was told. Inside was a .38 Smith & Wesson revolver.

"Close it," Morgan said.

Again, Gaspari did as directed.

"Touch that drawer again, and I'll shoot you without hesitation. Understand?"

The fat man nodded.

"I'm here because of Desmond Ashdown."

Gaspari started to say something, thought better of it, then lowered his chin to his chest.

"It's payback time."

"Oh, shit," Gaspari mumbled, not lifting his head. "I'm sorry."

"It's too late for apologies."

"I won't do it again."

"Look at me."

The fat man's head remained down, but he lifted his eyes to the detective.

"Where are the photos?"

Gaspari pointed to his computer.

"Download them to a disc."

"A disc?" he asked, his face scrunching into a look of disbelief.

"Don't be a smart ass. Use whatever you have. Download them and then delete them. Understand?"

"The thumb drives are in there," he said and pointed to the top drawer, the one with the revolver.

Morgan leveled the gun at him. "Nice and slow. Just like before."

Gaspari slowly opened the top drawer, removed a couple of thumb drives, then closed the drawer. He slowly lifted his hands in surrender.

"Get started," Morgan said.

He stepped behind Gaspari and watched him work. As quickly as he could, the man moved the files. The function was slow and later interrupted when the computer said the first thumb drive was full. Gaspari removed it and replaced it with the second drive. He continued the process until all the pictures were copied. He pulled the second thumb drive from the computer and handed them both to Morgan.

"That's all of them," Gaspari said.

"Now, delete those files."

Gaspari nodded and turned back to his computer. He highlighted the folders and hit the delete button on his computer. He turned to Morgan and said, "Done."

Morgan smirked. "Nice try. Go to your Trash bin and delete those files permanently."

The big man sighed and turned back to his computer. His mouse hovered over the recycle bin. He right-clicked the icon, then permanently deleted the files in the recycle bin. "Are we good now?"

"Where's the money?"

"What?"

"The money. Ashdown paid you forty grand. Where's it at?"

"I don't have it."

Morgan cocked his head.

"I spent it."

He lifted his gun. "That was your only hope of staying alive."

Gaspari's shoulders slumped. "The safe."

"Get it."

The fat man pushed his chair back, then slid to the floor on his hands and knees. Underneath his desk, built into the floor, was a safe. Gaspari spun the dial back and forth, then pulled it open. He removed several stacks of bills.

"How much money is there?" Morgan asked.

"About seventy thousand."

"I said forty."

"What?"

"Forty thousand is what is owed to Desmond Ashdown. Give that to me. The rest, that's yours. I'm not a thief."

Gaspari's eyes bounced around as he tried to comprehend what was occurring. He divided the pile quickly and put forty thousand to the side. "That's Mr. Ashdown's money." Morgan took notice of how polite the fat man was concerning Ashdown.

The detective put the money into his jacket pockets. "Put the rest back into your safe."

Gaspari did as instructed, closed the door, and turned the lock. He climbed back into his chair.

"Now, here's the deal," Morgan said. "You will never contact Mr. Ashdown again. Clear?"

"Yes, sir."

"Our business is done."

Gaspari raised his hands and lowered his eyes. "Yes, sir," he said, his voice wavering. "I'm sorry I put your client in this position."

"He's my friend," Morgan said. "I go the extra mile for my friends."

The fat man turned his head and pulled his arms back toward him as if expecting a bullet.

Morgan hesitated a moment, then walked to the front of the store. He pulled the cord and illuminated the *Open* sign. Then he spun the lock, pulled the door, and stepped out onto the street. The detective tucked his gun back into its holster and headed for his car.

***

Inside his car, Morgan sent a short text to Desmond Ashdown.

YOUR PROBLEM HAS BEEN HANDLED.

It felt good to have resolved one of the issues in his life.

***

Before heading home, Morgan drove along Sprague Avenue. He searched every spot where Joey Greene might be. He even took another detour behind the abandoned industrial building but did not find her. Several more calls and texts had gone unanswered. She occasionally was slow in responding, but she never ignored him like this. He was now thoroughly worried.

He turned north and stopped by her house. He let himself inside again. Nothing had changed since his last visit.

Morgan was no longer concerned about Lieutenant Culkin finding her and asking her questions. His worry had changed to something darker.

Something had happened to Joey Greene.

***

At his apartment, Morgan pulled out his laptop and plugged in the first thumb drive and copied the pictures to his computer. He then repeated the process with the second thumb drive. When all the files were moved over, he set about looking at what he had taken from Ricky Gaspari.

The files were all categorized by the last name, followed by a first name. He ran his finger down the list of names.

There were twenty-two folders. Most were names he didn't know. He saw *Ashdown-Desmond* listed first and opened the folder. There were more pictures than the ones sent. In these pictures, he could see Jenna/Ellen's face. These were all the snapshots from their moment of blackmail. He could see in some of the photos Ashdown was flaccid and not performing sexually.

He backed out of the folder and looked at the list of names again. He didn't see another name he knew until he came to *Millhouse-Terrance.*

Terrance Millhouse was a local defense attorney who had earned the nickname Terry Grindhouse with the way he treated police officers on the stand. Morgan clicked on the folder, expecting to see Millhouse in a compromising situation with Jenna/Ellen or another girl like her. Instead, what he saw caused him some confusion.

Millhouse sat naked in the corner of a room, watching a white woman with two black men. While the two men tangled with the woman, Millhouse pleasured himself. The photos seemed to have been taken at the same angle and covered most of the room. By the look on his face, Millhouse enjoyed the moment.

There was a knock at the front door, but Morgan didn't bother to move. Instead, he backed out of the Millhouse folder and began to move through the various folders of people he didn't know, wondering if he would find another face he recognized.

A second knock was followed by Alyssa's voice saying, "C'mon, Jimmy. I know you're home."

In the first file, it showed another woman with a man in a similar situation to Ashdown. The gray-haired man with a slight belly was flaccid. His eyes seemed unfocused in the photographs.

Morgan Googled the name on the folder and learned the man was Chief Financial Officer of a local tech company. He was also on the boards of several non-profits.

Alyssa knocked again. "Jimmy, are you in there? Are you asleep?"

He continued through the files. Jenna/Ellen was in three of the twenty-two folders. She had not been Gaspari's full-time girl. Maybe she was only his most recent. Some of the men in the photos appeared to be drugged, but some seemed willing participants. There were some, like Millhouse, who seemed to be a part of some sort of swingers group where they watched women, presumably their wives, have sex with other men.

Was one of these other men associated with Gaspari?

Did he have an in with a swingers' club somehow?

Whatever it was, Ricky Gaspari had himself a nice con going.

Chapter 28

The next morning, Morgan returned to HQ and scanned the hot sheet again. He looked for any mention of the murders of Yaban Karga and Stephanie Zentgraf. There was nothing. Two days now and no mention of their deaths. There were officers on the scene who knew about the murders, so it seemed strange Crime Analysis hadn't disseminated the news of the homicide to the rest of the department.

He thought about picking up the phone to call Dallas Nash to ask if there was indeed an information lockdown concerning Karga but, at the last moment, he stopped himself. A call from Morgan would seem odd, and even Nash—a cake-eating attaboy—would grab onto his line of questioning and dig deeper. There was no need to bring more attention to himself.

Besides, Sergeant Bynum was at his desk and would overhear the conversation. The office was too quiet since the rest of the team was in the field. Senai and Earley watched the neighborhood of flags while Thorn and Strange were bird-dogging any leads they could about The Eight.

He considered running Ricky Gaspari through the system but, with only him and Bynum in the office, it was too risky. The sergeant could look over, ask what he was doing, and he'd have to come up with some story. He would have done it if the office were full. More people in the office allowed him to work in anonymity. It was a strange phenomenon, and one he knew better than to challenge now.

Morgan's thoughts then drifted to Delaney and Burkett and their investigation into the drive-by shooting of Regina Baird, Tremaine Brown's girlfriend. He could quickly call on them, of course, but a walk over to the Major Crimes division would give him a chance to bump into Nash. He could then go on a fishing expedition with the man that wouldn't look so suspicious.

He pushed back from his desk and stood.

***

Morgan took a route that led him first by the desks of Dallas Nash and Glenn Higgins. Neither man was there. He stood for a moment, hoping either of them would suddenly walk around the corner. The longer he remained, though, the more awkward he appeared, and the less likely it would seem to anyone that he was *just* happening through on his way to see Delaney and Burkett. He relented and pressed on toward the other detectives.

As Morgan approached them, they were standing next to one another, each with a cup of coffee. Quinn Delaney wore a dark suit with a white shirt. His tie was pulled loose. Marci Burkett was in black slacks and a red blouse. They immediately stopped talking when they saw him.

"Detectives," he said.

"Morgan," Delaney and Burkett said in unison.

"Do that often?"

"Enough," they said together.

"Weird. Listen, any update on the shooter of Regina Baird?"

Delaney leaned against his desk. "Why do you ask?" Suspicion was clearly in his tone.

"Hey, man, you braced me about it. Then you interviewed Alyssa to make sure I was where I said I was."

"Nice girl," Burkett said. "A little young, don't you think?"

"You suggesting I go for an older woman? Someone like you?"

Burkett rolled her eyes. "Ick."

"You're the one flirting, sweetheart."

"I wouldn't flirt with you."

"Keep telling yourself that."

"You are so vile," Burkett said.

Morgan smiled and looked at Delaney, who wasn't enjoying the banter.

"You want something?" Delaney asked.

"Some insight into the case."

Delaney's gaze slid to Burkett, whose cup was about to her lips. She lifted her eyebrows and tilted her head. She lowered her cup and said, "We've arrested a shooter."

"You have?"

"We have," she said with some satisfaction.

"Who?"

Burkett twisted her lips as she thought.

"If it's a rival gang member, I can help," Morgan said.

"That's okay," Burkett said. "We'll take it to SIU."

"We both work gangs," Morgan said. "How can it hurt to have us both in your corner?"

Burkett looked at Delaney, and something passed between them. They both nodded, and Delaney said, "Jakeem Fields."

Morgan looked at the two Major Crimes detectives. "You serious? No way. He's a Giant. And he's a kid, for Christ's sake. He's like fifteen."

"Fourteen," Delaney said.

Morgan continued, "It doesn't make sense."

"What do you mean?" Burkett asked. "He's a banger. They do things like this."

"The Giants and the Dead Boys are not at war. Did he give you a reason for the shooting?"

"He did not," Delaney said, then sipped his coffee. "That's what we need SIU to tell us. Or, since you're claiming to be an expert, maybe you can fill us in."

"Can I talk with him?"

"No," the two detectives said in unison.

Morgan frowned. "How did you ID him?"

"He turned himself in," Delaney said.

"*What?*"

"He showed up at the front desk and turned himself in," Burkett said.

"Was this before or after you suspected me?"

"What do you think?" Delaney said. "We didn't screw with you just to screw with you. That's not how we operate."

Morgan believed him. Delaney and Burkett might be the Glory Hounds, but they played the game straight, especially with other cops.

"Don't you think it's strange that he turned himself in?"

"He copped to it," Delaney said.

"That means he's taking the fall for someone else. You get that, right?"

Burkett shrugged. "He's given us everything, including the gun. We're pushing him, but he's holding to his story."

"Did he tell you why he shot at Brown?"

"He said it was over territory," Burkett said, putting her empty coffee cup on her desk. "And that he pulled the trigger. He refused to say much more than that."

***

As he walked down the hallway to leave the Public Safety Building, Morgan heard someone yell, "Morgan, wait!"

The detective stopped and turned to see Lieutenant Neil Culkin. He wanted to ignore the man but making a scene with an Internal Affairs lieutenant in the hallowed halls of the Spokane Police Department was begging for trouble.

When Culkin neared, he hissed, "What did you do with her?"

"Who?"

"You know who."

Morgan shook his head. "I don't know what you're talking about."

"Josephine Greene, the prostitute. What did you do with her?"

"I didn't *do* anything with her," Morgan said.

"Of course you didn't." Culkin clicked his tongue against his teeth and brushed past Morgan on his way toward the chief's office.

Morgan pulled his phone from a pocket. There had still been no answer to his texts, but that didn't stop him from sending another.

JOEY, WHERE ARE YOU?

***

Morgan left the Public Safety Building and walked a block east to the Gardner Building.

For decades, the low-profile building housed the city's and county's evidence warehouse. When a new warehouse was built, the city converted the Gardner Avenue structure into a multi-use office building. They then moved many functions to this location. Even some departments that had once been housed in the Monroe Court Building were relocated here.

One of the units shifted to Gardner was the Special Investigations Unit, the department's brain trust on all gang activity. In respect to governmental empire building, the CTF was supposed to hand all gang-related work to SIU. However, gangs touched most criminal activities, so CTF often stepped on the toes of the SIU detectives. It did not go unnoticed, nor unforgiven, by the SIU leadership, who saw Morgan as perhaps the most frequent transgressor.

The detective entered the building and ignored the receptionist behind the bulletproof glass. The Gardner Building had more security than the Public Safety Building, where the municipal court and its administrative offices were. Morgan wondered what that said about society's concern for the safety of its judges and their staff.

He pressed his ID badge against the entry pad near the steel interior door. The lock noisily released, and he yanked open the door. He headed straight for the office of Sergeant Trevor Hackworth.

The man was hunched over his desk with a brown, felt-tip pen in his hand. The fluorescent lights gleamed off his bald head. Hackworth had previously been a member of SWAT before eventually leading SIU. He only left SWAT when it interfered with his pursuit of gangs, his one true love.

Morgan knocked on the open door to Hackworth's office. The big man looked up. As he did, his eyes narrowed, and a frown creased his lips. "Morgan," he said, as if cursing.

"What's going on with the Giants?"

Hackworth put the cap on his felt-tip pen and tossed it onto his desk. Then he crossed his arms over his thick chest. His tongue dragged over his teeth but remained under his lips. His head tilted to the side as his tongue continued its hidden glide.

Morgan watched the man's antics with patience. Hackworth might look like a dumb jock, but he was a born intimidator. This was a delay tactic. It was something to buy Hackworth time to think and to allow Morgan to feel uncomfortable.

Since he knew the play, Morgan shoved his hands into his pockets and leaned against the doorjamb.

"Gangs are our territory," Hackworth finally said.

"So I've heard. What's your take on the Giants?"

"They're on their way out."

"How so?"

Hackworth tapped a finger on his desk before answering. "It's like any fraternal organization. If you don't grow, you die. The Giants haven't recruited very well. Look at the Dead Boys. They're growing. The 509 is growing. Even the Wasted Souls MC has pulled a handful of recruits. All the gangs are growing except the Giants. They're slowly fading away."

Morgan's eyes drifted around Hackworth's office, taking in the man's various awards and accommodations.

"Why are you asking about the G?" Hackworth asked.

"I get the feeling something's going on with them."

"What do you know that we don't?"

"Delaney and Burkett just arrested the shooter of Tremaine Brown's girlfriend. Jakeem Fields."

Hackworth chuckled. "Fields? How would the Glory Hounds even know about that baby gangster?"

"He walked into the department and turned himself in."

The sergeant's chuckle turned into a full-throated laugh. "Then you know it's bullshit."

"That's what I said."

"If Fields is admitting to it, it's because the Giants are hiding who did it."

"I agree."

Hackworth thumped his desk with the tip of his finger. "Delaney and Burkett should let us run with this."

"Yeah, I don't know," Morgan said. "I don't like the Hounds any more than you do, but they know what they're doing. They've earned their reputation for a reason."

"The same way you earned yours?"

The detective's eyes narrowed at Hackworth's accusation.

The sergeant smiled after having scored a point in this game of back and forth. "I hear you arrested Dontari Brown on his warrant."

"And?"

"We were holding off on that until Parker and the county were done with their investigation into the rookie's shooting."

"Why?"

Hackworth shrugged. "Because we're team players."

"If you knew where Dontari was, you should have grabbed him. A warrant is a judge's order, so you were disobeying—"

"I know what a warrant is, smartass."

Morgan grinned. "Just admit you didn't know where he was."

"Gangs are our territory," Hackworth repeated. "Therefore, you should have looped us in."

"What's the harm? We did you a favor by grabbing him. Now he's in jail, so you know where he is. See? Over at CTF, we're helpers."

"That's what you do, huh? Help? Did you get any intel from him before you booked him?"

"We didn't need any from him. We booked him and went about our way. You're welcome."

Hackworth shook his head, then waved his head dismissively. "Get the fuck out."

"The Giants are up to something," Morgan said.

"We'll look into it," Hackworth said, his head bowed over his paperwork. "If they shot at Tremaine Brown, it was the desperate act of a dying crew."

Chapter 29

The door opened before he could knock. Tremaine Brown stood in black jeans and tan boots. His low-slung tank top revealed tattoos on his chest. A bandage covered the wound in his shoulder where he'd been shot.

Before Morgan could say anything, Brown asked, "Who arrested my brother?"

The detective thought about lying, but instead said, "I did."

Brown sneered. "Yeah. That's what I thought."

Morgan remained silent.

"I went and saw him yesterday. He's still in lock-up, you know? He said some plainclothes officers snatched him on that rinky-dink warrant he had."

"Assaulting an officer isn't a rinky-dink charge."

Brown made a sucking sound through his teeth. "Did you do this because of that shooting with the cop?"

"No."

"Bullshit."

"A lot of people have been saying that to me lately."

"That so? Then I'll say it again. Bullshit."

"I did it for his girlfriend."

That gave Brown pause. He lowered his head as he thought. "Dontari's girl? Leigh?"

"She's a friend of my friend. When your brother hits her, she tells my friend. That makes my friend worried. When my friend worries, that makes me worry. When I worry, well, you see how that works, right?"

Brown searched Morgan's eyes. "Why didn't you tell him to stop?"

Morgan's brow furrowed. "Do you think me telling your brother to stop anything would make a difference?"

Brown rubbed his face with both hands before stepping back from the detective. "My brother wouldn't listen to you any more than he listens to me."

"I hope he does listen to you," Morgan said, "because when he gets out, he either stays away from her, or I'll toss him back in the can. You know who will win that battle."

Brown gave Morgan a sideways glance, then asked, "Are you here for some reason beyond threatening my family?"

"There's always a reason."

"Of course, there is."

"I want you to squelch the beef with the rookie."

Brown pointed at his shoulder. "You mean the motherfucker who shot me? Why would I do that?"

"Because I'm asking."

"You gotta do better than that."

"I've got something for you. Something you want to know."

"Yeah? Like what?"

"Major Crimes arrested a suspect in your girl's death."

Tremaine Brown's face flattened, and he pulled his lips back from his teeth—a tiger about to bite. "What do you know about it?"

"All I know is they grabbed the shooter," Morgan lied. "I'm still looking into it."

He could have told Brown about the baby gangster who admitted to the shooting and his gut feeling the whole thing was a sham. It would have fired up Brown and sent him off after the Giants. That was something he didn't want to occur.

"Tell me who that shooter is, and I'll consider squashing the beef. Until then, the rookie stays in the crosshairs. If I read about Gina's shooter in the papers, then any leverage you think you got is worthless, and I'll let the system take the rookie down. Got it?"

The detective stared at Brown.

"Now, get the fuck outta my house."

As he walked back to his car, Morgan realized his paying respects to Brown's dead girlfriend did little to help him.

He spat on the sidewalk.

Being nice rarely paid the dividends he hoped.

Chapter 30

It was almost midnight when Morgan parked his pickup nearly six blocks away from the neighborhood of flags. He walked toward the houses his team had surveilled for several days.

He had left Alyssa sleeping in his bed. She showed up uninvited—he hadn't invited her over once yet, he realized—and proceeded to tell him she wasn't happy with how he treated her. He listened to her complaints and, when she was finished with her rehearsed monologue, he asked if she wanted to stay or leave. Morgan wouldn't apologize for how he treated her—never for that. It was the push and pull, and it was working as it should.

Before leaving, he considered kicking her out of bed, but it wasn't worth the hassle. Besides, he hoped she would still be there when he returned.

The rest of the team had already called it a day several hours ago. If the CTF had more guys, they could pull around-the-clock surveillance. Or, if he wasn't so stubborn and was willing to ask for help, he could get additional manpower to watch this block. Or maybe get the authorized overtime to pull the surveillance. There was a time they could work all the hours they wanted, but those years were gone with budgetary constraints.

To get any help or possibly squeak out a few extra hours, he would have to reveal what he knew about Yaban Karga and Stephanie Zentgraf's connection to these houses.

Perhaps that was the problem all along. Maybe whoever was inside the houses knew the cops were sitting on the block. Perhaps they knew they were being watched and weren't going inside or coming out while the police were around.

Whatever it was, the cops and their unmarked cars were the foreign bodies in an organism, which might have caused it to shut down in an abundance of precaution.

By walking in alone, Morgan hoped he would get to see something different.

When he arrived on Pacific Avenue, he located a tree opposite Magnolia Street and leaned against it. He wanted to pull his phone out and text Joey but doing so would backlight him. That was against the light discipline he'd been taught in The Corps.

Instead, Morgan remained quiet, watched, and listened.

Whenever his attention drifted, his mind spiraled into the problems he had been dealing with lately. He continually pushed the concerns away to remain focused on the neighborhood and the house with the flag fist.

He kicked himself for not running Ricky Gaspari's name before the end of the day. He'd make it a priority tomorrow, he decided. Morgan wanted to know more about the sweaty, greasy man. Maybe it didn't matter much anymore now that they'd reached a deal, but it still bothered him that he didn't have his ducks in a row before dealing with the man.

Finally, a white car pulled up to the little house he'd been watching. It was too far away and too dark for Morgan to make out more than that. Several figures walked out of the house, hurried across the front lawn, and climbed into the car. The car drove by where Morgan was standing in the shadows.

It was a white BMW 3. When the car turned northbound, he saw the dent on the driver's door. It was the same car he'd stopped earlier. The white sedan sped away.

Morgan wondered if anyone remained inside the house. He had his lockpick tools with him. He was confident he could get access if given enough time. Even if the picks failed, he could break a window, kick a door, or do something he hadn't thought of yet. If he wanted to gain entry, there was nothing to stop him.

The detective moved from his hiding place across Magnolia Street into the yard of the first house on the block. He stood behind another tree.

Nothing was moving in the neighborhood. If he took his time, Morgan figured he could get close to the little yellow house, assess his risk, then decide whether to take the gamble of entering on his own.

Almost ten minutes passed as Morgan stood in the heavy darkness of a shaded tree at night. The wait was agonizing, but it was a mental pain he'd been familiar with for decades. He'd first learned patience while on the battlefield. It was further honed as a patrol officer and later as a detective. Waiting was a skill Morgan knew, and letting anxiety or impatience rush a decision led to harmful, even deadly, results.

He checked the luminous hands on his watch. Another minute, Morgan decided, and he would creep one house closer.

Still, nothing moved in the neighborhood. A couple of houses were lit up, but none of the places with flags had lights on in them. They all were dark.

Morgan stepped into the open to move when the door to the little house opened. He froze.

A small figure appeared. It rushed down the stairs, tripped in the yard, and sprawled into the grass.

Morgan moved back into the thick shadow provided by the nearby tree. He rested his hand on the butt of his gun.

The darkened figure struggled to its feet and stumbled toward the sidewalk. It was a naked woman, and she was crying now.

As she continued to stagger forward, a chill ran down the detective's back.

He recognized her.

***

Morgan carried the frail body of Joey Greene in his arms and hurried toward his truck.

Her words were jumbled and slurred, leaving them mostly incomprehensible as she cried with her head buried into his neck.

She had been frightened before he stepped out of the shadows. When she saw him, she screamed. Then she realized it was him and lurched into his arms.

Blood was around her left wrist, but Morgan didn't bother to investigate further. He took off his jacket, put her in it, and carried her as fast as he could to his pickup. Even though she barely weighed a hundred ten pounds, taking her six blocks strained him. His shoulders ached, his back hurt, and his arms burned.

Morgan shuffled his feet as quickly as possible, but he was afraid he would trip and fall on top of her.

"Joey," he said, so she would stop her incoherent rambling. "You're safe."

She put her head into his neck and wrapped her arms tighter around him. Her words stopped then, but the tears didn't.

His arms felt as if they would soon fail him, but he wouldn't put her down. He couldn't.

His footsteps were heavy, and his breathing was haggard. When he finally arrived at his truck, he stopped and said, "I have to put you down."

She clutched him tighter.

He slowly lowered her to the ground, but she didn't let go of him. Her arms were clasped around his head, and her face was buried in his neck.

"Joey, please. I need to unlock the truck."

That registered somewhere inside her, and she let go. He stuck the key in the passenger side door, unlocking it. When he opened the door for her, she started to get in.

"Let me help," he said.

"No," she whispered. "I got it." The tears stopped then. She reached out and pulled the door closed behind her.

Morgan stared at her for a moment, then ran around to the driver's side and climbed in.

***

His badge expedited the patient check-in process at Sacred Heart. They rushed her to a private room, and Morgan remained with her.

In the bright light of the hospital, she looked like hell. Due to the life she lived, the little beauty she had was tamped down and muted, but all that was gone now. First, the run-in with the jerk in the SUV had blackened her right eye. Now, the left eye was swollen shut and her face bloodied. When she opened her mouth to speak, a couple of teeth were broken. Bruises covered her body.

Morgan considered the blood on her wrist and hand. He'd seen it before in his career. Someone had handcuffed her to something. It appeared as if she had pulled her hand out of the metal restraint to get free. In doing so, she tore flesh from the hand. It was only possible due to her small size. Had she been a bigger person, she probably would have never escaped the restraint.

"Got something to eat?" Joey asked. Her voice was soft and child-like.

"No."

"Haven't eaten in days," she whispered.

"When the nurse comes back, we'll get you something."

She nodded and pulled Morgan's jacket tight around her.

"What happened?" the detective asked.

Joey couldn't pull the jacket any tighter, but her hands gripped the garment as if she were trying.

"We don't have to talk about it right now," Morgan said.

Her tongue touched the broken teeth. She winced and closed her eyes. Lowering her head, she whispered, "I was checking on the house—the one you wanted me to look after."

Morgan opened his mouth to say something, but what could he say?

I'm sorry. That was lame.

I didn't mean for this to happen. Yeah, no shit, you didn't mean for this to happen.

What did you do that caused this? Nice work, asshole. Blame the victim.

Instead, Morgan closed his mouth and remained quiet.

Joey sat quietly for a few moments before saying, "I guess one of them noticed when I walked by one too many times."

Her hands relaxed on the jacket, and she shoved them into its pockets. She used her fists to keep it tightly wrapped around her.

Joey continued. "One of them came out and told me to take it elsewhere. I told him I went where I wanted to, when I wanted to, and that no man was going to tell me how to run my business." She fell silent for several moments before muttering, "He laughed at me."

"What do you mean?"

She looked up. "You know, a small one. Like he was happy we met, but I was wrong." She held up her bloodied wrist. "I learned that the hard way. He asked if I wanted to come in and party. I thought maybe if I could see what was inside the house, then that would help you."

"You didn't have to do that," he said.

Joey looked away. "I know."

As Morgan watched her, a hatred grew inside.

They remained silent for several minutes before she said. "They had some witch."

"Were they using?" Morgan asked.

Joey shook her head. "No."

"They're dealers?"

"Bigger than that."

"Distributors?"

"That's the word. Others would come to them for the drugs. Then they would take them to sell."

Morgan nodded. A piece to the puzzle had finally been put into place.

"They offered me a taste," Joey said. "That's when it started. As soon as I went flying, they started taking turns."

Morgan watched her. He expected her to cry now, but she didn't. Instead, her face hardened.

"How many days has it been?" he asked.

She shrugged. "No idea. It started after I last talked to you."

"Three days."

"Okay," she said.

Morgan said, "I'm sorry," and he meant it.

She wrapped her arms around herself again. "It's going to hurt getting back to normal. They've kept me high the entire time."

"Why did they hit you?"

She removed a hand from one of the pockets to touch her face.

"The first time was after I shit myself." She sniffed dismissively. "I didn't know what I was doing; they had me so high. One bastard beat me like a dog. Next thing I knew, I was being hosed off in a shower. They took me to the bathroom after that, sort of like you take a puppy. If I didn't go fast enough, he hit me."

"Did all of them hit you?"

Joey nodded. "A couple of them started hitting me just to hit me. Probably never got to hit a girl without her fighting back."

"Why the handcuff?" he asked, pointing to her injured wrist.

"I think I wandered off at some point. I thought I dreamt that."

The nurse had now been gone for several minutes, collecting the rape kit. She would return soon to collect samples from Joey.

"I need you to listen to me," he said and leaned forward. "Some people are going to come and ask questions."

Worry crossed her face. "Can't you ask the questions?"

"These people are specialists," he said. "It'll be okay. They're going to be Major Crimes Detectives. Maybe some rape advocates. They're going to want to know what happened to you. Do you understand?"

"I guess."

"When anyone asks what you were doing when they grabbed you, you just say you were in the neighborhood. Understand? Do not say you were doing this for me."

Her brow furrowed. "Yeah. Okay."

"I'm going to find the men who did this to you. Do you believe me?"

Her face relaxed, and she struggled to open an eye. "Do you promise?"

"Yeah, Joey. I promise. I'll find these men, but you have to say what I told you."

Tears streamed down her face.

"Now, this one is critical," Morgan said. "There is a lieutenant who has been looking for you."

"For me? Why?"

"He's with Internal Affairs."

"What does he want?"

"Do you remember the man in the Escalade? The man that hurt you?"

"What about him?"

"That man filed a complaint."

"About you?"

"Yes."

"But you were protecting me." Her fingers touched the torn flesh on her wrist.

"In the eyes of the department, what I did was wrong," Morgan said. "Do you understand?"

"I get it."

"When the lieutenant comes to you, tell him it was someone else."

"He can't arrest me, can he?"

"No," the detective said, "you'll be fine. If he threatens you with anything, he's bluffing. It's me he wants."

"I won't let him get you."

"I know. Just tell him some other guy helped you out."

She inhaled deeply, as if fighting back a sob.

"What's wrong?"

"It's nothing," Joey said.

"Tell the lieutenant it was a good Samaritan. Describe him like me, but it wasn't me. Get it? The lieutenant will show you a picture of me."

She wiped the tears from her cheeks. "I'll take care of it. I promise."

"Now, I'm going to reach into my jacket and pull out my notebook," he said. When she nodded, he slowly and carefully removed his notebook and pen from the inside pocket of the coat she wore. He also pulled out his lockpick kit and tucked that into his pocket. He opened his notebook and said, "Describe the men that did this to you."

Morgan diligently took notes and assigned characteristics to each man. As he jotted down the attributes to the fourth suspect, Joey said, "And this one had a funny way of talking."

"Funny how?"

"He always finished everything with uh-huh. Like he said, 'You like that, uh-huh?' or 'You're a crazy bitch, uh-huh.' The guy was weird."

Morgan laid his notepad on the foot of the bed and pulled his phone from his pocket. He searched through it for a moment until he found the photograph he wanted. He turned it toward Joey. "Was this the guy?"

Her eyes narrowed, and her lips pinched. "That was him. Definitely, that was him. That one beat me like a dog."

It was DeShaun Harmon's supposed cousin. Morgan cursed himself. He should have worked harder to get the man's name when they first met outside the convenience store.

The detective wished he had a picture of Bilbo to show her. He had known the man for many years now, and this didn't seem like anything he would have ever participated in. But the game changed people in terrible ways.

"Do you know the others?" Joey asked.

"No, but I'll find out who they are."

"What are you going to do when you find them?"

"I'll do what's right."

"What's that mean?"

Morgan tucked his phone away, leaned over, and lightly kissed Joey on the forehead, ignoring the stench that rose from her skin.

As he walked out, she repeated, "What's that mean, Morgan?"

The entire CTF team huddled around his desk. Each of them read a copy of Morgan's initial report, along with a search warrant signed by Judge Michael Crocker. He'd made multiple copies so they could speed up the process when the team arrived. He had not been home yet and, for a brief second, wondered if Alyssa had remained in his bed overnight. He had no way to communicate with her, as they had never traded phone numbers.

After finishing his brief interview with Joey Greene, Morgan called police radio and reported that he transported a rape victim to the hospital. He asked for a corporal to respond to photograph her injuries.

He left his jacket with her. Because it had her blood and potentially the DNA of one of her attackers, the corporal would take it into evidence.

Morgan then went straight to the CTF office and began the search warrant for the yellow house on Pacific Avenue. He completed it about four in the morning and woke the judge with a call as he drove to his residence.

Michael Crocker lived in a large home on Browne's Mountain. Standing in his doorway, he wore gym shorts and a plain white T-shirt. His usually perfect hair was mussed from sleep. At this early hour, the judge struggled to focus on the warrant. He was a man who lived a life of comfort and wasn't used to interruptions.

Crocker didn't even bother to ask him the standard affiant questions about swearing to the true and accurate nature of the warrant request. Instead, when he finished reading, Crocker signed in the appropriate places, shoved the documents back toward Morgan without further word and slammed the door closed.

Morgan returned to the office and made copies of the warrant. He wanted to be ready for the team when they arrived.

"These guys raped a prostitute?" Courtney Earley asked.

"That's right," Morgan said.

"Stupid," Adrian Thorn muttered as he read.

"Why?" Jeremiah Strange asked. "Because she's a prostitute?"

"No," Thorn said. "That's not what I meant. They could have just paid her and avoided all this trouble. They probably could have handcuffed her, too, if they gave her a bonus."

Strange smirked. "It's about power, man. You know that."

"I know but read the girl's identifiers. She's a hundred pounds soaking wet. What kind of power trip does someone get from doing that?"

"Who knows?" Strange said. "But paying for it wouldn't satisfy what these turds were looking for."

Nayla Senai listened to their back and forth.

Sergeant Bynum watched it all, lowered his head, flipped the report back to the beginning, and started over again. "There are no names in this report," Bynum said.

"She didn't get any," Morgan said. Technically, he wasn't lying. Joey hadn't learned any of their names. Morgan only knew one of them to be Bilbo's cousin, but he didn't have a real name or even a moniker. He held that information from his report. He thought about putting it in, but he could always get that info later by having Joey identify the cousin in a more legally appropriate way.

Senai tossed her copy of the paperwork on the desk. "How did you find her?" Her words were harsh.

"It's in the report," Morgan replied. He didn't like the way Senai studied him.

"I know that, but why were you down there on your own time? Why hadn't you checked out with dispatch?"

Morgan noticed the guys, including the sergeant, had all looked up from their paperwork. They were studying him, and he didn't like it.

"Are you accusing me of something, Nayla?"

"I'm asking you a question I think we should have answered. Why were you down there, *alone*, without checking out with radio? Why didn't you call one of us to join you?"

Morgan shrugged. "We've gotten nowhere during our normal rotation. We haven't involved any other units. I went down there to check out what's going on. I didn't think it needed an additional officer, nor did it warrant the hassle of requesting overtime."

Senai crossed her arms. "The girl reported seeing drugs and guns. She gave you a description of four black males but doesn't recall any names being spoken while in the house. How's that possible?"

"She was drugged." Morgan slowly stood behind his desk. "What are you implying?"

Senai glanced at Bynum, then returned her attention to the detective. "I'm not implying anything," she said.

Morgan crossed his arms. "Just say it, Nayla."

She glanced at the others on the team.

"Never lie," Morgan said.

Her eyes snapped to his. "Fine," she said and set her jaw. "I worry this might be bullshit. That the drugs and guns might be a fiction of some prostitute's imagination, and when we go into that house, there will be nothing there."

Sergeant Bynum stood then. "I'm not sure what's going on between you two, but does someone want to clue me in?"

Morgan pointed to the warrant paperwork. "If you think this is bullshit, Nayla, I'll wait. You can run up to Sacred Heart and interview my witness for yourself, or you can follow up with the responding corporal to see when those evidence photos will arrive. Either way, we'll wait."

Nayla pursed her lips. Earley, Thorn, and Strange had all moved slightly back from the two of them.

"But know this," Morgan said, "that woman was raped and beaten by whoever lives in that house. She escaped from them. If they have any brains in their heads, they're going to figure out the situation they've put themselves in, and they're going to disappear like that." He snapped his fingers. "We only have a short window to get into that house and find out what's going on."

Nayla lifted her hands in mock surrender. "I'm part of the team. I only want to know what we're doing is right."

"Of course, it's right," Morgan said. "I wouldn't ask you to do something that wasn't."

Bynum looked between Nayla and Morgan. "Are we good, or do the three of us need to have a counseling session?"

"We're fine," Senai said flatly.

Morgan searched Senai's eyes before agreeing, "We're fine."

Bynum said, "So we're going into the house to look for her clothes and evidence of the rape?"

"Correct," Morgan said.

The sergeant continued, "You have a basic description of four black males who attacked her."

"We detain whoever is in the house," Morgan said, "and photograph them. We then take a photo array to her. Let her point out who attacked her. If there are less than four, maybe we get one of them to rat on the others."

"Did she say anything about the flag?" Earley asked.

Morgan shook his head. "She never saw them doing anything with a flag. She was kept drugged and in a back room."

Sergeant Bynum eyed his team. "Then it's settled. We're a go."

Chapter 32

Nayla Senai sat in the passenger seat and kept her eyes straight ahead. She hadn't said anything since getting into the car. Initially, she tried to ride with the rest of the team in the GMC Yukon, but Morgan called out to her and said, "Nayla, you're with me."

She reluctantly accepted.

As they left the parking lot of the Monroe Court Building, Morgan let her sit in silence. When they passed through downtown, though, he asked, "What was that back there?"

"What do you mean?"

"You called me out in front of the team."

"You told me to. You said, don't lie."

"That's different from calling me out. I thought you were my partner."

She turned and looked out her window.

"What is it?" Morgan asked.

"You do things that are… questionable."

"Like what?"

"Really?" She faced him. "Do you want me to list them?"

Morgan became silent then. They left downtown and continued east on Sprague Avenue. As they approached the turn on Magnolia Street, Morgan noticed a fire up ahead and the flashing lights of fire trucks and police cars. He continued onward.

"You missed your turn," Senai said.

Ahead, a patrol car with its emergency lights whirring blocked oncoming traffic. An officer stood in front of the vehicle, redirecting traffic. Behind the car, two fire engines were parked in the street. A team of firefighters battled a blaze from inside the Better Kitty Adult Bookstore.

"Good riddance to the flesh peddlers," Senai said.

"Yeah," Morgan muttered. "Good riddance."

It was a problem for another time, he thought. He wanted to know what happened, but he couldn't spend the mental energy trying to solve that problem. He spun the steering wheel, headed south, and took several side streets before pulling up behind the rest of the team.

They had parked a block away and around the corner. Courtney Earley, Adrian Thorn, and Jeremiah Strange had already exited their vehicle and put on ballistic vests. Earley carried a shotgun while Thorn and Strange appeared somewhat bored by the whole experience.

After parking, Morgan and Senai opened the trunk and put on their ballistic vests. Morgan tugged at his until it felt tolerable. The idea that the vest once felt reassuring had faded into his past, along with a concept that combat boots were once comfortable.

Morgan grabbed a portable radio, turned it on, and clipped it to his belt. Then he called dispatch with his cell phone. It was answered on the first ring.

"Radio, this is Annie."

"Annie, this is Jim Morgan."

"Hey, Jim."

"CTF is executing a search warrant," he said and then provided her with the address.

"Copy," the dispatcher said. "Is Sergeant Bynum with you?"

"He's on the way. We didn't want to announce this over the radio in case other ears were listening."

"I understand. Not my first rodeo."

"We'll be on the data channel." Annie was a professional, and he didn't need to break it down for her like a rookie. "Thanks for being there when we need you."

"Be safe, Jim," she said and hung up.

His phone rang almost immediately, and he answered. It was Bynum.

"I'm not going to make it," he said. "I got hit."

"Hit?"

"A car ran into me. I got to fill out the report."

Morgan sighed. Just what he didn't need right now—a delay. "Want us to wait?" he asked.

The team glanced at him.

"No," said Bynum. "You've done this before. If it looks bad, don't jump until I can get there and get you more support."

"Understood."

He shoved his phone into his back pocket and turned to his team. The four of them looked at him expectantly. "Bynum was in an accident," he said.

"Is he all right?" Senai asked.

"He's fine. Just a fender bender, but he's not going to be with us."

"Won't be the first time," Thorn said.

"And probably not the last," Strange added.

"Okay," Morgan said. "Here's how this will work. Courtney goes first. I'm second, with Senai bringing up our rear. Doc, you and Adrian take the rear of the house."

Strange nodded. There was no argument from him this morning. It was about being team players now.

Everyone knew the location of the house as they had all sat off it at some point during the previous week. "Let's go," Morgan said.

The five of them climbed back into their cars for the short trip to the little yellow house. Morgan and Senai were in the Dodge, the rest of the team following them in the faded Yukon. There was no further discussion as he started the engine, dropped the car into Drive, and accelerated from his spot along the curb.

The Charger raced around the corner and stopped a couple of houses away. He quickly came to a stop, slammed the gear into Park, and exited the car. He hurried toward the front of the little yellow house, knowing Senai was behind him. As they climbed the porch, he noticed the flag with the fist was missing from the window.

He took a position to the left of the door, Senai tucked in behind him. Earley was on the other side of the front door.

Earley pounded on the front door. "Spokane Police Department," he yelled. "Open up. We have a warrant."

For several seconds, there was no noise behind the door. Earley pounded again and repeated his announcement.

When there was no response, he looked at Morgan.

The detective stepped in front of the door, pulled his gun tight into with chest, and kicked the door near the knob. It popped inward, splintering at the lock. There was no hesitation as Courtney moved into the house with the shotgun at the ready. Morgan button-hooked to the left, and Senai followed him in.

The three of them moved through the house and searched room to room. At that moment, they weren't trying to find evidence linked to the rape of Joey Greene but rather to secure the residence.

As he passed through the house, Morgan mentally registered items to come back and examine further. In the front room, there were several folding chairs and bags of trash. The nearest bedroom was immaculate, not a single item inside. In the back room, he saw a bare mattress lying near a radiator.

Finally, the three of them—Morgan, Senai, and Earley—said in quick succession, "Clear." Except for them, no one was inside the house.

"Big man," Morgan said, "let Doc and Adrian in."

Courtney walked off.

Morgan returned to the small bedroom to look at the mattress. There was blood on it in several places. He sensed her by his shoulder before she spoke.

"Is this how the victim described it?" Senai asked.

"Yeah."

She left him then.

Morgan imagined Joey handcuffed to the radiator. He visualized her frail body, receiving an unbelievable amount of punishment for days. He fought to control his anger and snatched the radio from his belt. "Ida seventy-seven," he called.

"Seventy-seven," dispatch responded.

"We're code four at our location. Start a corporal for photographs and fingerprints."

He moved out of the way so Earley, Strange, and Thorn could enter the room with the mattress.

"I'm stepping outside until the corporal arrives," Morgan told Senai.

"You okay?"

He grunted a non-committal response and went outside. As he stood on the sidewalk to the house, his attention drifted to the place across the street. Its white Seahawk flag remained hanging in the window.

He then checked out the house to its left to discover its flag removed. Morgan struggled to remember what had hung in its window and decided that it was the Tabasco flag.

Morgan walked to the sidewalk to look at the house next door to one the CTF had just raided. Its flag, which Morgan remembered was a University of Washington flag, had also been removed.

The detective scanned the neighborhood once more. All the flags had been removed except the Seattle Seahawks flag. He focused on the house and noticed the flag moving slightly.

Had someone looked out from behind it?

Morgan didn't hesitate. He sprinted across the street, up the stairs to its small porch, and stood to the left of the doorframe. He pounded on the door.

"Spokane Police!" he yelled. "Come to the door."

Nothing happened. Had he imagined the flag fluttering? Was he making a mistake?

Movement from across the street caught his eye. His team was exiting the yellow house and walking toward him.

"What the hell, Morgan?" Earley yelled.

The detective pounded on the door again. "Spokane Police! Come to the door."

The flag moved slightly. He saw it this time.

Someone was inside this house.

He pounded on the door again.

How could he justify kicking this door while his team crossed the street? There were no exigent circumstances. They would see him do it. He would be outside of department policy, and he would have no way of explaining what he did.

Would his team back an illegal entry?

The time was now, he decided. He couldn't worry about it any longer. He would explain his actions later.

Morgan quickly stepped in front of the door and prepared to kick it.

A shotgun blast rang out and exploded a hole in the wall where the detective had previously stood. Wood and siding flew everywhere. Splinters and debris sliced through the skin on his arms.

Morgan dove from the porch to the dead grass in front of the house. He landed on his side. Something dug deeply into his hip, and he yelled in pain. He frantically low crawled to the edge of the porch then drew his gun.

More shots rang out, exploding window glass from the opposite side of the house.

"Hell!" Earley yelled.

Morgan turned to see the big man fall in the middle of the street. He clutched his shoulder as he writhed in obvious pain. Thorn and Strange crouched near him and fired back at the house.

Senai hunched down and returned fire as she ran across the street.

Morgan pulled his police radio from his belt. He keyed his mic and yelled, "Ida seventy-seven!"

There was no response. From the house, gunfire continued.

Again, Morgan depressed the radio's transmit button and hollered over the noise, "Ida seventy-seven!"

Still no response.

It took another fraction of a second for him to realize the radio was broken. He'd landed on it when he jumped from the porch—that was the stabbing pain in his side. Now, he was without communication.

When Senai neared, he grabbed her and yanked her closer. "Call radio! Get back-up."

Morgan clamored by her then and crawled toward the steps. He looked up to see a black male standing in the doorway with a shotgun in his hand. The man racked a round and shot across the street. It was too far for an effective shotgun blast, but it still could do some damage. Morgan, however, was only a few feet away from the shooter at the bottom of the steps.

The detective scooched back out of sight and glanced over his shoulder to see Earley, Strange, and Thorn were no longer in the street. Strange stood behind Morgan's car and fired back into the house.

Morgan peered up the stairs. Several feet above him, partially hidden by the doorway, the shooter continued to search for members of the CTF. The man's forehead was slick with sweat, and his eyes were wide with excitement.

Due to the difference in height, the shooter failed to notice Morgan. The detective shot upward, striking the man in the chest. The shooter tottered backward into the house, discharging his shotgun into the ceiling.

"Rumble!" someone yelled.

"What happened?" another screamed.

All the shooting from inside the house stopped.

"They got Rumble!"

From inside the house, the gunfire began again, but without the booming shotgun the man Rumble had wielded. The shots now came only from the corners of the house.

A hand touched his leg. Senai said, "Help is on the way."

"Let's go," Morgan said and quickly clambered up the stairs. In a moment, Senai's comforting hand rested upon his shoulder.

The detective could see where the shooters were inside the house since the barrels of two assault rifles stuck out of windows. The men were in the far corners of the house. One was in the room, just off the front door. Due to their locations, the angle was too sharp for either shooter to get Morgan or Senai.

As rounds continued to be fired from the front window toward his teammates, the detective switched his gun to his left hand. Morgan leaned into the front room. He exposed as little of his body as possible and saw another black male firing an AR-15. Several magazines were at his feet.

Morgan aimed and squeezed the trigger.

The shooter collapsed. The man never once sensed his executioner was nearby.

The detective considered entering the house and grabbing the AR-15, but he didn't know how many rounds were still in the rifle nor where an additional clip might be. Once he entered the house, he would be without cover or concealment.

It took only a few seconds for the remaining shooter to become aware he was the only man firing.

"Max?" a voice yelled. It sounded like it was coming from the bottom of a well.

Morgan dropped to a knee and pointed his gun on the hallway that he suspected led to the other room. Senai remained tucked behind him. Her hand rested on his shoulder—a non-verbal signal to let him know where she was.

The two detectives didn't need to communicate with words, which was good, because Morgan could barely hear anything now. This was partially from the adrenaline dump he was experiencing and the gunshots from him and the others.

A couple more rounds came from the backroom before the shooter yelled, "Max, you okay?" He sounded so far away.

Morgan and Senai remained silent.

The detective struggled to hear anything. He thought he could hear sirens in the distance, but he wasn't sure. There was a constant whining in his ears now, and every other noise sounded as if he heard it through cotton. Briefly, Morgan turned his left ear toward the hallway, hoping to hear something—*anything*.

A round fired from above him, and it set off a further high-pitched squealing in Morgan's ears. He jerked his head toward the interior of the house in time to see a body collapse in the hallway. An AR-15 skittered away as the man hit the floor.

Morgan blinked several times, understanding how lucky he'd been to have Senai behind him. She patted his shoulder, indicating it was time to move. Morgan stood, pulled his gun back to his chest, and moved through the house.

It took only a few seconds for the two detectives to clear the residence. When they were done, they confirmed three shooters—all dead. No one else was inside.

As they moved back through the small two-bedroom house, Morgan noticed more guns stacked together. He also saw two open cardboard boxes. Morgan paused by one of the boxes and removed a small plastic package from inside. On it was the same fist that had been on the package he'd taken from Laszlo Nagy. The other box had differently packaged bindles.

Senai motioned toward the outside, and he nodded. She left the house.

Morgan checked the faces of the three dead men. He expected to know all of them. He based this supposition on Bilbo's cousin, identified by Joey as one of her rapists. However, the detective had never seen any of the three men in the house. If they were involved in any criminal activity, he'd never run across them. Had the Giants recruited new members—men with the courage to engage in a firefight with the cops—without the CTF knowing? Glancing at the boxes of drugs and the number of weapons they'd just found, he found that concept highly unlikely.

Morgan stood in the middle of the house and pondered what had just occurred.

Four men had repeatedly raped Joey Greene in the house across the street. Three men were now dead in *this* house. They had to be connected. Morgan knew precisely which man was missing, though, and he wasn't going to let him get away.

He went outside to check on the rest of his team.

Chapter 33

Detectives James Morgan and Nayla Senai sat on the curb, watching the activity between the two houses. It would officially be termed an officer-involved shooting, but Morgan knew what it really was—a clusterfuck.

There were three dead men with automatic weapons and illegal narcotics. That alone was enough to make the situation hairy for anyone involved, but an officer had been shot.

After dragging him out of harm's way, Adrian Thorn applied pressure to Courtney Earley's wound while Jeremiah Strange provided suppressing fire. It didn't appear Earley's injury was life-threatening, but it didn't matter. As soon as the scene was secured, Thorn and Strange tossed the big man into the team's Yukon and rushed him to Deaconess Hospital.

While Morgan watched Officer Sean Thayer string tape for an inner perimeter around the house with the Seahawks flag, he realized he hadn't figured out what the flags were truly about. He now had a suspicion, though.

The gang was selling guns and drugs. Based upon the fist stamp, he suspected some of the packages contained heroin, and some may have contained cocaine. They didn't have time to do a field test kit to determine what types of drugs were there. If that were true—if there were two different types of drugs, they could have stored the heroin in one house, the cocaine in another, and the guns in the third. Doing that would allow the gang members to keep an eye on them without having anyone or any product too far away. They could pick up and deliver all to practically the same place. It wasn't a place for junkies and dealers to go. It was a warehouse system for the gang. At least, he now had a theory that he could work to verify or debunk.

But that was for later.

As his hearing slowly returned, the ringing did not fade. He wondered how long that would remain.

Sergeant Bynum approached, and it was clear he was upset. He scowled as his head swiveled back and forth. He was looking for someone to blame, or he was afraid to see someone aiming the blame at him. A leader doesn't encounter a scene like this and not worry about his career.

"Why didn't you wait?" Bynum asked. His voice was low, and his eyes darted around the scene. "You didn't have to go to the other house."

"It was my call, Ken," Morgan said. "There's no one else to blame."

Bynum studied him before responding. "Someone has to stand with me when the brass wants an accounting because you know that's coming."

"I'll be there," the detective said.

The sergeant shook his head. Morgan knew he wasn't exactly the best wingman in the event the brass came calling.

Bynum said, "They've invoked the OIS protocol."

"And?"

"County is sending a team out to lead the investigation."

"Who's shadowing?"

"Nash."

Feeling some relief, he nodded. Even though Dallas Nash was a cake-eating attaboy, Morgan knew the man was a professional. Due to his seniority, Nash was the unofficial leader of Major Crimes. If anyone was going to look over the shoulder of some county detectives, Morgan would be happy it was Nash.

"What do we do now?" Senai asked.

Sergeant Bynum watched the arriving news vehicles. "You wait for the chief to make a show of checking on you. After that, the county detectives will want to collect the clothes you're wearing and take your guns for ballistics testing. You'll be issued a new gun when you return to duty."

Senai glanced at Morgan, who nodded once in return.

Bynum continued. "After you're finished with all that, you'll immediately be placed on a seventy-two-hour leave of absence from the department. When you come back, you'll be interviewed about the incident. I'm sure the union will advise you of this, but I'll say it, anyway. Don't talk about the shooting until then. Even if the chief asks, which he knows he's not supposed to, you don't say boo until you return. Got it?"

***

Officer Sean Thayer drove Morgan to the Public Safety Building. Neither man spoke until they were upstairs in the locker room. The rookie was to collect Morgan's clothes and gun, then immediately deliver them to the county detectives for placement into evidence.

After a visit to the john, the detective removed his ballistic vest and tossed it on the wooden bench near Thayer's leg. With gloved hands, the younger officer picked up the vest and tucked it into a brown evidence bag, then set it to the side.

As Morgan untied his shoes, Thayer looked around the corner of the locker room, assuring they were alone. "You okay?" he asked.

Morgan stepped out of his shoes. "You a therapist?"

"No. I mean—"

"Relax, kid. I'm fine." Morgan kicked his shoes toward the rookie, who picked them up and shoved them into another brown bag.

The younger officer remained silent as Morgan pulled his shirt over his head and tossed it near another evidence bag.

"What about you?" the detective asked. "Feeling better now that you're back in rotation?"

Thayer shrugged. "I've been second-guessing myself about the shooting."

"Don't." Morgan unbuckled his belt, then shoved his jeans to his ankles. "Believe what you did was right."

"I do, but did I shoot him because it was right, or did I shoot him because he was a moolie?"

After the detective tossed his pants on the bench, he crossed his arms. He stood only in a pair of plaid boxer shorts.

Thayer grabbed the jeans and stuffed them into the bag. "Fucking Black Lives Matter, right?"

Morgan's quickness surprised the rookie. He shoved Thayer into the nearest locker, which caused a racket. The younger officer bounced off the wall of metal, dropped the paper bag filled with Morgan's pants, and lifted his hands in preparation for a fight.

"The fuck, Morgan?"

"Don't ever talk like that."

Thayer's face scrunched in disbelief.

The detective pointed at him. "Don't you ever talk like that again."

Thayer glanced around, then up toward the ceiling. He whispered, "Are they listening?"

"You need to get rid of that thinking. Don't even let that shit in your head."

The younger officer smirked and picked up the brown bag. "This coming from you. I've heard about your reputation."

Morgan tapped his bare chest. "My reputation maybe, but you don't know anything about me, except I'm trying to help you."

"Shoving me is helping?"

"Listen," the detective said, "I don't know why you shot Tremaine Brown but let me give you another piece of advice. If you begin your career by thinking of people in terms like moolies, spics, or fags, you're going to end up in a very dark place. You don't want to be there."

Thayer remained silent, but his face reddened.

"There are plenty of dark places this job will take you. Don't put yourself in one before you even get started."

Morgan turned to his locker and removed a pair of gym shorts. He pulled them on as Thayer continued to stare at him. The younger man's face contorted into a glare, and he noisily rolled down the tops of the three brown paper bags.

"Whatever," the detective muttered. "Think about it how you want. It's no skin off my back." Morgan reached back into his locker for a wrinkled T-shirt. He slipped it over his head. "What do I know?"

Thayer collected the three bags and stalked out of the locker room.

Morgan was left alone.

Chapter 34

Morgan caught a ride home with another patrol officer. He had to. The Dodge Charger was part of the larger crime scene and would be confiscated as evidence.

Shortly after the boys fled the scene for Deaconess, Morgan noticed bullet holes in the side of the car. He knew what that meant. The city-owned vehicle would be locked down in the evidence warehouse while a forensic team and other detectives combed through it, looking for fragments of the rounds fired at his team. If Morgan wanted to avoid another disaster, he needed to act fast.

While patrol cars continued to arrive to secure the scene, Morgan casually opened the trunk. He watched Senai direct the arriving officers to various locations. He straightened the crumbled Jack in the Box bag and removed the remaining packages of heroin from the fast-food bag. It would be easier to explain the packages being in his pocket than being inside his trunk.

He could always say he picked them up inside the house. They might not match the chemical make-up of whatever was actually in those boxes, but he could explain that away with another lie. Morgan shut the trunk and eventually sat on the curb.

The entire time he spoke with Sergeant Bynum and Nayla Senai, he had the last couple of packets in his pocket. He wasn't worried now—he'd handled the problem. While the rookie escorted him to the station to take his clothing, Morgan commented a couple of times that he needed to take a leak. The younger officer never even questioned him when he detoured toward the restroom after arriving at the station. Morgan wrapped the drugs in a wad of tissue, tossed them into the toilet, and flushed.

Then he walked into the locker room and gave his clothing to Thayer.

One bullet dodged. Morgan smiled sardonically. One *metaphorical* bullet dodged. He'd avoided plenty of real rounds today.

Morgan showered slowly. His muscles relaxed underneath the pulsating hot water. When he finished, he dressed in a clean pair of jeans, a black T-shirt and running shoes. The rookie had taken his only pair of ankle-high tactical boots. Morgan made a mental note to get a new pair.

The day had flown by, and it was almost five. Morgan grabbed a beer from the kitchen, ignored checking on the pool activity below, and turned on the five o'clock news.

The top story was the shooting at the Pacific Avenue house. The banner at the bottom of the screen read— DEADLY POLICE SHOOTOUT.

As he listened to the report, it was clear the department had not shared much information yet. He almost felt sorry for the newscasters as they struggled to portray the incident accurately. Almost.

The footage showed detectives and officers examining the exterior of the house.

When the newscast switched stories, it moved to the fire at the Better Kitty Bookstore. There was film footage of firemen fighting the blaze. A new banner appeared at the bottom of the screen—BODY FOUND AT SCENE OF FIRE.

Morgan's cell phone vibrated. It was Vivian.

"Morgan," he said.

"Are you okay?"

"Why wouldn't I be?"

"Your picture is on the internet with the story."

"Have they identified me?"

That would be unlikely, he knew. The department wouldn't identify officers involved this early after an incident. They would want to complete their initial investigation and let the officers' families deal with the event before they announced who was at the scene. Usually, the media respected that policy.

There was a knock on the front door.

"No," Vivian said. "There was a picture with you in the background. I figured you were involved somehow. Are you okay?"

"I'm fine, Viv."

"Well," she started and paused, as if choosing her words carefully. "I'm glad. I wouldn't want anything bad to happen to you."

A surge of happiness ran through Morgan when he realized she was worried about him.

There was a second, more persistent knock at the door.

"Viv, can I call you back?"

"Anytime."

Morgan ended the call, got up from his chair, and walked to the front door. When he opened it, she didn't hesitate before jumping into his arms. She pressed him against the wall, and she pressed her lips hard against his.

"Hey, now," Morgan mumbled into her open mouth. "I'm fine."

Alyssa pulled back. Her brow furrowed in an inquisitive nature. "Huh?"

"The shooting. I'm okay."

Her mouth closed slightly, and she blinked several times. "There was a shooting?" she asked.

"I thought you heard."

The redhead stepped back and studied him. She wore a white shirt, pink shorts, and white sandals. "Are you hurt? You look fine."

"That's what I've been saying," Morgan said. "I'm fine."

She attacked him again, kissing and groping as she moved about his body.

Previously, he failed to respond to this type of advance from her. He wanted the chase—the push and pull. But this evening, he responded immediately. He grabbed her and roughly spun her around, pinning her against the wall. Alyssa yelped, but she didn't resist.

Morgan controlled her as he kissed the back of her neck. Perhaps it was the simple joy of being alive after surviving the gun battle that made him feel this way. Whatever it was, he felt real joy, and she responded accordingly.

He picked her up and carried her into the bedroom.

***

It was still light out when Morgan awoke with Alyssa in his arms. Her breathing was soft and rhythmic, and she felt warm. He quietly rolled away from her and stood. She remained sleeping, her naked body on display. All the bedding, including the sheets, was on the floor.

Morgan studied her for a moment. She was a beautiful woman, and he had been right at his earliest assessment of her. Her pleasant paleness was enjoyable to the touch.

He padded out to the living room where he had left his cell phone. There were more than thirty text messages. Most of them were from guys on the department wanting to know if he was okay or asking to get the scoop on the shooting.

There was a text from Adrian Thorn letting him know Courtney Earley was doing well and out of surgery at Deaconess Hospital. He responded by text and said he would get to the hospital as soon as he could.

It was a text from Joey Greene that gave him pause. He studied it for several moments.

THAT COP WAS HERE ASKING ABOUT U.

Morgan walked back into the bedroom and quietly dressed. He didn't wake the now softly snoring Alyssa.

Chapter 35

Courtney Earley sat upright in his hospital bed. On either side of him stood Adrian Thorn and Jeremiah Strange. They seemed to be involved in an intense conversation when Morgan arrived. The three of them immediately stopped talking and turned to the detective.

"How you feeling, big man?" he asked.

"Better," Earley said.

"How bad is it?"

"Hurts."

Thorn and Strange intently studied Morgan. They didn't bother to hide their anger.

"What's with you guys?" Morgan asked.

They shared a glance, then turned to Earley, who looked at them both. He shook his head and said, "Lieutenant Culkin was here."

"Of course he was," Morgan said.

Strange crossed his arms. "The man's after you."

"What about it?"

"Did you do something we need to be aware of?" Thorn asked. "I mean, are you going to drag us down for some of your legendary Morgan bullshit?"

"Relax, Adrian," Earley whispered.

"I haven't done anything," Morgan said.

"You haven't?" Strange's lip curled after he spoke.

"What do you call that cowboy bullshit from today?" Thorn asked. His cheeks reddened. "The shit that got Courtney shot?"

"Take it easy," Earley muttered.

"I did what I thought was right," Morgan said. His face warmed as he spoke. "It wasn't illegal, and it wasn't out of protocol."

"It wasn't safe," Strange snapped.

"It was stupid," Thorn barked.

"It was right," Morgan said. "If you two idiots—"

"Shut up!"

The three of them looked at Earley, who was now wincing in pain. "Just shut up," he whispered. "Culkin is the problem. Not Morgan. He did his job. He didn't shoot me. Some piece of squeeze did."

The four of them remained silent for some time. The only sounds in the room came from the hum of the fluorescent lighting and the beeping of the medical equipment monitoring Earley's vital signs.

"What did Culkin want?" Morgan asked.

"Dirt," the big man said.

Morgan exhaled in frustration.

"We didn't have any to give him," Earley said.

"Believe me," Thorn said, "after that bullshit today, if I had something to give, I would have."

"Me too," Strange added.

Earley shook his head. "We're cool, Morgan. These two just need to calm the fuck down."

Strange looked away, and Thorn rolled his eyes.

"Thank you."

"But you better check on Nayla," Earley said.

"Why?"

"She was with us when Culkin came by. After the lieutenant's full-court press, she was really upset. She bailed right after he did."

***

When Morgan left Deaconess, he drove directly to Sacred Heart Hospital. Spokane's two main hospitals were less than a mile apart and in almost a straight line.

Joey Greene was in the process of being released and stood next to her bed in a pair of oversized sweatpants that must have been donated by a women's charity.

"How are you doing?" Morgan asked.

"I'm doing."

"Ready to go home? I can give you a ride."

She looked away for a moment, then nodded. "That would be nice. I got some paperwork I need to finish, but yeah, that would be nice."

It took another thirty minutes for the hospital to out-process Joey. Morgan gently held her by the upper arm as they walked outside and passed the *No Parking—Police Vehicles Only* signs.

"Where's your car?" she asked.

"I'm driving my personal rig."

When they arrived at his pickup, she paused and considered it. "This was what you were driving when you found me."

"What about it?"

"It's a hillbilly truck."

"No, it's not."

She shook her head. "It is, Morgan. I didn't realize you were a redneck."

He turned to her. "Joey, if there's one thing I'm not, it's redneck."

"Why? Because you like me?"

"Stop talking," he said.

He helped her into the truck, closed the door, and walked around to the driver's side. The truck lurched forward. They drove for several minutes in silence before Morgan asked, "Did you watch the news?"

"No."

He turned onto Sprague Avenue.

"Why?" she asked him.

"We executed a search warrant on the little yellow house, the one where …"

He didn't finish the thought, so Joey did it for him.

"Where I was raped. I'm a big girl, Morgan. You can say it."

"It didn't go as planned."

Joey shrugged. "It figures. They'll get away with it, huh?"

"We killed three of them," he said.

She slowly faced him.

"The fourth is still out there, Joey, but I know who he is."

Neither of them spoke until they got to Joey's house. Morgan stopped his truck, got out, and helped Joey into her home.

When he got her situated on her couch, he asked, "Do you need anything?"

"Are you holding?" she asked.

"I'm sorry," he said, and he meant it. "If I had anything, I'd give it to you."

"I know," she said.

"Want me to sit with you for a while?"

"This ain't the movies, Morgan. I don't need you to hold me."

"You sure you're okay?"

"I'm going to take a shower, then smoke some weed. How are you sitting here going to do anything except slow me down from getting what I want?"

The detective nodded, then turned to leave.

"Hey, Morgan?" she said as he stepped out the door.

"Yeah?"

She inhaled as if she were about to say something but paused. Then she exhaled and nodded several times. Finally, she said, "You're a good man," and slowly closed the door.

***

He'd just started his truck to leave Joey's house when his phone rang.

"Morgan," he said after answering it.

"I've received another demand," Desmond Ashdown said. His words were fast and slurred, like he'd been drinking. "You promised it was done."

"It is. It was."

Morgan's phone beeped in his ear that he was receiving an incoming call. He pulled it away and looked at the screen. The new call was from Nayla Senai.

"They're threatening me, Morgan." Ashdown's voice sounded small as it came from the earpiece. "They're threatening me *again*. I'm paying you for this to be over."

"I'll handle it," he said and hung up on the man to answer Senai's call.

Chapter 36

They met at the Yoke's Fresh Market on North Foothills. Morgan pulled into the parking lot, saw Nayla Senai standing next to her Toyota Camry, and drove slowly to her.

When he slipped out of his truck, he said, "This is clandestine."

"Lieutenant Culkin came by to see Earley at the hospital."

"I heard."

Senai glanced around the parking lot, then stepped forward. "He said there was an open door if we ever saw you do anything illegal or anything wrong."

"Wrong isn't illegal," Morgan said.

She sighed. "Unethical. That's what he's after."

Morgan frowned. "And?"

"I met with him."

He studied her for a moment before asking, "What did you tell him?"

"The truth."

Morgan shoved his hands in his pockets. "That's all I've ever said. Tell him the truth."

"I told him you push up to the line, but I've never seen you cross it."

She was bothered, but he kept his mouth shut. He sensed Senai didn't need his comfort. She needed something else.

"I lied," Senai said.

He remained silent.

"I've seen you do things that were unethical," Senai said. "Illegal, too. You dented that man's car. I didn't see it, but I know you did it. You intimidate people. You've made illegal entries. You lie to get things done. I can't prove any of it, but I know you do it."

"Then why didn't you tell him that?"

She shrugged. "Because you would never purposively hurt the boys or me. For that matter, you'd never hurt anyone in the department, even the ones you dislike. If the shit ever goes down, I can always count on you to be by my side. There are many on the department I can't count on."

"I would never hurt you or the team."

"But you do. You just don't see it."

Morgan's brow creased.

"Do you understand the value of your lies, Morgan?"

He wanted to look away, to stop this conversation, but he stared intently at her.

Senai continued. "Everything about us has value, positive or negative, good or bad, for us or for someone else. That value is in our actions and our words—even our lies. But our lies are the worst. They allow us to think they have value while they taint our souls and taint the souls of those we lie to. Even when it seems they do something positive, they are really negative. Do you understand?"

Morgan didn't answer.

Senai walked around to the driver's door of her car, opened it, and stood behind it. "Don't make me regret sticking my neck out for you." She dropped into her vehicle, pulled the door closed, and slowly drove away.

He stood in the parking lot for some time, thinking about Nayla's words.

Chapter 37

Morgan headed north on Market Street and drove by the Quick-E Mart convenience store on Bridgeport Avenue. When he saw the blue Impala lowrider parked out front, he flipped a U-turn and pulled into the lot.

DeShaun Harmon walked out while smacking a pack of menthol cigarettes against his open hand. Morgan intercepted him before he got to his car.

"Bilbo," the detective said.

The man glanced over his shoulder, recognized Morgan, and slowly turned around. His gaze ran the length of the detective as he continued opening the pack of Newports.

"What's so funny?" Morgan asked.

"Your ride's not here, and you're not wearing a badge or carrying a gun."

"I'm carrying. Never doubt that." He had one tucked into an ankle holster at that very moment.

Bilbo ripped open the pack of cigarettes and shook one free. "Sure, detective, but you ain't working, right? Which means this is off-book, or you're off the job. Which is it?"

"I'm on my way home, and I saw you. Simple as that."

"With you, nothing is as simple as that."

"Did you hear about the shooting at the house on Pacific?"

Bilbo's eyes hardened, and he stuck the cigarette in his mouth. "I wasn't part of that."

"Your crew was."

The smaller man shook his head. "That wasn't my crew."

"Yeah, it was."

"Do you like it when you get blamed for the things other officers do?"

Morgan smirked. "That's how it works."

Bilbo pulled a Bic lighter from his pocket and snapped it a couple of times before it lit. He inhaled deeply, then exhaled smoke away from the detective. "Whatever, Morgan. You're not arresting me, so what's this about?"

"Your cousin. He was supposed to be at the house, but he wasn't."

The shorter man pretended to study his cigarette. After a moment, he asked, "Why do you think he was supposed to be there?"

"I have my ways."

Bilbo sucked again on the cigarette and studied Morgan. After he exhaled, he said, "You're fishing."

"He raped a woman I know," Morgan said. "A woman I care about. She identified him by the photo I took. The one I took right here. Remember that?"

Bilbo flicked a finger against the cigarette even though there was no ash to set free. "I don't know nothing about that."

"We got the other three—"

"Meaning you killed the other three."

"Your cousin is still missing. I want him. Where is he?"

Bilbo shrugged.

"Not good enough."

The smaller man began to lift the cigarette to his mouth, but Morgan batted it from his hands. Bilbo remained still and refused to make eye contact with the detective.

Morgan leaned into his ear and whispered, "Where is he, Bilbo?"

"I don't know."

"How about I drag you around the corner and beat it out of you?"

Bilbo turned his head slowly and glowered at the detective. "Listen to what I'm saying. I don't know where he is. If I did, I would tell you, Morgan. No bullshit."

The detective stepped back and appraised Bilbo. "He's your cousin. You'd give him up that easy?"

The smaller man bent over and picked up his cigarette. He knocked the ash from its end and inhaled. As he spoke, smoke escaped from his mouth. "We're not cousins."

The detective nodded slowly. "No kidding. What's his name?"

"Kyler Moore."

"Where's he from?"

"Cali."

"California? Where?"

"Oaktown."

Morgan's pulse quickened. "Now that is a coincidence. Do you know who else is from Oakland?"

Bilbo inhaled on his cigarette.

"The Eight."

"That is a coincidence," the smaller man agreed.

"Do you believe in coincidences, Bilbo?"

Bilbo flicked some ash from his cigarette. "I don't know, man. Maybe."

"Is your cousin Eight?"

"He's not my cousin."

"Is he Eight?"

Bilbo shrugged.

"And the rest of the shooters?"

Another shrug.

Morgan leaned in and sniffed the smaller man. "Smells like bullshit. Gangs don't do co-ops."

"What do you want?" Bilbo asked. "They had the manpower, and we had the territory. Either we adapted, or we got wiped out. It didn't take a genius to figure that out. We came to an agreement that benefited both sides. They agreed to come under our banner so as not to raise any suspicion. While that occurred, we worked to establish a new business model."

"They what? Used your brand? Like a sneaker endorsement?"

"Sneaker?" Bilbo snickered. "How old are you?"

"Not too old to break your fucking jaw."

Bilbo held up his hands. "Okay, peace, man. Peace." He dropped his cigarette and ground it out. "Besides, Corporate America does that shit all the time. Why can't we?"

Morgan shook his head. "No way. That's not how a gang works."

"Says who? You? The police are telling the gangs how to operate now? No. Things change, or they die. It's a law of nature, Morgan. Even a thick-headed cop like you has to understand it."

Morgan considered what Bilbo had said—The Emerald City Giants were licensing their brand to a rival gang. "The guys in the house, the reason I didn't know them, they were all Eight."

Bilbo shrugged. "Each and every one."

Morgan crossed his arms. "Tell me about the flags."

"What about them?"

"What did they mean? Why cluster the houses together?"

Bilbo glanced away for a moment. Then he puffed his cheeks out with an exhale of air. "It was a tactical decision. The Eight bunched them together because they thought it was smart. Guys could move product from one house to the next, depending on the day. The product never stayed in the same house for two days in a row. The flags were the password. If you knew what you were looking for, you were golden. We could spot surveillance. It worked like a charm. I got to give it to them. It was a good idea until the cops moved into the neighborhood. We don't know how that happened, but we spotted them pretty quick."

"If you spotted us, why not move everything?"

"We liked the neighborhood concept. We'd been there almost six months before the cops found it."

"The Eight has been in town for six months?"

Bilbo nodded.

Morgan let that roll through his mind. He and his team had only heard of their move for about a week.

"We knew the days of that neighborhood were numbered," Bilbo continued. "The flags were too obvious, so we worked out a new scheme and picked a new area. You busted that house a day before everything was to be moved," Bilbo said. "That's why everything was in one place. They should never have done that. Had we got it out of there, you wouldn't have found it. You got lucky."

"I didn't get lucky. Your boys made a mistake. Like I said, she's a friend."

Bilbo spat on the ground. "Arrogant bastards."

"They did her bad."

The smaller man looked away, ashamed.

"Promise me you weren't part of that. I couldn't let it go if I knew you sanctioned it."

Bilbo's lip curled. "I ain't no saint, Morgan. You know that, but I would never do that to a woman. I got a mother, a sister, and a daughter. I don't need that kind of karma in my life."

"You guys were doing things smart until someone decided to shoot at Tremaine Brown, then rape a girl. Why?"

The smaller man turned his palms up. "The new partnership. They got some good ideas—the houses with the flags was one. But then they wanted to pick a fight with someone we got no business fightin'. Tremaine isn't a threat. The man stays on his side of the tracks, and we stay on ours. They let ego get in the way. It's stupid is what it is."

"Stupid is right. Let's talk about Yaban Karga."

"Who?"

"The Turk."

Bilbo's eyes flattened.

"Why kill him?"

Bilbo shook another cigarette free from his pack.

Morgan took a deep breath as he thought. Finally, he said, "I told the Turk the DEA was watching him."

The smaller man paused while lighting his cigarette.

"It was some bullshit," Morgan said.

"The DEA wasn't real?"

"A figment of my imagination."

Bilbo flicked his lighter and inhaled deeply.

Morgan continued. "So Karga relayed my story to your crew and spooked someone because he'd been getting his dope from your crew, probably from the neighborhood of flags." Morgan held a fist in the air. "As soon as he called, saying he was in trouble, someone gave the order to meet with him, make sure he wasn't followed, then they ended the relationship. They needed him to meet with someone he knew. Someone he trusted. Someone who's been in the game awhile. I'm guessing that was you."

Bilbo rubbed a finger under his nose but refused to say anything.

Morgan shrugged. "Water under the bridge, I guess."

Bilbo cocked his head.

"Who went after Tremaine?"

"We should have remained corporate," Bilbo said, wistfully. "Fly under the radar. Make allegiances where they're strategic. We don't need to fight with other brown people."

"So, you're confirming it was a Giant who killed Brown's girlfriend."

Bilbo shook his head. "No way. It wasn't a Giant. We had a peace with the Dead Boys. It was Eight all the way. Kyler. He wanted to remove Tremaine, and the man's girl was just a bystander."

"Then why send the baby gangster to cop to it?"

The smaller man shrugged. "The new world order. They sent the baby with no bones to claim the shooting. He gets juice by taking the heat for Kyler. When he gets out, he'll be eighteen and ready to do some real banging."

Morgan shook his head.

Chapter 38

She stopped as soon as she entered her apartment. "I know you're in here," she said.

"Then shut the door." Morgan stood in the kitchen, out of her line of sight, with a gun in his hand.

"I'll call the cops."

"Go ahead. When they arrive, we'll talk about how you killed Ricky and burned down the bookstore."

Morgan heard the door close. In a moment, her head peeked around the corner. When she saw the gun, her eyes widened.

"Relax," Morgan said. "I'm not going to shoot you. This was a safety precaution."

"For what?"

"To make sure you didn't come home with a gun. Or worse, a boyfriend."

Jenna/Ellen stepped into the kitchen then. She wore tight blue jeans with suede high heel boots. Underneath her gauzy tan blouse, she wore no bra, which revealed her dark areolas. Over her shoulder was a bucket-style purse.

"Boyfriends are overrated."

"Guns aren't," Morgan said. "Put the purse down."

Ellen slipped it off her shoulder and laid it carefully on the counter.

"Step back."

"I'll save you the trouble," she said. "There's a gun in there."

"The one you used to kill Ricky with?"

"How do you know I shot him?"

"I'm assuming. I didn't think the man would hang around while his building burned. It's a straight line to that assumption."

Ellen crossed her arms.

"You killed the man and took over his extortion scam. Desmond Ashdown received a text demanding another payment tonight."

Her forehead wrinkled in confusion. "Desmond?"

"I stopped by Ricky's, and we came to an agreement that he'd never bother the man again."

"I didn't know that."

"Had you never bothered Desmond, I wouldn't have cared if you carried on the scam."

"I won't bother him again," she said. "I promise."

"I know."

"How do you know?"

Morgan waved his gun.

"Oh," she said.

"Why'd you kill Ricky?"

"Because of what you said."

"How's that?"

"I figured he owed me a bigger cut. He was making ten times—fifty times—what I got paid, and I was the one having to get naked with these guys—be in the pictures. Didn't seem fair."

"Life's not fair," Morgan said.

"No, it's not."

"Ricky deleted the pictures," the detective said. "I saw him do it. I even made him delete them from his computer's trash can."

"It's called the cloud, grandpa. They were backed up there."

"He showed you how to access them?"

"He sent me a link."

"Then you killed him?"

"Why do you keep rehashing these questions like a cop?"

Morgan considered his gun. "I need to know if I can work with you as a partner."

"Partner?" she asked.

"I don't care what you do with the photos, and you can earn anyway you want."

"You want a cut."

"No," he said. "There are two people I'm interested in. Their photos must be fully deleted. Do you understand?"

"Yes."

"The first is Desmond Ashdown."

"And the second?"

"Terrance Millhouse. Have you done anything with his photos?"

Her brow furrowed, and she slowly shook her head. "No. Who is he?"

"Another friend. You don't need his pictures. Delete them."

"And the rest?"

Morgan slipped his gun into his holster. "I don't care what you do with them."

"What's your name?"

"You don't get to know that."

As he walked by her, she asked, "Are you a cop?"

Morgan stopped. "Would a cop be here?"

Ellen looked down and considered his question. "Probably not," she said.

"Stay out of trouble, Ellen, or I'll be back to renegotiate our partnership. You won't like the new terms."

Chapter 39

When he returned to his apartment complex, he parked his truck and got out. He lingered in the darkness for a moment and replayed the day's events.

For a moment, he remembered the brief encounter with Alyssa. He wondered if she was still in his bed where he left her. He doubted it but, if she were, that would be a pleasant diversion from the evening's events.

When he stepped onto the curb, he noticed a patrol car at the end of the parking lot. He slowly moved that way, his head swiveling side to side, his senses on alert.

This was a nice community, and it was odd for an officer to visit. Occasionally, a vehicle was prowled, but that was a rarity and would not require a patrol response. Perhaps it was a domestic violence call, but only a single officer seemed to be on the scene.

Morgan continued walking until he was in front of the building where Vivian Basler lived. He looked up toward her apartment, and the front door was open. Morgan climbed the stairs—two at a time.

He peeked into the apartment, and a young, uniformed officer was talking with Vivian. He handed her an incident report card and said, "Call us if he returns."

When the officer stepped out, he nodded to Morgan and passed by. The detective thought about introducing himself to the graveyard officer and asking what had occurred. Morgan quickly decided getting to Vivian was more important. He stepped into the apartment and closed the door.

"What's going on, Viv?"

"Leigh's boyfriend showed up."

"Dontari Brown? He's out of jail?"

"I guess," she said with a shrug. "I don't know how he knew where I lived, but he showed up angry. He searched my apartment for her."

"Did he hurt you?"

"He only scared me," she said with a dismissive wave. "He said I put the thoughts into her head about leaving him, and if she followed through with it, he'd be back. I'd be sorry then."

"That's when you called the police?"

She nodded.

Anger burned in Morgan's chest. "I'll take care of this, Viv. You don't have to worry."

"Thank you, Jimmy."

As Morgan watched her, his heart ached. "Want me to stay awhile?" he asked. His words sounded like a schoolboy hoping to do homework with a girl he had a crush on.

Vivian's smile was kind. "That's okay, Jimmy. I'm fine. I'll lock the door and go to bed with my phone. I've already left a message for Leigh to watch out for Dontari."

"All right," Morgan said. He did his best to hide his disappointment.

Vivian hugged Morgan and kissed the side of his cheek. She smelled wonderful. When they broke their embrace, he turned and left.

***

When Morgan got back to his apartment, Alyssa was in the kitchen, wearing one of his T-shirts and nothing else. Her hair was pulled back and tied with a rubber band.

"I was wondering when you'd get back."

"You didn't go home?"

"Did you want me to?" She pouted.

As Morgan studied her, he smelled the lingering effects of Vivian's perfume in his nose. He slid his hand into Alyssa's, and he led her into the bedroom.

"Well, hello there," she said with a giggle.

He turned the light off, slipped the T-shirt over her head, and pretended he was making love to Vivian.

Chapter 40

He waited for twenty minutes before he was escorted back to the man's office. He didn't have an appointment. He'd shown up unannounced at the ninth-floor office in the Lincoln Building. While he waited, he enjoyed the view from the lobby windows.

The receptionist opened the door to Terrance Millhouse's office and waved him in.

Millhouse stood behind his desk. "Detective Morgan, right?" he asked as he approached with an extended hand.

"That's right."

"I have an appointment in a few minutes, so we'll need to make this quick."

Morgan handed a manila envelope to Millhouse and watched as the man removed the photos.

Terrance Millhouse had earned his nickname "Terry Grindhouse" because he tore up officers whenever they appeared in court against his clients. He might look like a kind man, but behind his mild-mannered façade was the mind of a courtroom killer.

The same man every cop feared from the witness stand suddenly looked small and frightened. As he quickly moved from picture to picture, his hands shook. Finally, he stopped, shuffled the photos together, and stuffed them back into the envelope.

"What do you want?" the attorney whispered.

"Relax, counselor. I'm not here to squeeze you."

Millhouse inhaled, swallowed, then exhaled. For a man whose career was built on words, he seemed incapable of finding any at that moment.

Morgan pointed at the envelope. "I stopped those from being used against you."

The attorney's brow crinkled. "Why would you do that? We don't know each other."

"I was helping someone else in the same situation when I found those. Maybe I'm wrong, but I'm guessing that's your wife with some friends. If that's true, that's nobody's business but your own."

For a moment, Millhouse studied the envelope in his hand. Then his eyes moved back toward Morgan. "Nobody works for free."

The detective shrugged. "An Internal Affairs lieutenant is coming after me."

"And there it is." Millhouse smacked the folder into the open palm of his other hand. "Quid pro quo."

"Quid pro quo," Morgan repeated.

"You call me," the attorney said, "and I will be there. If there is ever a conflict of interest that stops me from helping you, I will request a favor from a friend. I'll stand over their shoulder to make sure you get whatever help you need. Is that fair?"

"That's fair."

Millhouse considered the envelope again. "Are there any other copies of these pictures?"

"No," Morgan lied. "Those are the last."

Terrance Millhouse walked over to a paper shredder that sat near his desk and removed a photograph from the envelope. He quickly glanced at the picture, then slipped it into the shredder. It noisily destroyed the evidence of his fetish. Then he reached into the envelope for another.

"Thank you for bringing this to my attention, Detective."

Morgan let himself out and left the attorney alone in his moment of sacrifice.

****

After leaving the offices of Craven, Knadler, and Millhouse, he walked several blocks to Indaba Coffee. He ordered a black coffee, then sat with his back to the wall, watching three male patrons enter. It was apparent they were meeting for a mid-morning break.

He listened to them order fancy drinks—a Natatorium Delight, a Staccato, and a Cortado. All of them sounded pretentious, and none of them made sense. They were chubby young men, each wearing overly tight slacks, tight button-up shirts, and tight smiles. Their haircuts were short and primped with overuse of hair products. Next to them, Morgan looked like an out-of-work longshoreman.

He believed these three to be a young girl's fantasy of what today's men should be. However, they would be a grown woman's disappointment when she realized an entire generation of men had been neutered.

Morgan watched the three with obvious disdain. One of them caught his eye, tried to look tough for a fleeting moment, then happily turned away when the barista announced his name.

"Robin, your coffee is ready."

The detective sipped his coffee and watched the men as they huddled together. The three loudly talked and laughed like peacocks trying to attract interested mates.

Noise from the street entered the café when Desmond Ashdown opened the door and stepped inside. The man wore a dark suit, blue shirt open at the collar, and no tie.

He searched the establishment, then walked directly toward Morgan. He did not bother to get a coffee.

Ashdown dropped into the seat across from the detective. "What's going on?"

"It's done," Morgan said.

"You said that before."

"That's why we're meeting face-to-face. I want to assure you it's done. There will be no further screw-ups."

"What happened?"

"Let's call it a miscommunication between partners."

"A miscommunication?" Ashdown's voice rose. "Are you kidding?"

"Take it easy. Things happen. It's done now."

"You guarantee it?"

Morgan nodded. "I do now."

Ashdown did his best to look around the coffee house casually, but it was an act. He reached into his jacket pocket and placed an envelope on the table. Morgan picked it up and opened it.

"I didn't think you counted the money in public."

Morgan continued to flip through the bills until he reached ten thousand. When he was satisfied, he put the envelope back on the table. "This isn't the movies. You trust but verify."

Ashdown stood. "Thank you for your help."

"Remember our deal."

"I've no idea who you are," Ashdown said.

Morgan lifted his coffee cup in a silent toast and watched Ashdown hurry from the café.

***

His next stop was the Public Safety Building. Even though he was still on his mandatory seventy-two hour administrative leave following a shooting, he had someone to see. He entered the building and headed straight toward the office of Internal Affairs.

It was a two-person office, staffed by a lieutenant and a sergeant, but only Lieutenant Neil Culkin was behind his desk.

"I heard you've been asking about me," Morgan said.

Culkin looked up at the detective, then leaned back and crossed his arms over his chest. "Are you coming to confess your sins?"

"You don't look like a priest."

"Not even close. I don't give absolution."

"Should I contact my union rep?"

"What for? You came by voluntarily. I haven't asked you anything."

"But you've been asking my team about me."

"And they closed ranks around you. Even the prostitute protected you for some reason."

"You found her?"

Culkin's smile was full of disbelief. "Like you don't know. She claims the person who saved her was not you, but some john who was jealous she was spending time with our complainant. She described him. He sounded oddly like you, but she swore it wasn't you. When I asked for his name, she said it was 'John.'" Culkin shrugged. "Tell me how you did it, Morgan."

"Did what?"

"How did you get everyone to back up your lies?"

"Lies?" Morgan leaned against the doorframe. "I don't know what you're talking about."

"You're a slippery son of a bitch."

"The same could be said of you, lieutenant."

"That's insubordination."

"Not really. But even if it were, you'd have to prove it first."

Culkin studied him the way a boy does when he burns ants with a magnifying glass. "Keep playing it fast and loose, Morgan. One of these days, it's going to catch up to you, and I'm going to be there to bring you in."

The detective stiffened. "Is that an accusation? Or are you just slinging mud?"

"You're dirty."

"Sounds like mud, lieutenant. Where's the actual accusation?"

"I've got my eye on you, Morgan."

The detective clicked his tongue a couple of times inside his mouth. "Okay, lieutenant. I'll be on my best behavior."

Chapter 41

Morgan pulled into the parking garage of Northtown Mall and drove to the top level. He spotted the Monte Carlo waiting at the far end of the lot. He pulled in next to it and rolled down his window.

The Monte remained quiet with its heavily tinted windows rolled up. Morgan developed a bad feeling a gun was aimed at him from somewhere behind the darkened windows. He leaned away from the sleek, black car.

The detective heard them before he saw them. Two cars pulled in next to his truck—one on the passenger side and one behind him. Since his truck was pointed into the wall, he was now boxed in.

He'd made a fatal error.

Morgan's gun was under the hip he was leaning on. He twisted slightly to reveal its holster and quickly pulled the gun free. His heart beat wildly, and he looked over the lip of his window to see if there was any movement.

The darkened window of the Chevy slowly rolled down to reveal Tremaine Brown behind the wheel. He watched Morgan with curiosity. Beside Tremaine sat his brother, Dontari, who angrily stared straight ahead.

Morgan glanced through the back window as he asked, "The hell is this, Tremaine?"

"I needed to make sure you wouldn't do anything stupid."

"Like this?" Morgan said, glancing around. A Ford blocked his rear, and a Buick was in next to him. Both cars had darkened windows, so he couldn't see who was at the steering wheel. "This looks like a stupid decision. People are going to get hurt."

"*This* is a precaution," Tremaine said. "I brought Dontari here for a reason."

"Our truce is about to get royally fucked over at this moment."

Tremaine looked at his brother. "Tell the man."

Dontari shook his head, then looked at the detective. "I'm leaving."

When Dontari looked out the front windshield again, Tremaine turned to Morgan. "He's not happy about the exile."

"He's running on his bond?" the detective asked.

Tremaine shrugged. "The cost of doing business."

"You threatened my friend, Don. I can't let that go."

Dontari scowled at Morgan. "Ain't shit you can do about it, is there? I'll be out of this city before you leave this parking garage."

"Get out," Tremaine said.

His brother flicked a hand at him, exited the Monte Carlo, then climbed into the Ford. It sped away before Dontari closed the door. The Buick backed up and followed the other car out of the parking lot.

"Dontari is gone, Morgan. He won't bother Leigh, either. Your friend has nothing to worry about anymore."

"Where's he going?"

Tremaine shook his head. "You don't get to know that. All that matters is he's out of the five-oh-nine, which means he's out of play for you."

Morgan looked down at the gun in his hand. He didn't care about Dontari. He only wanted to make sure he never bothered Vivian again. Leigh Gaston was an offshoot of that concern, but she didn't figure much into his equation. If Dontari never bothered Viv, Morgan would consider it a win. He tucked the gun into his holster, sat upright, and faced Tremaine.

"So why are we here, Morgan? You called for this parlay."

"Gina's shooter."

Tremaine's eyes hardened. "What about him?"

"The guy that's in lock-up is the wrong guy. The detectives just don't know it yet."

"How's that?"

"He's a baby taking a fall for the real shooter."

Morgan handed him a paper that had two photographs. Under each picture was a name and physical description. One was of Kyler Moore, and the other was of DeShaun Harmon. "The younger one was the shooter. He's Eight."

Brown looked up. "What?"

"The Eight have been in town for a while now, operating under the banner of the Giants."

"Straight?"

"The Giants sold their brand just like corporate America."

Tremaine tapped Kyler Moore's face. "Why'd this one try to take me out? We've been cool with the Giants."

"Attack your enemy while they're sleeping. It's war."

"It's business," Tremaine muttered. He put his finger on the second photo. "I know Bilbo. How's he involved?"

"He ordered the shooting." The lie came quickly for Morgan.

Tremaine eyed the detective. "*Bilbo* greenlit me? Why?"

"After the corporate merger, he ended up a middle manager. What do you think he's going to do? He's got to make some noise to get noticed. This merger wasn't supposed to be known until it was too late. The Eight are moving up along the I-5 corridor, with Seattle being the long play. They were supposed to take over Spokane now, then the Tri-Cities and Yakima. Seattle would fall eventually when they had it surrounded."

Tremaine stared at him, dumbfounded. "They're playing this shit like it's World War Two."

"Your truce with the Giants went away the moment The Eight decided to enter the fray."

"Shit," Tremaine said, staring back at the two pictures.

The two men sat quietly. Tremaine seemed lost in thoughts of revenge. Morgan was lost in his web of lies.

Finally, Tremaine turned to him. "You know what I'm about to do?"

Morgan knew. He couldn't get justice for Yaban Karga without exposing himself. Identifying Bilbo as the finger for the shooting put him into Tremaine's crosshairs.

"No innocents," Morgan said. "Just players."

"Fair," Tremaine said and handed Morgan back the photos of the two men.

Morgan tossed the paper onto the passenger seat. "One last thing," he said, pulling his gun from his holster.

"What's that?"

"The rookie."

"What about him?"

"Drop the lawsuit."

Tremaine smirked. "That could be a big payday. Why should I drop that for you?"

Morgan lifted his gun over the lip of the window.

Tremaine stared into the barrel. "It's not the first time I've stared down a gun, Morgan. And you know they have cameras on this parking lot, so you're not going to shoot me. You could have made your point without the piece."

"Maybe, but at least this way there is no confusion."

"And what's the confusion?"

"Me and you. We have a deal. I'll work with you if you work with me. It's gotten both of us a long way, but never forget it's blue versus you. I'll never cross that line. If you go after one of my brothers, that means I come after you."

"Motherfucker's a racist."

"But he's still blue."

Tremaine leaned toward Morgan and the gun. "You came after my brother. How is that any different?"

"Your brother had a warrant, and I did it right. And I told you about it. There was no profit in it for me. What you're doing is all about profit."

"Everything is about profit."

Morgan shook his head. "However you twist it won't matter in the end. Me and you, or blue versus you. It's simple. Do we have an understanding?"

Tremaine turned forward, started his car. "We have an understanding," he said.

Chapter 42

That afternoon Morgan lay by the apartment's pool, sipping his second can of beer. The sun was beyond its zenith, and he was afraid he might melt if he didn't get in the water soon. Once he finished this beer, he would, he decided. The warmth of the rays on his skin was moving from enjoyable to uncomfortable.

Alyssa dropped onto the lounge chair next to him. He turned to face her and smiled. Her bikini top barely contained her, and he wondered if wishful thinking could cause her to spill out.

"You're home early," she said.

"I'm on administrative leave."

"What's that for?

"Administrative stuff."

She grabbed his beer, took a sip, then handed the can back to him.

"You okay?" she asked.

"Yeah."

"Want to go up to your apartment?"

"Inna bit," Morgan mumbled, then took a sip of his beer.

She *tsked* once, then reached into the floppy bag she brought along. She pulled out a bottle of lotion and tossed it onto Morgan's stomach.

"I need to put some sunscreen on, or I'll burn like crazy."

She spun around and lay on her belly. Morgan sat upright and grabbed the bottle before it fell to the ground. He set his beer on the concrete and studied Alyssa. She looked away from him and pushed her butt higher into the air.

He opened the bottle and thought about squirting the lotion into his hand. The mental image of caressing her soft skin careened through his slightly inebriated brain.

There was absolutely no chase involved, but he knew that wouldn't matter this afternoon. She'd gotten into his nose now, and he would be hers for a while until she was ready to move on to someone who would be husband material or, at the very least, someone she could take home to daddy.

He tossed the bottle of lotion onto her back and stood.

She flipped onto her side and angrily looked up. "The hell, Jimmy?"

"C'mon," he said glumly.

"Where are we going?"

He cast a shadow over her. "Where do you think?"

She giggled and sat upright. "You're so easy to figure out, James Morgan."

He slid his hand into hers, yanked her to her feet, then led her back to his apartment.

The chase was over.

The push and pull had ended.

She had won.

Did You Like the Book?

I love when friends and family recommend a book for me. I'll often give it a read just because the recommendation came from someone I trusted. That's probably how we all are.

If you enjoyed this story, I'd truly appreciate it if you would tell your friends and family or leave a review at where you got the book.

All writers need feedback on their work—not only to help other readers discover them, but so they know they're delivering the goods with their stories.

Thanks for reading and hope to see you again!

About the Author

Colin Conway is the creator of the 509 Crime Stories, a series of novels set in Eastern Washington with revolving lead characters. They are standalone tales and can be read in any order.

He also created the Cozy Up series which pushes the envelope of the cozy genre. Libby Klein, author of the Poppy McAllister series, says *Cozy Up to Death* is "Not your grandma's cozy."

Colin co-authored the Charlie-316 series. The first novel in the series, *Charlie-316*, is a political/crime thriller that has been described as "riveting and compulsively readable," "the real deal," and "the ultimate ride-along."

He served in the U.S. Army and later was an officer of the Spokane Police Department. He has owned a laundromat, invested in a bar, and run a karate school. Besides writing crime fiction, he is a commercial real estate broker.

Colin lives with his beautiful girlfriend, three wonderful children, and a codependent Vizsla that rules their world.

Find out more about Colin at colinconway.com.